PRAISE FOR
THE GHOST OF GRANNY APPLES MYSTERIES

"Delectable . . . [An] appealing ghost story."
—*Publishers Weekly*

"Likable characters and steady suspense . . . [Sue Ann Jaffarian] makes paranormal activity seem plausible. One of the best cozy authors for light chatter and low-key humor."
—*Library Journal* (starred review)

"A unique voice."
—*Kirkus Reviews*

"Another charming entry in a series that remains fun while seamlessly incorporating an incorporeal spirit who feels real and whose love of pop culture is always welcome."
—Kings River Life Magazine

"Officially proves the vivacious Jaffarian is the literary heir apparent to Lucille Ball! . . . An eclectic mix of laugh-out-loud fun, heart-touching moments, whimsy, and rapid-fire page turning . . . [Jaffarian] deserves a standing ovation."
—The Book Resort

"A pleasant mix of cozy and paranormal."
—The Mystery Reader

"[Jaffarian's] plot is fabulously soapy and complex; the mystery . . . is twisty, turny, and thoughtfully constructed; and Emma's investigation is refreshingly thorough and logically undertaken."
—Smitten by Books

continued . . .

The
GHOSTS of
MISTY HOLLOW

SUE ANN JAFFARIAN

BERKLEY PRIME CRIME
New York

BERKLEY PRIME CRIME

Published by Berkley

An imprint of Penguin Random House LLC

375 Hudson Street, New York, New York 10014

Copyright © 2016 by Sue Ann Jaffarian

Penguin Random House supports copyright. Copyright fuels creativity, encourages diverse voices, promotes free speech, and creates a vibrant culture. Thank you for buying an authorized edition of this book and for complying with copyright laws by not reproducing, scanning, or distributing any part of it in any form without permission. You are supporting writers and allowing Penguin Random House to continue to publish books for every reader.

BERKLEY is a registered trademark and BERKLEY PRIME CRIME and the B colophon are trademarks of Penguin Random House LLC.

ISBN: 9780425282083

First Edition: December 2016

Printed in the United States of America

1 3 5 7 9 10 8 6 4 2

Cover art by Robert Crawford/Lindgren & Smith

Cover design by Diana Kolsky

Book design by Kristin del Rosario

Acknowledgments

My undying gratitude to my agent, Whitney Lee, and all the good folks at Berkley, especially my editor, Kristine Swartz, who take my words and bring Granny Apples and all her friends to life between the delightful covers of a book.

A special acknowledgment to Heide van den Akker, my dear personal friend and an avid reader. Poor Heide listened to many hours of plots points and twists and maybes and maybe nots as this book took shape, and who in return gave wonderful advice.

Trust me, sometimes being the close friend and confidant of a writer can be pretty boring. We're talking snoozeville, folks.

· CHAPTER ONE ·

GINO Costello, the famous crime writer, came down the front steps of the farmhouse, taking them two at a time, to greet his guests.

"Uh-oh," said Emma to Phil, who was behind the wheel of the rental car. "He's not alone."

"That's his wife on the porch, isn't it?" Phil asked.He brought the car to a stop next to a black SUV parked in front of a large garage just off a circular drive. On the other side of the SUV was a white compact sedan.

"I think so, but I'm not talking about her."

"Uh-oh," echoed Phil with a groan as soon as he understood what she meant. "Can't we even get settled before ghosts start pestering you?"

"They're not pestering me, Phil," Emma said. She was still looking toward the large porch that ran across the front and down both sides of the two-story white farmhouse.

"But they're definitely here." She started unbuckling her seat belt.

"Friendly or disturbed?" Phil asked.

"Not sure yet," she answered as she continued to check out the hazy apparitions. "So far I count three possible outlines of ghosts. One is coming toward us with Gino and is more distinct. He's male and fairly young. It's almost as if they were waiting for us along with our host."

Gino came to a stop next to the car. The big burly man with the thinning dark hair was clearly excited about their arrival. The spirit floated beside him, and gave Emma a hesitant wave.

"The spirit with Gino just waved at me," Emma said to Phil. "Guess that means friendly."

Phil shook his head. "Let's hope he stays that way." He couldn't see the ghosts, but knew their presence meant that Emma would probably get little rest during this visit. "Wait till Granny gets here," he said to Emma. "It will be a real ghost convention, like an early Halloween."

Emma was barely out of the car when Gino engulfed her in a big bear hug. His soft flannel shirt smelled of cigars and wood smoke. "It is so good to finally meet you guys," he said. "I feel like we're long-lost family." Although they'd never met, Emma had been in contact with Gino several times over the past year. Both their daughters, Kelly and Tanisha, resided in Boston and had become very close friends. Gino had even helped Emma out with a recent matter she'd been investigating.

"It certainly feels that way, Gino," Emma said with a broad smile while keeping an eye on the ghost. She wondered if the spirit was going to embrace her, too. It didn't, but it did step forward. As the ghost's facial features came into focus, she saw she was right, the ghost was a young man, maybe in his twenties. He was studying her, assessing her. He waved again, barely moving his hand. "Can you see me, ma'am?" he asked.

Without being too obvious, she turned her head toward the ghost just behind Gino's left shoulder, and looked him straight in the eye, giving him a small dip of her chin to let him know she could see him.

In response, the spirit nodded back quickly. "So you can also hear me." It was more of a statement than a question, but the spirit seemed greatly relieved when Emma gave him another nod. "Welcome to Misty Hollow," he said with a slight bow, then scampered up the porch to the hazy outlines of the other spirits to give his report: a full-blown medium was in the house.

Phil came around the car. Gino held out his right hand to him. "I understand," Gino said, pumping Phil's hand with gusto, "that congratulations are in order. Tanisha tells me you two got engaged this summer."

"Yep," Phil answered, putting an arm around Emma's shoulders. "Emma's finally agreed to make an honest man out of me."

"Speaking of which," Gino said, "let me introduce you to my better half." He indicated a woman on the porch who had made no move to greet them.

Gino's wife was standing to the right side of the large black-lacquered front door. The small gathering of ghosts was huddled to the left of it. She didn't know the spirits were there and they seemed to Emma disinterested in her. As the three of them walked up the steps, Emma glanced over at the ghosts. She could still only make out the young man. The others appeared to be clusters of dust shimmering in the fading sunlight, but Emma knew better.

"This is Vanessa, my wife," Gino said, introducing them when they were on porch. "Honey," he said to his wife, "Emma Whitecastle and Phil Bowers. Emma is Kelly's mother."

"I know who she is," Vanessa said, bored impatience plastered on her perfectly made-up face. "You're Grant Whitecastle's ex."

Emma cringed but tried not to show it. She really disliked being considered an appendage of her ex-husband, especially now that they had been divorced for several years. Grant Whitecastle was a flamboyant daytime TV talk show host known for his temper, nastiness, and disrespect for others. Emma had her own TV show. It explored paranormal topics in a serious and informative fashion and, even though it was on cable and only aired once a week—unlike Grant's show, which was broadcast daily on a major network—Emma had built her own solid following and reputation away from him. She preferred to stay out of the limelight and the tabloids, while Grant seemed to encourage them.

Emma did a quick study of Vanessa Costello and realized the woman had intended to make her uncomfortable. She'd been around many women like Vanessa when she was married to Grant. They were rich and spoiled and any other woman who showed any independence or individuality around them was game for sport. Vanessa had purposely made the comment to let Emma know she viewed her as nothing but the ex-wife of a famous man— a dime-a-dozen commodity. Emma also knew how to stand her ground, something she'd learned in her long years as a Hollywood wife. She smiled and looked Vanessa Costello in the eye, conveying that she was not going to be easy prey. With cool politeness, she held out her right hand toward the woman. "Do you know Grant?"

Vanessa flipped her long, honey-blond-highlighted hair over her shoulder before taking Emma's hand and giving it a single dry, feathery pump. On her wrist hung several thick gold bracelets and a very expensive watch. Her thin frame was covered with black leggings and a long cashmere cowl-neck sweater in pale yellow. Emma guessed her to be in her early to midforties, just a few years younger than Emma herself.

"As a matter of fact," Vanessa said, "I met him once, years ago, at a friend's party in LA. Interesting man, to say the least, and very much like his media personality. I can see that Kelly takes more after you."

From her tone, Emma couldn't tell if Vanessa thought that a good thing or not, and decided in Vanessa's world it was not. She knew that Kelly liked Gino quite a bit, but she'd never said much about Tanisha's stepmother, except that she'd met her a couple of times and not for long. Tanisha had never said anything to Emma about Vanessa, except that she existed. Emma was beginning to see why both girls had been so closemouthed on the subject, and why Tanisha looked to Emma as a surrogate mother. Tanisha's real mother, a college professor, had died in a tragic car accident when T was only thirteen. Her parents had never married.

Vanessa turned to Phil. "You're certainly a departure from Grant Whitecastle." She took Phil's offered hand, giving it the same limp shake.

Without a bit of hesitation, Phil grinned directly at the

woman. "Everyone says Emma traded up. After meeting the man, I tend to agree."

Off to the side, Gino stifled a laugh while Vanessa considered Phil and Emma for a few awkward seconds.

"This is a great old house," Phil said, breaking the short silence. "And the location is beautiful."

"Yes," responded Gino, "it is. The house was built in the early 1800s, but it has been totally modernized. Only the outside has been preserved as it was originally. I was told that about ten or twelve years ago the previous owner turned it into a B&B, expanding bedrooms and adding en suite baths in some of the rooms. There's a photo album in the living room showing the before and after photos. The place is called Misty Hollow."

"Was that the B&B's name?" asked Emma, remembering the greeting of the ghost.

"The B&B was called that, too, but Misty Hollow is actually the name of the property itself," Gino explained. "Out by the driveway entry there's a plaque bolted to a large rock with the name on it. The current owner closed down the B&B when he bought it and turned it into a vacation rental." He walked to the right side of the porch where it turned around the house. "The porch encircles the entire house and there's a small lake behind the property with a private beach and dock."

Phil and Emma followed him and could easily see a lovely lake beyond a span of newly mown lawn. The trees on the property were already partially ablaze with their fall finery of red, orange, and gold leaves. They were mixed with evergreens and birch. The view was as pretty and as inviting as any New England postcard.

"The place is usually booked solid through October,"

Gino continued. "I was lucky to get it, but I booked early. As you can see, the leaves are already changing. By the time you depart, most of them will be totally done. We're here at the perfect time for checking out fall foliage." He paused to drink in the scenery. "The current owner and his family spend a lot of time over the holidays here, as well as a couple of weeks during the summer. I heard about the place through a friend."

"How long are you here for?" Emma asked, her face still turned to the view as she appreciated the natural beauty.

"Five or six weeks, depending on how much time I feel I need," Gino answered. "We arrived about ten days ago. We're their last guests for the year so the owner was flexible with our departure date." He looked around and took a deep breath of the clean September air, clearly content with his surroundings. "I like it here. I think I'd like to stay the full six weeks, through the end of October." He paused, then added, "I actually wouldn't mind staying here through Thanksgiving. There's such a quiet peace to the place."

Behind them, Vanessa groaned. When Gino glanced at her, they exchanged looks. Vanessa's was pinched with distaste. Gino's was a look of frustration. "My wife," Gino said, returning his attention to his guests, "does not share my enthusiasm for rural Massachusetts. Actually, for rural anything."

"When you told Emma you were renting a farmhouse for a writing retreat," Phil said, trying to break the tension, "I expected a real farmhouse. This place is the size of a small mansion."

"That's what the owner calls it, and this was once a farm," Gino explained, "but over the decades parcels of land have been sold off and new homes built on them. There is another structure on the property even older than this one. It was the original farmhouse until this one was built after the original owner began to prosper and his family expanded."

"We need to speak, Emma," said the ghost who'd welcomed them. He'd returned to stand next to her during the introductions but had remained quiet until now. Emma shot him a short glance and nod, hoping it conveyed *later*.

Vanessa approached them. "If Gino had his way we'd be staying in that ramshackle place instead of here, which is primitive enough."

Even without going inside, Emma could tell that the house and its furnishings were anything but primitive. "I take it you prefer the city," she said to Vanessa with a forced smile.

"Don't most civilized people?" Vanessa answered, speaking through tight lips with an emphasis on each word. "There's absolutely nothing to do here."

"Phil and I both enjoy the country," Emma said. "He was raised on and still owns a small ranch in Julian, California; a former gold-rush town in the mountains north of San Diego. I was raised in Pasadena on the edge of Los Angeles, but also own a home in Julian."

Phil circled Emma's waist with an arm. "Emma and I divide our time between the city and the country. We get the best of both worlds."

"Tanisha raved about your place in Julian after her visit," Gino said. "I'm sorry we couldn't take you up on the invitation to come with her."

"Another time," Emma said pleasantly, though after

meeting Vanessa Costello, she wasn't sure she wanted to extend the invitation again. "Maybe we can get Jeremiah to come down, too."

"You know Jeremiah Jones?" Vanessa asked with a mix of surprise and distaste.

"Yes," answered Emma. "Gino was nice enough to put us in touch with him when we needed some help with something."

"I hear you've all become fast friends," Gino said, clearly pleased.

"We love Jeremiah," replied Emma, giving Gino a genuine smile. "In fact, he's agreed to join us in Julian again this Thanksgiving."

Phil looked at Vanessa, then at Gino. "You folks live full time in Chicago, don't you?"

"Mostly," answered Gino. "We also have an apartment in Paris, and we travel a great deal. We're practically nomads." He chuckled. "We spent a couple of weeks in Italy before coming here."

"Raphael invited us to his villa," Vanessa said, still looking bored. "That would be Raphael Brindisi."

"Yes, the Italian novelist," Phil said. "I'm well acquainted with his work."

"Phil is a voracious reader," Emma said proudly. "In fact, Gino, he's a huge fan of your books."

"More like a squealing fan-boy," quipped a ghost, but the sassy remark didn't come from the young spirit standing patiently with them. Emma glanced over to see the ghost of Ish Reynolds, better known as Granny Apples, the ghost of her great-great-great grandmother, standing off to the side. She shot Granny a quick warning look to behave.

"What?" the ornery ghost said. "It's not like anyone can hear me but you and Slim here." She indicated the young ghost who was now staring at Granny with a slack jaw. "Close your mouth, son, before flies get in there," Granny said to the other spirit. He snapped his mouth shut.

"So Kelly has told me." Gino beamed, continuing the conversation he could hear without any clue about the one he couldn't. "Speaking of which, I have something for you, Phil. It's inside, but why don't we get you two settled first?"

Just then a man came out of the house. He was tall and angular and dressed in jeans and a hunter green V-neck sweater over a white T-shirt. In his hand was a cell phone. "Gino, Neil's on the phone."

Gino turned to his guests. "If you'll excuse me, I need to take that. It's my agent." He turned back to the man. "Help these folks with their luggage, Leroy, then let's all meet in the library. I believe it's almost cocktail time."

Taking the phone with him, Gino entered the house through a door off the side porch. All eyes followed him, including those of the friendly young ghost who was politely keeping his distance and keeping his mouth shut. The spirit caught Emma's eye. "We'll speak later," he said and disappeared.

Emma glanced at Granny and with a slight tilt of her head indicated for her to follow the spirit. It was always a crapshoot with Granny. She might or might not get the subtle request, and even if she did, Granny might or might not agree to do it. Emma was pleased when Granny saluted her and said, "On it, Chief."

Leroy turned to Emma and Phil, holding out a courteous hand. "I'm Leroy Larkin, Gino's assistant," he told them. They all shook hands politely. He turned to Vanessa. "Which guest room would you like them in, Mrs. Costello?"

Vanessa had turned back to stare at the lake, her arms hugged tightly across her chest. At Leroy's question, she turned her head slowly toward them but didn't really focus. "I think Marta prepared the big blue room, but put them anywhere you like." Without another word, she headed across the porch and down the far steps toward the lake.

After she left, another wave of awkwardness fell over the now much smaller group. Leroy plastered a smile on his face and finally said in a forced perky voice, "You'll love the blue room. It's one of my favorites."

The blue room was indeed blue. The walls were covered with wallpaper of small blue medallions on a powder blue background peppered with blue teardrops and flecks of gold. In addition to the bed, there was a good-sized sitting area with a love seat, wing chair, and tiny coffee table positioned by French doors. The furniture was upholstered in period fabric to match the room.

Leroy set Emma's bag down on the quilt-covered four-poster bed. "This is the second largest bedroom in the house," he explained. "The Costellos are in the largest suite on the other side of the main staircase. There are three other bedrooms on this floor between this room and the other. One is a smaller suite with a private bath, and the other two bedrooms have twin beds and share a bath. They are all empty for now."

"For now?" Emma asked.

Leroy nodded. "At least until Tanisha and Kelly come. I was told they will be here next weekend. They wanted to catch you before you went back to California."

Emma beamed with excitement. "I'm so glad the girls are coming," she said to Phil. "I was worried Kelly wouldn't be able to make it with school just starting."

Phil smiled, pleased with her delight. He put his bag on the bed next to hers. He turned to Leroy. "Where's your room? Are there more bedrooms downstairs?"

"There is one roomy bedroom and bath off the kitchen," Leroy reported. "The people who converted the house into a B&B years ago turned that room into a handicap-accessible room. Smart move on their part." He pointed toward the window. "There's also a nice guest-house in the back, facing the lake. That's where I'm bunk-ing." He let out a low snort, his large eyes bulging in humor. "Out of the fray."

Before they could make any comment, Leroy contin-ued. "As soon as you like, come on down to the library," he told them. "It's the second room to the right of the front door, next to the formal living room. We're very casual around here. So don't feel the need to dress up."

"I should go down and help Vanessa in the kitchen," Emma said to Phil.

Leroy let out another half snort, snagging it by the tail before it was fully birthed. "No need," he told Emma with a tight smile. "Vanessa flew Marta in for our time here. That's their cook and housekeeper in Chicago. Marta is staying in the room by the kitchen." For a few awkward seconds, Leroy hung around, like a bellhop expecting a tip. Finally, he said, "Well, if you folks need anything, just ask."

"Thank you," Phil told him.

Without another word, Leroy left, closing the painted white door behind him.

Phil unzipped his bag. "Did you know Kelly was coming?"

"Last I heard it was iffy," Emma said. She slipped out of her leather jacket and started unpacking her own bag. "She said she had so much to catch up on after her trip with Quinn this summer and with her final year starting." Emma plopped down on the wing chair. "I can't believe my baby is about to graduate from college, Phil."

"Well, school's not out yet," he said with a laugh. "And she'll be going to grad school next year, won't she?"

"She's not said a word about it in a long time." Emma blew out a gust of frustrated air. "Every time I ask her about it, she evades the question or says it's under control. She won't even tell me if she's applied anywhere. I called her father and he said he's even more in the dark than I am. Grant did say that he offered Kelly a job with his production company if she decides she wants to get into show business."

Phil was hanging a shirt in the closet and stopped. "I don't recall Kelly ever mentioning the entertainment field."

"She hasn't, except to say she'd rather scrub toilets in a prison first." Emma and Phil exchanged laughs.

"Now that sounds like our girl," Phil said, and finished hanging his shirt.

Emma smiled, pleased at how close Phil and Kelly had become. It had happened naturally over time, with Kelly turning to Phil for fatherly advice and comfort when her own father couldn't put his narcissism aside. Emma stood back up and pulled clothes from her bag and placed them in the antique dresser, on top of which sat a very modern television. "I talked to her a couple of days ago," she said to Phil. "I told her if she didn't make it here this week, then we'd shoot up there for a short visit before we left."

"I can't wait to hear about her adventures with Quinn and his crew," Phil said.

Dr. Quinn Keenan was a dashing archeologist who'd once been a guest on Emma's show and was now a good friend. He traveled the world and had a strong interest in paranormal activities in all cultures, especially ancient ones.

"Me either," said Emma with excitement. "She said she had a lot to tell me."

Phil slipped into the adjoining bathroom to put away his shaving kit. When he popped back out, he said, "Maybe I should take one of the other bedrooms one night so you two can stay in here all night gabbing."

Emma went to him and wrapped her arms around his waist. "Would you do that for me?"

He kissed her and patted her bottom gently. "As long as it's only for one night."

"Deal," Emma said, kissing and patting him back. She pulled away. "In spite of what Leroy said, I'm going to change my top, brush my teeth, and freshen my makeup. I feel grimy from flying all day."

"Not a bad idea. I feel road weary, too." Phil pulled one of his shirts back out of the closet. "Too bad we weren't in a hotel." He pulled the jersey he was wearing over his head, removing it. "Then we could order room service and not leave the room until morning."

"I feel the exact same way." Emma took her toiletries into the bathroom. She emerged a minute later holding a toothbrush and toothpaste. "Especially since there seems to be so much tension between the Costellos." She applied some toothpaste to the brush. "Do you think Vanessa is angry because we're here?" She stuck the brush into her mouth and started brushing her teeth.

Phil walked past her and grabbed his own toothbrush out of his kit. He rinsed it under the faucet, then held it out to her. "No," he said as Emma applied some toothpaste to it. "I'm thinking she's mad because she's here instead of in Italy." He chuckled and stuck the brush into his mouth. Together they brushed their teeth, spit, and rinsed using heavy tumblers set on a small counter above the sink. After, Phil washed his face while Emma touched up her makeup.

While he was drying off, Phil said, "I don't think Vanessa is the type who enjoys country vacations, especially six-week ones that might turn longer, no matter how charming her surroundings."

"I'm beginning to see why Tanisha hardly mentions her."

Emma went back into the bedroom and replaced the heavy sweater she was wearing with another lighter one in pale yellow. Remembering Vanessa was wearing a similar sweater, she then switched it out for one in sage green with a V-neck that showed the top edge of her lacy camisole. "This place is charming, isn't it?" she asked as she checked her attire in the full-length mirror on the back of the closet door.

Heavy dark blue drapes framed the French doors that were covered with sheer white panels. Emma went to them and opened one, letting in chilly air. The doors led to a small balcony with two chairs and a view of the lake. In the growing darkness, she could see the dock at the end of the property line. A wide path led from the house down to the dock, with a smaller path branching off from the left to a small cottage. The paths were indicated by very low lights set along the path just above ground level. The dock was also lined with well-spaced lights. It extended into the inky lake like a jewel-encrusted finger. Across the dark water, lights from other properties twinkled like low-hanging stars. "This is so lovely," she said. "I can't wait to see what it looks like in the morning." She pointed to the small cottage. "I'll bet that's the guesthouse where Leroy's staying."

Phil came up behind her. "It's all very romantic." He snuggled her neck with his lips. "Are you sure we can't stay in here until morning?"

She closed the door and pushed him back playfully. "I'm sure."

Emma went back into the bathroom and ran a brush through her short blond hair, then fluffed it back up with her fingers. "You know," she said through the open door, "this might be a great place to rent for Kelly's graduation next year. It's not close to Boston, but it's not so far that we can't get to Harvard for the ceremony. We can put the whole family up here quite comfortably for a week of vacation. Maybe two weeks. I know my parents would love it. We'd even have room if my cousins come out or your sons, and for Tanisha if she wants to join us."

Before Phil could say anything, a voice came out of the air. "That's an outstanding idea, depending on the ghost situation."

Emma gave the ghost a big smile that Phil caught. Emma turned to Phil. "Granny's here."

"So I figured," he said. He pulled his clean shirt over

his head then waved in the direction Emma indicated. "Hey, Granny." The ghost waved back, even though she knew Phil couldn't see her.

"Yeah," the diminutive pioneer ghost said to Emma with a frown. "I felt their presence when I arrived. It was like wading through mud to get a fix on you. I followed Slim but the rest vaporized at the sight of me. Are they friendly, confused, or on the surly side?"

"I'm not sure yet, Granny." Emma left the bathroom and sat back down on the chair. She removed her boots and slipped her feet into comfortable suede flats. "The one you call Slim seems to be acting as their spokesperson and indicated that we would speak later. He seems very polite. From what I could tell, he's kind of young and dressed in farm clothes."

Granny nodded in agreement. "That's what I saw, too. Before he disappeared he told me they need to speak with you. That it's important."

Emma gave it some thought, then asked, "Do you know, Granny, if they knew ahead of time if I was coming, or if a medium specifically was coming? Or are they just greeting every new person, hoping to make a connection?"

"That's a good question," the ghost answered, "but like I said, Slim told me nothing except that they needed to speak with you."

"Granny, at some point tonight why don't you try to make contact with him again, or with the other spirits around here, and see what's up before I meet them formally."

"You got it." Granny disappeared.

Her shoes changed, Emma stood up. "Okay," she said to Phil, "Granny doesn't know any more than I do about the ghosts that were waiting when we arrived, but she's going to try and find out anything she can before I have a meet and greet with them."

"I hope that clambake can wait until tomorrow," Phil said with concern. "You're pretty pooped tonight."

"I hope so, too," Emma said with a weary smile. "And I'm thinking it's going to take a lot of my remaining energy and patience to get through dinner with Vanessa Costello."

"Yep. Tonight should be a real picnic if she's in the same mood as when we arrived," Phil noted in agreement. He turned to Emma and held out his arm to her. "You ready to go downstairs, darling? There will be alcohol."

Emma took his arm and straightened her shoulders. "Thank goodness for that."

· CHAPTER TWO ·

THEY found Gino and Vanessa waiting for them in the dark-paneled library. Vanessa was curled up in a corner on a large leather reading chair the color of dried blood. In one hand she held a half-full wineglass and with the other she flipped through a fashion magazine on her lap. Gino was bent over, tending to a fire in the stone fireplace. The tinkling sound of ice being dropped into heavy crystal competed with the crackling of the growing fire. They turned and noticed Leroy behind them at a built-in wet bar, fixing a drink. He poured amber liquid over the ice and brought it to Gino, who straightened and took it.

"What can Leroy get you folks?" Gino asked. "We have a nice selection of brandy, wine, beer, and scotch. Name your poison."

The library was a huge room with French doors facing

the lake, like those in their room. Instead of a balcony, the doors lead out to a humongous deck. Like in their room, the floor was highly polished hardwood covered with lovely rugs. Floor to ceiling bookshelves crammed with games and books of all types lined the wall opposite the French doors. An immense oak desk covered with books and papers was situated in front of the shelves. The room's floor space was dominated by an assortment of leather chairs and two sofas that faced each other. Cozy afghans were neatly folded and scattered over the backs of the furniture. In a corner near the fireplace was a game table and chairs. Over the fireplace, a large flat-screen TV had been mounted to the wall. The room was clearly meant to be the gathering spot for the house.

"I'll have what Gino's having," Emma said to Leroy.

"Make that two," chimed Phil.

"This room is fabulous," said Emma, taking a seat on one of the large sofas. Phil wandered over to the bookshelves and checked out some of the titles.

"It's the largest room in the place, outside of the kitchen," Gino told her. "There's a formal parlor next door, to the left just as you come in the front door, but it's rather fussy in decor. Across the hall from the parlor is the formal dining room. The kitchen is massive and has a less formal dining area."

Leroy handed Emma her drink and she thanked him. He crossed over to Phil and delivered his scotch to him. "Leroy told us," she said, "that there is another bedroom downstairs that is handicap accessible, as well as a guest-house at the rear of the house. Seems like the people who renovated the place thought of everything."

"Pretty much," Gino answered. "The accessible room is just off the kitchen. I think it was once a large storeroom, but now it's as nice as the other rooms. Marta is staying there. Marta Peele is our cook and housekeeper from Chicago. Vanessa insisted on bringing her here with us."

Vanessa looked up from her magazine long enough to shoot her husband a pointed look. "Like you fought me on it. You and I wouldn't survive more than two days on our own cooking, and you know it."

Gino grinned and shrugged. "It's true, my dear. We would have wasted away or been forced to dine on poor Leroy here."

Emma cast a look at Leroy to find him biting his lip, but she wasn't sure if he was holding back laughter or a snide remark. He was a difficult read. He came away from the bar with his own drink. "You folks will have to excuse me," he said to Phil and Emma. "I hate to eat and run, but right after dinner, I'll be heading out to meet a friend."

"Out in this Godforsaken place?" Vanessa asked, showing real interest for the first time.

"It's a friend from college," Leroy explained. "He lives near Boston. I'll be staying the night."

"Why not leave now?" Vanessa asked. "You won't get there until late if you stay for dinner."

"Because my friend works until 9," Leroy explained with a tight smile. "But he has off tomorrow." He turned to Gino. "Are you sure you don't need me back early tomorrow?"

"No problem. Stay tomorrow and enjoy yourself," Gino told him with enthusiasm. "We've been working hard for the past week. Besides, I'll be picking Emma's brain most of tomorrow."

With a salute to Gino that reminded Emma of Granny, Leroy perched on a stool at the bar. "Thanks, Gino."

After a few moments, Gino said to Phil, "Like I said before, Phil, I have a little something for you." When Phil looked at him with curiosity, Gino added, "It's on the coffee table in front of where Emma is sitting."

Phil left the bookcase and went to the coffee table. On it were several books, a large photo album, and a stack of coasters. He picked up the book on top of the others. It had Gino's name on it. "This?" he asked.

"Yep. That's an advance copy of my new novel," Gino told him. "My editor and his wife stopped by for a couple of days on their way to Maine, and brought that with them. It won't be out for several months. When Kelly told me how much you enjoy my books, I thought you might like it."

Phil looked down at the book like a kid looking at his favorite chocolate bar. "Wow! Thank you." He showed it to Emma with a wide, goofy grin plastered on his face. He opened the book and saw that Gino had inscribed it:

To Phil, may this be the start of a beautiful friendship—Gino.

Under that was Gino's full autograph.

Emma laughed. "You just made his day, Gino."

"Day?" gushed Phil. He looked up at Gino, still wearing the grin. "You just made my month."

Gino smiled. "Glad you like it." He pointed to the photo album on the table. "That's the photo album I mentioned earlier. It chronicles the history of this house, including all the renovations. There are even old photos of the original farmhouse not too far from here. Pretty interesting stuff." From her chair in the corner, Vanessa snorted.

Leroy cut his eyes quickly to Vanessa, then looked over at Emma and Phil. "It is pretty fascinating," he told them. "I'm hoping Gino includes the old place in his next book." He glanced up at Gino like a dog trying to please his master. "It's kind of creepy, Gino. You really should use it." Again, Vanessa snorted.

Emma put her drink down on a coaster. Picking up the album, she placed it on her lap and started flipping through it. As Gino had said, it was a pictorial history of Misty Hollow. Some of the photos were labeled or had comments neatly typed and affixed to the page. The first page was a lovely photo of the farmhouse as it was now, followed by a page with an aerial view of the property, showing the large house with its various outbuildings scattered around the property surrounded by thick vegetation and wooded areas.

Emma turned the book toward Phil. "This is pretty cool, honey. Check it out." Phil sat on the sofa next to Emma and they balanced the large photo album across both their knees.

"Look," Emma said, pointing at the aerial photo. "There's the guesthouse and there's the dock." She moved her index finger. "That's where our room is, looking out in this direction. And there's the road we came in on."

"This is very interesting," Phil said. He pulled out his reading glasses for a closer look, then pointed to a building on the outskirts of the property. "Is that the old farmhouse?" he asked, looking up at Gino.

Gino came and leaned over the album. "Yes, that's it. The current owner uses it mostly for storage. He's fixed up the outside and painted it to match the rest of the buildings, but inside I understand it's still pretty rough." He pointed to a small road that started to the left of the garage. "That road leads to it. It's well worth seeing. I'll take you there tomorrow when it's light out if you want. Although I'm sure it will have some electricity and lights if he's using it for storage."

Emma flipped through the album. It seemed to go back in time instead of starting with the earliest history. There were several photos of the place in various seasons, including one in which the yard in front of the dock was set up for a wedding and reception.

"They rent this place out for weddings?" Emma asked.

"Yeah," said Gino. "On their website they advertise the grounds for weddings and other events. The current owner told me the place hosted a lot more parties when it operated as a B&B, but since it's now a private vacation rental, they don't rent the grounds separately very often, so not to disturb their guests."

"Beautiful place for a wedding," Phil remarked.

The next several pages showed a backward progression of the big remodel in various stages, ending with photos of what the house looked like originally. Before the renovation it was a very large house with many tiny rooms upstairs. Walls had been broken down to merge rooms into the large suites and adjoining private bathrooms. Downstairs had also been a collection of small rooms. It looked to Emma like only the parlor and dining room had been left alone, while the library/den, where they were now, had been carved out of two rooms.

"It appears that the kitchen was always huge," noted Gino. "But then I suppose back then the kitchen was the focal point of activity. Still, they gutted it and totally modernized everything. They also expanded the porch in the back to make a nice-sized deck."

"This is quite impressive," said Phil. "Yet on the outside, it still looks the same, just spruced up."

"The garage is totally new," Gino said. "In the older photos you'll see that there was a barn or stable set back a little farther, between this house and the old farmhouse. It's now gone. It was torn down and the big garage that's there now was built closer to the house when the major renovations occurred."

Sure enough, in some of the photos there did appear to be a large but dilapidated barn along the small drive between the two houses but closer to the old house. As Emma stared at the photo, an odd feeling came over her, like the humming of an old tune heard coming from another room. She touched the barn in the photo but got no signal or response, just the feeling that she was hearing something no one else could.

She turned a few more pages until there appeared the same house but in an older photograph. It appeared to be an original, not a copy, as its edges were rough and brown. On the steps, people were gathered, standing in graded levels. In the very front, two straight-back chairs had been placed and in them sat an old couple. A few children sat cross-legged on the ground by the chairs, with children and adults of various ages standing or sitting on the steps. Two of the women held infants. The men wore stiff collars and formal suits with jackets. The grown women wore long skirts and the young girls pinafores. The young boys wore pants with suspenders and white shirts. Again Emma felt, rather than heard, a low hum. She studied the photo closely, especially the photo of one of the young boys in suspenders seated on the stoop next to a girl of about the same age. There was a strong family resemblance among most of the people in the photo. Those who didn't carry the same facial traits had probably married into the clan. But there was no doubt in her mind that she was looking at a multigenerational photograph—a formal family photo with everyone in their Sunday best. Under the photo was the caption:

The Brown family circa 1880.

"Were the Browns the original owners?" she asked Gino, pointing to the family photo.

"I'm not sure, but I think so," Gino answered. "From what I can gather from the photos and in talking to the current owner, someone in the Brown family owned it until the mid-1980s, when it was sold to the people who renovated it into a B&B. The current owner bought it and did more renovations in 2009. But those were mostly cosmetic—new paint and wallpaper sort of thing."

"Isn't that when they built the guesthouse?" asked Leroy. "I thought I heard the guy who leased it to you say something about that."

Gino gave the topic some thought, then answered, "I

believe he said it was originally some sort of outbuilding, and the B&B people converted it into a guesthouse during their renovation."

Emma paged through more of the album until she reached the old farmhouse. In these photos it didn't look abandoned but like the hub of family life. It was also two-story, like the newer house but not nearly as large, and it did not have a grand front porch. Two women were standing in front of it dressed in work clothes, posing awkwardly for the camera. Nearby, a group of young children played. The camera seemed more focused on the children, capturing their smiles and horseplay. Like the other photo, this one was also brown and partially faded. The caption read:

Old farmhouse circa 1870s.

Emma also got a humming sense when looking at this photo, but it wasn't nearly as strong as with the other picture. After viewing all of the photos, she went back to the one with the large family in front of the bigger house and scrutinized each face, always coming back to the boy in the suspenders. He seemed so familiar.

"Emma," she heard in a low whisper. "Emma." Snapping her eyes open, she jerked her head up to see Phil staring at her with concern. She looked at Gino, then Leroy and Vanessa. All three were also watching her. "You okay, Emma?" her host asked.

She giggled slightly. "Between the drink and the long day, I must have dozed off. Sorry."

"Nothing to be sorry about," Gino said reassuringly.

"Dinner will be ready in a few minutes. We have no plans for tonight, so feel free to turn in early."

Vanessa snorted. "Turning in early is all there is to do here."

Gino shot her a dirty look, then turned back to Emma and Phil. "T told me that you guys are vegetarian."

"Her," Phil said, pointing at Emma, "not me. I enjoy a good steak or rack of ribs when the boss here lets me."

"I do eat fish and seafood," Emma answered after giving Phil a playful swat, "but please don't trouble yourself with anything special."

"Vanessa doesn't eat meat either," Gino said. "Marta is cooking up some local seafood for tonight, along with a roast chicken." He turned to his wife. "Isn't that right, dear?"

As if hearing a cue, Vanessa uncurled her legs and stood up. "I'll go see if dinner is ready."

Gino watched her as she walked from the room, then sat down heavily on the matching sofa across from them. "I must apologize for Vanessa's behavior," he said in a low voice. "She did not want to come here, especially after all the parties and fun she was having in Italy. I should just send her back there or let her go home. If I don't, Leroy and I might not get any work done."

"Oh I'm sure we'll manage, Gino," Leroy said with a crooked grin as he swirled the ice in his drink. "We always do."

Emma gave Gino a small, understanding smile. "I'm sure it's difficult spending a lot of time in the country when you're not used to the slower pace."

"Back in Chicago, we hardly see each other," he

confessed. "She's always on the go with friends and I'm buried in my work."

"Speaking of your work," Emma said, moving the conversation away from the Costellos' domestic problems, "how can I help?"

"You're tired," Gino said. "Tomorrow morning after breakfast I can give you a tour of the place and tell you what I'm thinking for my new book."

"Does it involve Misty Hollow?" Phil asked.

"Not specifically," Gino said, "but it does take place in a sleepy New England town like this one."

"Please," Emma encouraged him, "tell us the plot and how ghosts or the paranormal fit in."

Gino took a big slug from his drink and leaned forward, eager to talk about his latest creation. It was then Emma saw the resemblance between Gino and his daughter. Tanisha's mother had been African-American. At first glance, T and Gino didn't look anything alike, but now Emma saw it. It was in the eyes. T had gotten her father's teardrop-shaped smoky eyes.

"Basically," Gino explained with barely contained excitement, "it's about a local serial killer who has been plaguing the countryside for years, but his kills aren't close together enough so as to rouse panic. People go missing here and there in a wide radius and no one suspects the real killer or that it's the work of a serial killer. They seem like random disappearances and no bodies are ever discovered. The killer is a seemingly nice guy, a quiet and solid family man, pillar-of-the-community type."

"It's always the quiet ones," quipped Phil.

"Yeah," Gino said with a laugh, "a real stereotype. Maybe I should make him loud and obnoxious." They all chuckled, and Gino continued. "There's this big, old, dilapidated farmhouse on the edge of town that everyone thinks is haunted and that's where this guy stashes the bodies. He never kills close to home and not close enough in time to spread any suspicion to him or his town, but he transports the bodies back to this spot. He's very possessive about them and wants to keep them near."

"Is the farmhouse really haunted?" asked Phil. He shot Emma a sideways glance before adding, "In the book, I mean."

"No, it's just a local legend," Gino explained, "but strong enough to keep people away until someone from out of town buys the old place and starts fixing it up. This unnerves the killer and he does everything he can to stop it, which starts unraveling his secret."

"This is very different from Gino's other books," Leroy said with enthusiasm. He shimmied his shoulders in an exaggerated shiver. "I can't wait to see where it goes."

"So how can I help you?" Emma asked again, still unclear of her role. The photo book was still on her lap, but closed now. She stroked it as Gino spoke. She still heard the low humming but it was more faint, more like a memory than a viable sound or sensation. "If the house isn't really haunted, it seems you could make up anything you want to fit the story."

"Because," Phil answered for Gino, "Gino is known for his thorough research and realism, even though his books are fiction."

Gino touched his meaty nose with an index finger and

with his other pointed at Phil. "Bingo." He stood up and paced as he continued talking. "Even though the haunting is a hoax perpetrated by the killer, I don't want my readers to know that until near the end. I want them to feel the eeriness of the place. I want them to fear the ghosts who supposedly inhabit the old farmhouse, which will not be nice like this one, of course. I want my readers to be terrified of the ghosts." He stopped and looked at Emma. "I want you, Emma, to guide me in setting that feeling so I get it right."

"Boy," said a voice from thin air, "what this guy knows about spirits would fit into a thimble and still leave room for two squirrels and their nuts."

Emma shot a look in the direction of the familiar voice but saw nothing. She turned back to Gino. "I hate to break your bubble, Gino, but spirits don't exactly operate the way you see them portrayed in movies, especially the scary ones."

Phil caught Emma's glance off into nothing and sensed that Granny was nearby. "Besides," he said to Gino, "I thought you didn't believe in ghosts."

"I don't," Gino was quick to respond, "but I think including them in the book as a red herring would be great." He came back to the sofa across from them and perched on the arm, leaning forward, hands clasped between his knees. "Listen, Emma, I mean no disrespect to you and your field, and I know a lot of people do believe in things that go bump in the night. That's why what I write has to sound plausible to them."

"You do know that your own daughter strongly believes in spirits, don't you?" Emma asked. She didn't know yet what Tanisha had mentioned to her father about being able to sometimes hear spirits, so she left it at Tanisha's belief. Emma also knew that Gino's friend Jeremiah Jones was a medium and had not told anyone but Phil and her.

"Yeah," Gino answered with a nod. "I know after that problem with the body in her apartment she got totally on board with ghosts and all, and of course her friendship with Kelly has certainly cemented it."

"Kelly is not a bad influence on your daughter," Emma said, bristling like an annoyed cat. "And I really don't think T is easily influenced by anyone."

Gino leaned back and held up his hands, palms out in defense. "I didn't mean that the way it sounded, Emma. I've come to love Kelly almost like my own, just as you two have nearly adopted my daughter. Kelly has had a very positive impact on T. She's a lot more sociable these days, believe me. And she seems to want to have a closer relationship with me. She visits often now. Before, I practically had to bribe her to come home. I attribute her change of heart to your family's influence and I'm very grateful." He lowered his hands. "As for the ghost part, T has always had one foot in that mud puddle. My grandmother Nonnie was a true believer in the spirit world and claimed she could see and hear them. When T would come to visit, she'd spend hours with Nonnie listening to her stories."

Emma exchanged sidelong looks with Phil, then said to Gino, "I believe that medium skills are most often genetic. My mother can hear and speak to them, but cannot see them. Kelly is like me, but not as developed. Three generations right in a row, and who knows how many others have been like us in our family but never realized it or told anyone." She didn't say anything further, deciding to see if her veiled suggestion sunk into Gino's head.

"Is this guy thick, or what?" snapped Granny, pacing behind the sofa Gino was sitting on. "Just come out and tell him, Emma. Tell him his daughter is a ghost buddy like you."

In response, Emma looked at Granny and gave her a slow, almost imperceptible shake of her head.

Granny stopped pacing and stood with her arms crossed in front of her, a deep frown on her fuzzy face. "Fine, but I think he needs to know, and coddling this old bear won't do him any favors."

For almost a full minute the four of them sat there, Phil and Emma on the sofa, Gino still perched on the arm of the other sofa and Leroy by the bar. Only the crackling of the fire broke the silence. Gino turned and looked at the fire. He got up without a word and went to it. Picking up the poker, he stirred the embers and logs until it went from a simple fire to a bigger, warmer blaze with sparks flying upward. After replacing the poker back into its stand, he turned to Emma. "Are you saying that Tanisha, my only child, might have inherited Nonnie's penchant for ghosts?"

Granny threw her arms straight upward. "Touchdown!"

"I don't know if I'd call it a penchant," Emma responded, trying not to scowl at Granny. "We think of it as a gift, or a skill or talent."

Gino returned to the sofa, but didn't make any move to sit. "So T can see and talk to ghosts?"

"Oh wow!" exclaimed Leroy. "Now that's *really* interesting." Gino shot his assistant a scowl and Leroy shut up and took a long drink from his glass.

"So far," Phil said, "we've only witnessed her hearing or speaking to them. And she can sense their presence."

"But it's only been scattered in her case," Emma added. "Like a static phone line. It could expand over time or might always be limited. There's no way of knowing."

Gino rubbed a large hand up and down his face as he digested the information. "For how long? And why didn't she say anything?"

"It started with that body the girls discovered," Emma told him. "As for why she's kept it from you, I don't think she has. Didn't she mention it when you came to the girls' assistance in Boston? And didn't you brush it off?" Emma tried hard to keep accusation out of her tone.

Gino crossed his arms over his powerful chest and looked up, blowing air at the ceiling in frustration. "Yeah," he admitted, "she did say something, but I thought it was just something she fantasized in the emotion and excitement of what had happened." He looked back down at Emma. "And honestly, I thought Kelly had put the idea into her head. I'm sorry."

"Gino, don't apologize to me," Emma told him. "Apologize to Tanisha, and listen to her. Whether you personally believe in spirits or not, believe in her."

A short, stout woman with a dour face and tightly curled short gray hair entered the room. She wore a light blue uniform with an apron and rubber-soled shoes, and looked to be in her late sixties or early seventies.

"Mr. Costello, dinner is ready," she announced in a thick European accent.

"Thank you, Marta," Gino said to the woman. "By the way, these are our guests, Emma Whitecastle and Phil Bowers. Emma is Kelly Whitecastle's mother."

Marta nodded at them in greeting, touching a crucifix hanging from a chain around her neck when she looked at Emma. She quickly turned her attention back to her employer. "Mrs. Costello said to please excuse her. She has a headache and has retired upstairs."

"She's not eating?" asked Gino.

"She has asked me to bring her a tray," the housekeeper told him. Seeing Gino had nothing more to ask, the woman turned and left.

"I'm sorry Vanessa won't be joining us," Gino said to Emma and Phil. "But at least now we can continue this conversation and I can tell you more about my book over dinner. Vanessa really dislikes me talking about my work over meals. She says the violence and crime bother her digestion." He paused, then added, "Unless you would rather we discuss the weather?"

"I'd love to hear more," Phil answered with the eagerness of a true fan.

"There goes fan-boy again," said Granny. Emma started to giggle, but held herself in check.

"Me, too," added Emma with a look in Granny's direction. "But I am sorry Vanessa isn't feeling well."

"I'm sure she'll be fine," he said as he directed them to the dining room.

Emma gently moved her head in the direction Granny was hovering, trying to convey to the ghost to follow them. When they were in the hallway, Emma asked where the downstairs restroom was located. Leroy directed her down a short hallway. "It's to the left, under the staircase, right before you get to that open door that leads to the kitchen."

"I'll just be a minute," she told the men and headed in the direction Leroy had indicated, hoping Granny had gotten her message and came with her.

The downstairs powder room was well appointed and roomier than she'd expected, with a sloping ceiling that followed the line of the wide staircase above it. It contained a toilet, a sink and cabinet combination, fresh towels, and scented soaps. The lower half of the room was paneled in white-painted wood with vintage wallpaper above. Under the lowest part of the sloping roof was a small two-shelf table on which was a silk flower arrangement with a few magazines on the lower shelf. Above the sink was a mirror with a silk ivy garland draped across the top and hanging down on either side. Looking around, Emma was sure at one time the room had been a very large storage area.

"Granny," she whispered into the air. No sound followed. "Granny," Emma said again, "where are you?"

"Keep your shirt on," a voice said. "I'm right here."

Emma relaxed. "Good. I was worried you didn't get the message to follow me."

"You have to admit," the ghost said, finally coming into view, "it was pretty vague."

"Did you find out anything about the ghosts hanging out here?" Emma asked.

Granny shook her head. "Only that they are busting

their buttons to talk to you." The ghost sniffed in annoyance and crossed her arms across her chest. "Apparently, I'm not good enough."

"Don't be hurt, Granny," Emma said, trying to soothe the spirit's ruffled feathers, something she'd become used to doing. "They probably just want to say what's on their mind once instead of repeating it."

"Maybe," Granny said, somewhat mollified. "They don't appear to be a chatty bunch, not even Slim, who seems to have been nominated as their mouthpiece."

"Could you tell how many there are? When we drove up, all I could make out was a few outlines, but nothing definite."

"Not sure, because they didn't show themselves much to me either. But I think I could make out four, maybe five, besides Slim."

"Did Slim tell you his real name?" Emma asked.

Granny scratched her head as she tried to remember. Granny's hair was braided and wound around her head like a crown. "I think his given name is Blaine. At least that's what one of the others called him. I didn't catch any surname."

"Good work, Granny," Emma told the helpful ghost. "I think their last name might be Brown, or at least that's the name of the family that originally owned this property. Maybe later tonight I can connect with them, or sometime tomorrow. If you do see Blaine or the others again, let them know I'm looking forward to speaking to them." She paused, then asked with some concern, "You don't think they'll just pop into our room in the night, do you?"

"You mean like I do?" The ghost put her hands on her narrow hips in challenge.

"That's exactly what I mean," Emma shot back. "Let them know I will be seeking them out when it's convenient and I'm free to talk openly with them."

"Sure, I'll be your errand girl," Granny told her. "Got nothing else to do. There's not even any dogs or cats around here to play with."

"You sound like Vanessa Costello," Emma told her.

"Yeah, isn't she a pip? Easy to see why Kelly and T don't care for her much." Granny paused. "I'm not sure about that Leroy guy. The girls like to make fun of him. Not to his face, of course. T says he's always slinking around, kissing up to Gino. She calls him slimy Sam."

"He's Gino's assistant," she told Granny. "He's paid to help Gino in any way he can." Still, Emma could see where T would get that impression of Leroy. There was something smarmy about him. He seemed too eager to please, but that helpfulness appeared underlined by sarcasm and not genuine. Maybe, she thought, he didn't really like his job and it was his way of dealing with it.

Emma had an idea. "Granny, I have a little job for you, if you want it."

The sourness on the spirit's face melted away, replaced by eagerness. "Sure."

"Go upstairs and check on Vanessa. See how she's doing and what she's doing."

"You don't trust her, do you?" asked Granny. "Me neither."

"I don't know if it's a lack of trust, but I do think something more is going on with her besides not wanting to be here."

"Did she say something suspicious? Like drop a hint that she's a criminal on the run or something like that?" Granny got excited as her overactive imagination started running in all directions.

Emma laughed softly. "No, nothing like that. I'm just getting an odd vibration from her. I actually think she's more scared than cranky. See if you can find out anything."

"On it, Chief." Granny saluted and disappeared.

· CHAPTER THREE ·

AFTER a delicious dinner, Emma, Phil, and Gino convened on the big deck in the back. Both the deck and the front porch had a selection of painted rockers. The back deck also had two patio tables and chairs. The three of them each took a rocker. Emma had brought out one of the afghans from the den and wrapped it over her jacket and around her shoulders against the cool night air. The men were wearing jackets. They gently rocked while they looked out at the dock and dark lake, which could only been seen in the night as far as the dock lights would allow. To the left, to the water, was the guesthouse. Its outside light was on, as well as the low-set solar lights lining the path to it.

"That's where Leroy is staying, isn't it?" Emma asked, pointing to the small building painted to match the house.

"Yes," Gino said. "It's a real nice studio bungalow

with a kitchenette and bath. On the other side, the side facing the lake, there's a small deck with two rockers like these. The B&B owners booked it as the honeymoon cottage. The current owners sometimes book it separately from the big house, but since it was available I booked it for Leroy as a treat. Leroy was thrilled. He's a fantastic assistant, but I know he gets tired of being around us all the time."

As if on cue, Leroy emerged from the small cottage, a backpack slung over one shoulder, and headed up a narrow path that led directly past the house to the front. He was on his cell phone. They couldn't hear what he was saying, but his voice sounded high and strained. He lowered his voice when he spotted them on the deck, then ended the call. As he passed the house, Leroy called out in a cheery voice, "I'll see you guys tomorrow."

"Leroy travels with you?" Phil asked once Leroy was out of sight.

Gino nodded. "Most of the time. He was with us in Italy this trip. In Chicago, he has his own place not far from us."

"This reminds me of Julian," Phil said as he rocked next to Emma. "We don't have a lake on the property but Emma's place has several of these big wooden rockers on the front porch. On nice evenings we like to sit out there and enjoy the peace and quiet."

Marta came out of a side door bearing a tray of mugs with fresh decaf coffee and a full carafe for refills, along with sugar and cream. There was also a large plate of fresh cookies. She placed it on a nearby side table, then handed a mug to each of them. "If you don't mind, Mr.

Costello," the maid said, "I'd like to retire for the evening."

"If Mrs. Costello doesn't need you," Gino told her, "you go right ahead. We're good out here."

"Thank you, Marta, for the delicious meal," Emma said to her. The maid cut her eyes to Emma, but didn't look at her directly. She nodded, reaching instinctively for her crucifix.

"Yes, Marta," chimed in Phil. "Thank you. That roast chicken was outstanding." Again the maid nodded.

"What will you be wanting for breakfast?" Marta asked, not focusing on anyone in particular.

"Folks," Gino said to Phil and Emma, "any special requests?"

Emma answered first. "I'm good with just cereal and fruit and I can get that for myself, so please don't fuss, Marta."

Still without looking directly at Emma, Marta said, "It's no fuss, ma'am. Not at all. Mrs. Costello has requested oatmeal with raisins and cranberries. Would that suit you?"

"I'd love that," Emma told the woman.

"Marta has this incredible homemade granola that she puts on top of the oatmeal," Gino added. "I hated the damn stuff until I had it with her granola. She brought a big baggie of it with her."

"Sounds good for me, too," added Phil.

"All right, then," Gino declared, "oatmeal all around. And, Marta, could you also whip up some of those great apple bran muffins of yours? And I'll be wanting a couple of scrambled eggs. The oatmeal is great, but doesn't hold me until lunch."

"Consider it done. The usual time?" Marta asked.

Gino turned to his guests. "You folks can sleep in as long as you like, but generally I have breakfast between eight and eight thirty."

"Emma and I are early risers," Phil said, giving Marta a smile, "so that's good for us."

Marta simply nodded again without expression and went back inside. After she was gone, Emma asked, "How long has Marta been with you?"

Gino chuckled, "Seems like forever, but it has only been three or four years. We went through quite a few live-in housekeepers for a while, then Marta came and seemed to fit our lifestyle and stuck it out. She's quiet as a mouse, efficient as hell, and an excellent cook. She's even an excellent seamstress. Our place in Chicago is quite large and she oversees the cleaning people who come in. She also coordinates the catering and staff for any entertaining Vanessa does. I don't know what we'd do without her." A deep chuckle rumbled in his large chest like a truck over a gravel road. "I joke with Vanessa that if we ever divorce, she can have anything she wants, except Marta."

Emma gave Phil a sidelong glance, then asked, "And Marta doesn't mind traveling with you?"

"Usually she doesn't travel with us, unless it's a place like this where we rent a large house and set up shop for a while. As far as I know, she doesn't have any family left. She moved to the states from Germany when she was a young woman and married a man named Peele, who passed away many years ago. I believe he was much older than her and they had no children. At least that's what the background check we did when we hired her came up with." He took a sip of his coffee. "The only time we see her animated is when T visits. She loves that girl. And she's in hog's heaven when T brings Kelly along for the occasional weekend."

"Tanisha is pretty special," added Phil. "She's become the fourth kid in our family, along with Kelly and my two boys." Phil paused, then added, "I hope you don't mind? We're not trying to replace you and Vanessa by any means."

"Not at all," Gino quickly answered. "I'm ashamed to say it, but we don't provide her with a stable family influence like you two do. The last time she really had that was when her mother was alive. And she and Vanessa don't get along that well."

Gino pulled two cigars out of the breast pocket of his shirt and held them out, across Emma. "Phil, would you like a cigar? I love smoking one on occasion after a good meal." He grinned at Emma. "You can have one, too, Emma. I know some ladies like them."

Emma crinkled her nose. "No thanks, but Phil enjoys one once in a while."

"That I do," Phil said, taking one of the offered cigars. Gino got up and offered Phil a light. After Phil was puffing away, Gino lit his own cigar and remained standing, leaning against one of the posts.

"Getting back to T," Gino said, "like I said before, since coming to know you folks, she's been a lot more keen on having a relationship with me. I thank you for that. After her mother died, I sent her off to boarding school. I was in a rocky marriage to my third wife and travelling a lot, like I do now, and couldn't make a real home for her. Then she went off to college. After, it seemed like we were strangers in an awkward dance. You know, locked together but not able to look each other in the eye. I thought I'd lost her until that incident that brought her and Kelly together. Now T makes a real effort to stay connected to me. I visit her as often as I can in Boston, just the two of us without Vanessa, and T tries to get to Chicago more than just on holidays now."

"She's a wonderful young woman," Emma said. "So bright and passionate."

Gino nodded. "Yeah, no thanks to me. She got all her good stuff from her mother. Janelle was an incredible woman." He sighed, then said in barely a whisper, "She was the love of my life, but I messed that up good. Sometimes when I look at Tanisha, I'm so reminded of Janelle that I physically ache inside."

Tanisha had once shared with Emma that Gino had wanted to marry her mother, but her mother didn't approve of his lifestyle and didn't want to be wife number three. Gino had gone on to marry someone else and had since divorced her and married Vanessa. Emma looked up but couldn't see the top floor of the house because of the roof over the deck.

Gino caught her glance. "Don't worry," he told Emma, "Vanessa is out cold from a sleeping pill. I checked on her after dinner. Besides, she wouldn't care. She hasn't said anything, but I'm pretty sure she has one foot out the marriage door, and a good part of the fault falls on me." He puffed on his cigar, then added, "That will make me a four-time loser in the matrimony department.

Is it any wonder my daughter looks to others for role models?"

"He's right about all of that," said Granny. Slowly the ghost started to materialize next to Gino. "Vanessa is sound asleep and from what I saw, they are not sharing the same room. He has the smaller suite next to her room."

Emma glanced quickly off to Gino's right, to where Granny was standing, to acknowledge the spirit, but said nothing.

"When I went up to check on her like you asked," Granny said to Emma, "she was sitting by the window, crying. Then that Marta came in with a tray of food but Vanessa hardly touched it. After just a few bites, she took a pill and went to bed." Granny shook her head. "I'm not real fond of that woman, but I feel bad for her and for Gino here. She's troubled and he seems at a loss over what to do about it."

Emma glanced at Gino and saw that he was looking out toward the lake. She turned her eyes back to Granny and mouthed, "What about the ghosts?"

"What?" Granny asked. "I didn't hear that."

Discreetly, Emma pointed at Gino, hoping that Granny picked up that she couldn't say anything out loud. Phil saw the gesture and started chuckling, knowing that Emma was trying to communicate with Granny and that Granny was being stubborn about it. He stuck the cigar between his lips to stifle the noise.

"The ghosts?" Emma mouthed again with silent emphasis on the last word.

"Oh," Granny said, spreading her arms open with enthusiasm. "You want to know about the ghosts."

Emma nodded with quick, short jerks of her chin, then stopped suddenly when Gino turned around to face them.

"I did see that Blaine again," Granny said, moving closer to Emma, "and told him you would seek them out as soon as you can but it might not be until tomorrow. I also told him not to pop in on you in your bedroom. That you hate that."

Emma smiled her thanks to the spirit. Next to her, Phil rocked and smoked, a knowing grin plastered on his face.

"Well," Gino said, straightening and putting out his cigar. "I'm going to turn in. You folks feel free to sit out here as long as you want."

"Thanks, Gino," Phil said. "I'd like to sit a few more minutes and finish my cigar." To emphasize his words, Phil happily waved the tobacco in a salute. "And thanks again for the book. I'm really looking forward over the next few days to seeing how you research and develop an idea."

"Yes," said Emma, turning her attention to Gino. "We can get to work right after breakfast."

"Sounds good," Gino confirmed.

"By the way," Emma said just before Gino went inside. "Is it safe to take a run along the road we came in on? I like to run in the morning before breakfast."

"Should be," Gino answered. "It might be pretty damp in the morning, but you shouldn't be bothered by anyone and traffic should be sparse. You may see a few animals stirring about, mostly fox and deer and small critters, but nothing dangerous. The small path by the garage that leads to the old house might be a good start. I walked it the day before yesterday. A ways past the old house, it circles back to the main road, giving you a nice loop. Just turn left when you hit the asphalt and you'll be heading in the right direction to come back here. I'm not sure how far it is exactly, but I'd say at least a two-mile loop."

"Great," she said with a smile.

· CHAPTER FOUR ·

IT was barely sunrise when Emma and Phil donned their running clothes the next morning. The big farmhouse was quiet. Before the run, Emma went into the kitchen to snag a banana for each of them from the bowl of fruit she'd spied after dinner and was surprised to see Marta already bustling around the big gleaming room.

"Good morning, Marta," Emma said to the housekeeper, who was busy chopping a hunk of beef into cubes with a meat cleaver.

Marta glanced up briefly from her work and muttered a "good morning" back, but didn't look directly at Emma. She went back to chopping the meat. Emma was sure that had Marta's hands not been occupied, she would have reached for her crucifix. "I am sorry, Mrs. Whitecastle, but coffee is not ready yet. I didn't expect you so early."

"Nothing to apologize for, Marta." Emma went to the

big fruit bowl and picked two bananas. "And please call me Emma."

"That would not be proper, Mrs. Whitecastle, and Mrs. Costello would not like it." Finished with the butchering, Marta turned her cleaver loose on a pile of peeled vegetables that included potatoes, turnips, onions, and carrots, deftly reducing them into nearly identically sized chunks.

"What are you making so early in the morning?" Emma asked.

"Beef stew for lunch. It has to cook for a long time to be good, so I must start now. Mr. Costello likes my stew." Again she glanced at Emma without making eye contact. "But don't worry, I will make a nice vegetable stew for you and Mrs. Costello. But it doesn't need to cook as long."

"That sounds wonderful," Emma told the woman with a smile.

"Would you like breakfast now?" the wary housekeeper asked. "I can start the oatmeal in a few minutes."

"No, Marta. Phil—" she started to say, then changed course to the more formal tone preferred by the housekeeper. "Mr. Bowers and I are going for a short morning run first. I just came in to get some bananas for a little energy boost. We'll eat breakfast after, with the Costellos."

"You run every morning?" the housekeeper asked in a monotone as she poured olive oil into a large, heavy stew pot on the stove and turned a flame on under it. "If so, I make sure you have bananas. Runners like that, yes?"

"Thank you, Marta. That would be very nice."

Out on the porch that faced the driveway, Emma found Phil lacing up his running shoes. She handed him a banana. They ate in silence while listening to the woods around them bustle with early morning life. By the time they were finished, daylight had broken.

"This really reminds me of Julian," Phil said when they were done, "except that the vegetation is more lush here. And I love how the house is surrounded by thick woods. At home we can't have that due to fire hazards."

"They get a lot more rain here than we do," Emma noted. "And we don't have near as many trees that turn color in the fall. Gino was right, we did come at peak fall foliage time." She took a deep breath of the damp air, redolent with earthy richness. "Funny how it smells so alive, when the leaves are really dying." The air was heavy with moisture, as Gino had said it would be. "I love morning smells and sounds," she said. "It's like a rebirth every day, no matter where you are."

"Give me your peel," Phil told her. "I think I spotted covered garbage and recycling bins at the side of the garage when we drove in yesterday." They got up and walked toward the garage. After stashing the peels in the garbage, Phil and Emma started off down the small road at a slow jog.

They hadn't gone far when they came across a clearing covered with low vegetation and wild grass. They stopped and looked around. "I'll bet this is where the old barn used to be," Phil said. He left the road and walked around the area.

"I think you're right," Emma said. "From the aerial photos in the album, it would have been right about here."

"It's almost like a small meadow," Phil noted, "but look at the tree line." He pointed to the surrounding trees, a thick mix of maple and birch. "It has an unnatural shape to it, too even and defined, and the few trees in the clearing are much younger." He moved closer to the woods. "And there are lots of small boulders in the wooded area and none in the clearing. I'm pretty sure this area was cleared on purpose."

Emma smiled as she watched Phil. Before meeting him, she knew very little about the outdoors and plants and animals, except for the potted plants and shrubs used to landscape homes. He had taught her a great deal about wildlife and nature in their time together, and she'd been a very willing student.

"Sh," Emma said sharply. Her smile dropped from her lips as she went on alert.

Phil turned to Emma and saw that her eyes were closed. She stood perfectly still, except for her breathing, which was deep and measured, her chest rising and lowering with slow deliberation. Just as he became alarmed, worried that she was having another of her out-of-body experiences, she opened her eyes. "This is definitely where the barn was," she said.

Phil returned to her. "Did you see anything?"

She shook her head. "No, but I got the same sense of humming that I had last night when I looked through the album." Before they had gone to bed, Emma had told Phil about the photos and how some of them had produced a sound, like the ghost of a long-ago tune.

Emma left the path and walked into the clearing where Phil had been. As she went deeper into the area, the humming got stronger. She held her arms straight out to her sides, as if balancing, and said into the air, "Show yourself. I know you're here. We mean you no harm."

Phil watched carefully from the dirt road but did not move closer. As always, he was ready to protect Emma.

The humming around Emma grew stronger and for a minute she thought she could see the shimmering outline of a spirit in the early morning light. "Is that you, Blaine?" she asked, remembering the name Granny thought belonged to the young farmer. She continued keeping her arms straight out. Her mentor, Milo Ravenscroft, a noted physic and medium, once told her that this posture showed unfamiliar spirits that you meant them no harm, nor were you afraid of them. It was an open, vulnerable position, and it had worked for Emma in the past. Still, she received no answer. She stayed that way, facing the unclear spirit, hoping it would show itself, when she began seeing the outline of another spirit, then another. She couldn't tell if they were male or female, only that they were near her. They came closer, then backed away, then approached again, only to retreat. Each time, the damp morning air around Emma grew chillier until goose bumps rose on her arms under the lightweight running jacket she was wearing. The shadowy spirits did this several times, coming and going, like waves on sand, until they backed away one last time and disappeared.

When Emma lowered her arms, Phil rushed to her side. "What happened?" he asked.

Emma took a few deep breaths. "There were several here. I couldn't see them clearly, just hazy outlines. I don't even know how many, but I think it was at least four or five." Emma looked around, trying to see if they were still close, but she saw and sensed nothing but a light breeze moving in the trees. "The trees branches are moving from a breeze. The presence of several spirits could cause that," she said to Phil.

Phil pointed to the woods on the other side of the road. "Those branches are moving, too," he noted, "so either it is just a breeze, or we're surrounded by a flurry of ghosts." He pointed up. "The treetops are moving, too, so my money's on a natural air current."

"Yes," Emma said, "I think our visitors are gone. Let's keep moving. I'm dying to see what, if anything, turns up at the old farmhouse."

When they were back on the road, Emma said, "Let's walk, Phil. I want to make sure I don't miss anything."

"You got it," he agreed, taking her hand.

They walked along the path at a quick pace, Emma keeping alert for any further signs of spirits. Phil looked the area over, too, but kept a close eye on Emma. They hadn't walked far when Emma brought them both to a halt. "There," she said, whispering. "Just to the left of the path is a spirit shimmer."

"Are you sure?" Phil whispered back.

Emma nodded, then said out loud. "Please show yourself. We're here to give you help, if you need it."

"Relax," came a familiar voice from their left side. "It's me."

Emma's shoulders drooped as she let out the breath she'd been holding. "It's just Granny," she said to Phil.

"*Just Granny*," the ghost parroted with indignation as she came clearly into view.

"You know what I meant, Granny," Emma said to her. "We encountered some spirits earlier on the path, but they didn't materialize or say anything. Have you seen any?"

"Not a soul," the ghost answered. "Not even that Slim guy." Emma turned to Phil and shook her head to convey Granny's answer.

"Granny," Phil asked, "have you been to the old farmhouse yet? It should be right around here, just past the clearing we passed."

"I didn't know there was one," Granny answered. "Remember, I can't go places I haven't been before unless someone I know is there to draw me."

Emma related the answer to Phil and quickly brought Granny up to speed on the photos and the humming sensation. "We're heading there now, Granny. Gino said the present owner uses it as storage."

"I checked in on Vanessa again this morning," Granny told them. "She's pretty sick."

They'd just taken a couple of steps when Emma stopped abruptly. Tethered to her by their hands, Phil stopped, too. "What do you mean, Granny?" Emma asked. "How sick?"

"Green as pea soup," the ghost reported. "She hardly touched her food last night, but she's puking like crazy this morning. And she's pale as a ghost, if you know what I mean." Granny gave Emma a knowing look.

"What?" Phil asked.

Emma let the words sink into her skull, then asked Granny, "Are you saying that Vanessa Costello is pregnant?"

"What?" Phil asked again with surprise.

"Maybe, or maybe it's just a bug," Granny said.

"Did she look pregnant, Granny?" Emma asked.

"If she is, she's not far along in her time."

"What?" Phil asked a third time, now with impatience.

Granny cocked a thumb in Phil's direction. "Better fill him in," she told Emma. "He's beginning to sound like some old fart who needs a hearing aid."

Emma turned to Phil, still unsure of what to think about this possibility herself. "Granny says that Vanessa was vomiting this morning and looks pale."

"Maybe it's food poisoning and not a pregnancy," Phil suggested. "Then again, she's probably in her forties, so a pregnancy is not out of the realm of possibility."

"True, or she could be starting menopause. Some women start earlier than others and get sick from it." Emma gave it more thought. "Gino thinks Vanessa is about to leave him. Having a baby could change everything."

"Providing she keeps it," added Phil. "She might not at her age and if the marriage is about to end. This could explain her surliness last night. She might be trying to decide what to do." He paused. "If Vanessa is pregnant, I wonder if Gino knows?"

Emma shook her head with sadness. "I'm guessing he doesn't. Vanessa was drinking before dinner last night. I only saw her slowly sipping some wine, but mixing alcohol with sleeping pills is definitely not good for a baby. If Gino knew about the pregnancy, I think he would have stopped her. Or again, she's not pregnant."

"Well," Granny said with pursed lips, "if she is pregnant, I'm thinking it might not be Gino's bun in Vanessa's oven."

Emma turned quickly to the ghost. "Why would you say that, Granny?"

"After she got sick this morning, Vanessa called someone. I couldn't tell who, but it definitely was not a business call. She was keeping her voice pretty low and sugary. She was miserable, but putting on a brave face for whoever was on the other end of the call."

"What about Gino?" Emma asked. "Did you see him?"

"He was still asleep, as far as I could tell," Granny reported. Emma passed Granny's comments along to Phil.

Phil paced back and forth on the path. "This is none of our business, Emma," he said, coming to a stop in front of her. "The Costellos are in the middle of some serious marital issues and I'm not comfortable being here. Nor am I comfortable using Granny to spy on them, even though it is convenient."

"I like the spying part," Granny said getting huffy. "Just call me double-o-ghost." Emma did not relay those words to Phil.

"Me either, Phil." Emma reached out and stroked Phil's upper arm. "Maybe I can give Gino all the background he needs today and then we can beg off the rest of the trip, say we need to get back. We could leave tomorrow and swing up to see Kelly before heading home."

"I can certainly say something came up at my office, but aren't Kelly and Tanisha coming here in a few days?" Phil asked, remembering what Leroy had told them.

"I can call Kelly," suggested Emma, "and warn her about the drama going on here so they don't make the trip. At least Kelly might be able to stay clear of it." She pulled her cell phone out of her pocket and looked at it, hesitating instead of calling. "Although it is pretty early to call." Emma thought about sending Kelly a text, but changed her mind. She wanted to talk to Kelly in person.

"Aren't you guys forgetting something?" asked Granny. Her arms were folded in disapproval and a schoolmarm scowl was carved on her face. When Emma turned her attention back to the annoyed ghost, Granny added, "The ghosts?"

"Granny," Emma said with frustration, "I can't help them if they won't show themselves."

"True," Granny replied, "but at least take the time to meet Slim and see what he has to say. You've only been here a short time."

"It's true," she said to both Phil and Granny, "we haven't been here long and I still need to help Gino with his questions. Maybe today the ghosts of Misty Hollow will tell me what they want and it will be an easy fix."

Phil snorted and grinned at Emma. "When has it ever been an easy fix, darling?"

Knowing Phil was right, Emma didn't make a comment. Instead, she started walking in the direction of the old farmhouse. "Come on," she called back over her shoulder, "we might as well finish our walk. Maybe the ghosts will show up somewhere along the way." Even though Phil couldn't see her, Granny gave him a shrug as they started off after her.

They came across the old house within a few steps and encountered no spirits along the way. The house was set back from the small road in a clearing behind a patchy stand of birches. Leading up to it was a wide paved driveway. Brush and bushes had been cleared from around the house, making it look even more forlorn. On the edge of the clearing, trees in their fall glory rustled gently in the breeze. They might have missed it, except for Emma hearing the humming as they got closer.

"See how the trees are much smaller and younger on this side?" Phil was pointing to the right. "I'll bet at one time this was all cleared out over here, joining the property around the old barn with this patch."

They stood at the beginning of the drive, staring at the old house. As Gino had told them the night before, the farmhouse had been painted outside to match the big house where they were staying. At first glance, it looked like most old but well-maintained houses in New England. But unlike the other house, there was something sad and tragic about it. The windows, both upstairs and downstairs, were adorned with painted black shutters. They were the same shutters used at the big house, but these were shut tight, not open so that daylight could come through shiny clean glass and warm the inside. The front porch was meager and only a couple of steps above the ground. Emma recognized it from the photo in the album.

"They're here," Emma said. "The ghosts are here waiting for us."

"Can you see them, Emma?" Phil asked.

She shook her head. "No, but I can feel them." She turned to Granny. "Can you see them, Granny?"

"No," Granny answered, "but their presence is very strong."

Emma let go of Phil's hand and started slowly down

the drive toward the house, pulled by the energy of the spirits. The humming stayed the same, low and foggy in the back of her brain like a fading memory, but definitely a constant. Phil and Granny followed as Emma continued down the drive past the birches. She came to a stop in front of the door and waited, hoping a spirit or two would make an appearance, but none showed.

"Mr. Brown," Emma called out in a firm but not too loud voice. "Blaine Brown. Are you here?" They waited. Emma turned to Granny and raised her brows at the ghost.

"I got nothing," Granny said to Emma's unspoken question.

Granny floated up the steps. "If you want our help, you'll have to show yourself," she said to the building and any spirits that might be lingering. "This here is Emma, my great-great-great granddaughter. She has the gift." Granny pointed at Phil. "That's Phil, her man. He can't see or hear us, but he's a friend to those on the other side just the same."

When there was no response, Emma stepped up on the porch and tried the door. It was locked. Phil had followed her up the short few steps and was trying the shutters. "They're tight as a drum, too," he reported. "Let me go around back and see if there is another entrance." Phil hopped off the porch and went around the side of the farmhouse.

Emma stepped back off the porch and studied the two-story structure. Holding her arms out, palms up, she said to the building, "Mr. Brown, you said you needed to speak with me. Here I am."

"There's one," said Granny in a loud whisper. She

pointed off to the left of the porch where a hazy image hovered.

Emma turned toward the image. "Mr. Brown? Is that you?"

"No," said a voice behind her. "I'm over here, Mrs. Whitecastle."

Both Granny and Emma turned and saw nothing, but Emma recognized the voice from the night before. "Mr. Brown," she said to the empty air, "it's very nice to meet you. Please call me Emma." She pointed to Granny and made the formal introduction.

"Folks call me Blaine," the ghost said, starting to come into view.

"Blaine," Emma said, trying out the name. She smiled at the spirit. "And who is that over on the porch? I see one spirit, though there might be more."

"That's my grandmother, Abigail Brown," Blaine told them. "A lot of my kin are around, but we're the only ones here right now." He looked toward the fuzzy image on the porch. "It's fine, Nana Abby. This is Emma Whitecastle and her kin Granny. They're here to help us." As he said the words, the image grew stronger, revealing the spirit of a woman of advanced age in a long, dark, simple dress with long sleeves. Her hair was white and worn smoothed back into a bun fastened at the back of her neck.

Emma studied the woman with curiosity. There was something very familiar about her face. She turned to Blaine. He also looked familiar. She thought about the photos back at the big house. Was Abigail one of the seated old women in the photos? Was Blaine one of the young boys? "I've seen a photograph of the Brown family taken in front of the big newer house," she told them. "You were both in it, weren't you?"

"I've seen that old photograph," Blaine said. "Nana Abby is in it, but she was much younger. I wasn't born yet."

"Then there is a striking resemblance between you and one of the boys in the picture," Emma told him. "He's seated on the steps next to a girl of about the same age."

"That would be Chester," Abigail explained in the slow, warbled voice of an old woman. "Blaine's uncle. My son. There is an uncanny likeness between them. Everyone said so from the moment Blaine was born. Blaine's father was just a babe in arms when that photo was taken."

Immediately, Emma's memory flashed to the young women holding babies in the photo. One of them must have been Abigail.

"The girl seated next to Chester is Clarissa, his twin," Abigail Brown continued. "That was taken on their eighth birthday. The entire family got together to celebrate." She sighed and her imaged faded in and out. "It was right before," she began, but didn't finish.

Blaine was about to add something when the front door to the house was yanked open with a groaning of wood. Phil stood on the threshold, dusty and pleased with himself. "I found a way in through the back," he announced. Abigail and Blaine faded as quickly as it took to snap your fingers.

"Don't go," Emma said to the air around her, both arms extended in a plea. "Blaine. Abigail. Please come back."

"It's just Phil," Granny called out to the retreating spirits, "Emma's man. He can't see or hear you, but we love him anyway."

"Oh oh," Phil said, looking about. "Did you finally make contact and I scared them off?"

"Yeah," Granny snapped, although Phil couldn't hear her, "and just when they were gettin' to the good stuff."

CHAPTER FIVE

ONCE again Emma sent out her plea. "Please come back, Blaine. I can't help you if you don't tell me what's wrong." Her voice was carried on the breeze and echoed by the trees. She stood still and Phil and Granny did the same. The three of them remained in place, Phil and Emma barely breathing as they waited for any sign that the Browns had returned.

"Over there," Granny finally whispered. She pointed over toward the end of the porch where a hazy apparition was pulsating with the regularity of a heartbeat but without any definition.

"Blaine?" Emma asked as she took a couple of slow steps forward. "Is that you?" The spirit lingered but didn't become any clearer or identify itself; then it disappeared.

"Whoever that was, he's gone." Emma took a deep breath and looked around the clearing in case any other spirits were present. She saw none. "I don't think they're going to return right away."

"I think you're right," Granny noted.

"I'm sorry," Phil told Emma. "I didn't know you'd made contact."

Emma walked up the short set of front steps to the narrow porch and the front door. "It's okay, Phil." She patted his cheek with affection. "If they want our help bad enough, they'll be back." She looked behind him into the dark old house. "Now show us what you found."

Phil, Emma, and Granny entered the shut-up old farmhouse. Overhead burned a small industrial light fixture that lit the center of the room but didn't do much to illuminate the corners.

"There is electricity in here, but it's not very bright. I found a switch by the back door when I entered, and another here." He indicated a small switch by the front door.

Emma turned to Granny. "Granny, why don't you see if you can locate Blaine or Abigail while we look around?"

"Gotcha," Granny said, then was gone.

Outside the old farmhouse might have looked like a smaller version of the larger and grander house, but inside they were nothing alike. The floors here were made of thick wooden planks, rough in texture and with almost no stain and polish. The walls were also simple and unadorned except for faded and peeling wallpaper. There was a big stone fireplace along one outside wall that was boarded up. Heavy discarded furniture had been pushed against it. Labeled boxes and other furniture were neatly stacked along the other walls spreading into the large room like fingers. Phil and Emma negotiated the small paths around them while dust and mustiness tickled their noses.

"Gino was right," noted Emma. "The owners are using this for storage. It doesn't look like any of this has been touched in years." She ran a finger along the top of an old table, cutting a path through the thick dust blanketing the heavy wood.

They moved forward. Besides the living room, the downstairs of the house was made up of a collection of smaller rooms, all neatly filed with boxes and furniture. Some were covered with dustcovers, but most were not. There was a roomy kitchen in the back with a large stone cooking hearth. In the kitchen, drop cloths covered most of the items stacked against the walls. Emma lifted one of the cloths to discover modern folding tables in both rounds and rectangles, and folding chairs in white wood.

"I'll bet these are what they use for weddings and other on-site parties," Emma said. "They're not as dusty as the other items."

Phil poked around some of the boxes. "None of it looks very old." He indicated the large back door, which he'd left open. "They must enter the place from the back where it's wider and almost level with the ground. The door was locked, but the lock wasn't fully engaged. A bit of jiggling and it popped open easily."

Off the kitchen was a narrow staircase leading to the second floor. "I wonder if they use the top floor for storage, too?" Emma stood at the bottom and peered up into the darkness. "I don't see any lights or light switches for the stairs or upper floor, though I'm sure there is one somewhere."

"It's a shame they don't fix this up and use it for a residence or even a rental," Phil said, rapping his knuckles on a wall. "It seems pretty sturdy."

"I don't see any indoor plumbing," Emma noted. "It would cost a pretty penny to put that in and rewire the place for proper lighting."

"We were very happy here," came a voice by the hearth. Emma turned toward it and saw Abigail. "A simple life, but a happy one."

Next to her was Granny. "Delivered as asked. She wasn't too far away. Now if you don't mind, I think I'm going to go back to the other house. I have a gut feeling Vanessa's about to bolt the barn."

Emma nodded to Granny, who disappeared. She then caught Phil's eyes and indicated with a slight tilt of her head the whereabouts of the other spirit. "How many of you lived here, Abigail?"

The ghost smiled. "That depends on what time you're asking after." She floated over to the door and looked out at the woods behind the house. "This house was built by my husband's father, Caleb Brown, shortly after he was married. The Brown family owned considerable property throughout the Commonwealth. My husband's grandfather wasn't rich, but better off than most. When my husband's parents married, they were given quite a bit of land in this area and named it Misty Hollow because sometimes a low fog covers the lake early in the morning. My father-in-law, Caleb, loved the land and settled here to farm and raise a family. My husband, Warren, had a brother and sister. As we all married, we all lived here, but as more children began arriving it became crowded and Caleb decided we needed a bigger house. He had the big house yonder built."

"It's a beautiful home," Emma told her. "I saw photos of it before the renovation."

"Aye, it is," Abigail agreed, "but Warren and I loved this one. Everyone moved into the big house but us. Our family stayed here but there was a lot of coming and going between the two." She smiled as she remembered. "The children often slept at one place or the other, not always in their own bed. Aunties, mothers, uncles, fathers—made no difference. We viewed the young'uns all as our own." She drifted back to the hearth. "A lot of meals were cooked here and enjoyed in this very kitchen."

Emma noted that Abigail was starting to fade. She glanced over at Phil, who was patiently leaning against the doorjamb waiting for her to update him. She turned back to the spirit, who was little more now than a collection of dust motes. "Abigail, what can I do to help you?"

"Blaine will explain. He's a good boy. Died too young in an accident and I lived too long." Even though her voice was getting weaker, there was no mistaking the sadness in it. "People should never outlive their children or grandchildren."

When Abigail was gone, Emma continued to stare at the place by the hearth, thinking about the ghost's words. Abigail had hit on a sensitive topic for any parent, but her words hit Emma in her heart firsthand. When she was little, her older brother, Paulie, had been struck by a car and killed. Emma had been nine at the time, her brother just eleven. It had been a tragic accident. Paulie had dashed into the street after a ball and the driver of the vehicle could not stop in time. Losing Paulie had nearly killed Elizabeth Miller, Emma's mother. The woman had been thrown into a depression that had taken years for her to climb out of, but even then the pallor of loss had hung over the entire family like a sticky film.

Taking a deep breath, Emma turned to Phil and quickly brought him up to date.

"Do you think they want you to look into Blaine's death?" he asked.

Emma went to the back door and stood next to Phil, but didn't look at him. Instead, she looked out at the woods behind the house, just as Abigail had. The wide-packed dirt driveway circled the house. Beyond that was a clearing of wild grass that had been recently mowed. At the edge of the clearing began the woods. It was full morning now and the earlier dampness was burning off.

"I don't think so," she answered. "Abigail said Blaine's death was an accident." She dug back through her recent conversation with Blaine and Abigail. "Just before you came out the door, they vaguely referenced something that happened shortly after the photo of the family in front of the big house was taken." She turned to look at him. "That's about all they've told me so far."

"Should we stick around and wait for Blaine?" Phil asked.

Emma shook her head. "No. Let's go back to the house. I want to look at those photos some more." She smiled at him. "And I'm hungry."

She turned back to look at the trees, some evergreen, some in the midst of turning colors. "This is really a beautiful place, Phil, but it has a feeling of tragedy hanging over it."

He stroked her arm. "Even I can feel that, darling. Melancholy hangs over this house like a second roof, in spite of what Abigail told you about them being one big happy family."

"I think they were happy here, Phil. Very happy. At least until something happened, and I'm almost positive it had nothing to do with Blaine's early death."

Phil went through the house to the front, relocked the front door, and turned out the lights. Back in the kitchen, he turned off those lights. As soon as they were both outside, Phil secured the back door.

"Something tells me we're not leaving Misty Hollow any time soon," he said to Emma as he jiggled the back door to confirm the lock was fully engaged.

Emma gave him a small smile of guilt, knowing he wanted to get away from the Costellos' domestic problems. "I feel like we need to make sure the Brown family is at peace about whatever is bothering them. Do you mind terribly?"

"Not really. It will probably only be a few days, and if we stay out of the drama between Vanessa and Gino, we should be safe enough. And the girls will be here soon. That will help."

· CHAPTER SIX ·

THEY headed back to the big house. Walking hand in hand, they took the same path back instead of making the full circle, saving it for another day. Overhead, a few scattered dark clouds moved across the sky as if in slow traffic.

"It's going to rain soon," Phil said. "I read on my phone this morning that they're expecting a storm to blow through. You can also feel it in the air." When they reached the clearing where the old barn once stood, they stopped and waited, hoping a spirit or two would show.

"They're here," Emma said to Phil in a whisper. "I can feel them."

"Here," he asked, indicating the clearing, "or following us?"

Emma stood still and closed her eyes for a minute. When she opened them, she said, still whispering,

"Maybe a bit of both. And it might not be Blaine and Abigail. I'm thinking many of the deceased Brown clan are keeping watch. Maybe many of the people in that very photo."

"This is new for you, isn't it?" Phil asked.

"New?"

"Dealing with a family of ghosts?"

Emma nodded, not sure how she felt about it. "Yes, if that's the case. I'll have to e-mail Milo and ask him if that's ever happened to him, but he's never mentioned it and it's not in any of his books."

"There you go again, darling, trailblazing." Phil squeezed her hand.

"Milo's said a lot of things have happened to me that have never happened to him."

"The student surpassing the master?" Phil suggested.

A short scoffing sound popped out of Emma. "Never in a million years could I gain the same level as Milo."

"Don't be so sure, Emma. In the few years I've known you, you've made great strides in the paranormal field." He eyed her with a mixture of concern and pride, unsure of which emotion should take priority at the moment. "Often without your consent."

A large black bird flew low overhead, winging from one tree to another. They both watched its graceful travel.

Emma shivered slightly, remembering some of her more harrowing adventures with spirits. "It's more like I have a similar but different set of skills from Milo. He told me shortly after our trip to Las Vegas that my talents seem to be more intimate. The spirits speak to him and come to him during séances, but they seek me out with more personal needs."

"You're a fixer," Phil said, glancing her way. This time it was amusement that glowed on his face like sweat.

Emma stared at Phil. "A what?"

"A fixer," Phil explained. "You know, someone they can go to in order to set things right. To solve their problems so they can move on."

Emma looked around the clearing, her eyes searching for any physical signs of the spirits she felt stirring about. "When I hear the word *fixer*," she said, not taking her eyes off the surrounding trees and shrubs, "I think of some scary guy who makes nasty problems go away for the rich and famous before the media finds out."

Phil chuckled. "You've been watching too much TV with Granny." He patted her arm and walked into the middle of the clearing, scanning the ground.

Emma followed him off the path. "What are you looking for?"

"Nothing really." He scuffed the surface of a few places with the toe of his sneaker, then walked a few paces in a straight line. "Just trying to get a feel for how big this barn was. From the size of the clearing I'm thinking it was large, and it looked to be a nice size in the photos, but you never know. Photos can be deceiving."

He toed the ground again and found another outline in the dirt to follow. He continued doing that until he was pretty sure he had an idea of the width and depth of the building. "Yep, it was pretty big. Larger than the old house, but that makes sense. Barns have to store tools, livestock, and food for the livestock."

Scratching his head, he looked around the clearing. "Emma, did you see any evidence of a well anywhere?"

"No, I didn't. Is that important?"

"Not really. I'm just curious. They would have used well water." Taking off his cap, he laughed and wiped a hand over his forehead. "What can I say? It's just the old rancher in me coming out. I love visiting old places like this and getting a sense of what it must have been like to farm or ranch without all the modern conveniences." He replaced his cap.

"Tell him the well was located between the barn and the house." Emma turned to see Blaine Brown standing next to her. "It's been locked up and out of use for many years." He pointed to the wide patch of brush separating the old farmhouse from the clearing. "It's in there. To the right a piece."

Emma gave Phil the directions to the well and he made a beeline in that direction, disappearing among the shrubs and trees.

When he was gone, Emma turned to Blaine. "I spoke with your grandmother back at the house. She seems very sad about your death. About outliving you."

The ghost nodded. "Nana Abby has suffered much loss in her life. When I died, everyone thought it might be the final blow, but it wasn't. She's the strongest person I ever met. She was the heart of the family."

"How did you die, Blaine?"

The ghost drifted over to where Phil had been scuffing the ground with his foot. "I fell to my death," he told her. "Right here. It was about this time of year and I was mending the barn roof. We'd had a lot of rain with more on the way. Pa and I didn't want to wait until the next storm passed before patching the leaks found in the last rain." Blaine looked up as if he could still see the top of the big barn. "My pa and I were almost finished when I slipped on a wet mossy spot and fell. I broke my neck when I hit the ground."

Emma briefly closed her eyes, picturing the tragedy. "Your father must have been beside himself seeing that."

"Yes, ma'am." He drifted back to stand beside her and looked directly into Emma's eyes. He had been a handsome boy in life, with wide intelligent eyes and a strong jaw. His hair had been dark and chopped short with a longer piece that fell over his forehead. His nose was narrow and straight.

"You were very young when you died." Emma resisted the urge to push the wayward lock of hair off of the ghost's face. She knew it would be useless to try, but the mother in her wanted to make the effort.

"Yes, ma'am. I had just seen my twentieth birthday." He looked away toward the brush, where they could hear Phil bumbling around. "I was courting Marjorie Woodbine over in Spencer and hoped to make her my wife the following spring." He turned again to Emma. "Can I ask you a question, Emma?"

"Of course."

Even though Blaine no longer breathed, he went through the motion of taking a deep breath before continuing. "I must have died as soon as I hit the ground because I saw my body, all crumpled up like old newsprint, where it fell. And I saw Pa. He was screaming down at my body and nearly fell hisself."

"I'm glad he didn't," she told him, trying to give him comfort during the painful memory.

"That's what was real peculiar," Blaine told her. "Next thing I know I was standing next to Pa on the roof, calling to him and trying to pull him back from the edge, but I couldn't. My hands could not grasp him. They went through him like he was made of water."

Emma gave him a smile swelled with compassion, understanding how frustrated Blaine must have been seeing his father nearly follow him in death. "Actually, your father was solid and you weren't. You'd already become a spirit. And very quickly, too." To demonstrate, she reached up in an attempt to push back the hair on his forehead. Her hand went through him as if he weren't there. "See? Like now."

"I finally understood that, but that wasn't the odd thing I was speaking of. I remember becoming so intent on saving Pa that I finally made one final grab for him and shouted his name. That time my hands did latch on to him and pull him back."

Emma's eyebrows shot skyward in surprise. She'd heard about and even witnessed spirits being able to move objects by whipping up the air currents that usually accompanied their presence, but never knew of a ghost being able to make physical contact with a living person or a solid object except in movies and on TV shows. "Are you sure you physically got hold of him?"

"Yes, ma'am." Blaine's face flooded with conviction. "For just a split second he was in my hands and I pulled him back from the edge of the roof. And he heard me holler to him. I'm sure of it." He went through the motions of another deep breath, determined to relay the memory correctly. "Then Pa sat down on the roof kind of dumbfounded and looked around up there, calling my name as if I were still there working away and not down yonder like a rag doll. I tried to put my arms around him and let him know I was there, but this time my hands and arms went right through him like butter on a summer's day, and he couldn't hear me calling his name no matter how loud I yelled it."

Emma briefly covered her face with her hands, then removed them lest Blaine misread her confusion for disbelief.

"After he collected hisself, he went down the ladder and tried to help me, but it was too late. He was totally grief-stricken and yelled for my mother, but at least he was on solid ground then and in no mortal danger."

The morning breeze kicked up a little more, carrying along with it the earthy scent of rotting leaves and the fresh scent of the country air. Overhead, the black bird darted among the trees again, this time followed by another; the birds joyfully getting in some fun before cold weather brought it to a close. Emma wrapped her arms around herself. Off in the bushes came the sound of shuffling and branches being broken, along with a few swearwords.

"Either your man is digging around like a bear, or a bear is digging around after him."

Emma laughed out loud at Blaine's comment, then turned to him, concerned. She found him grinning in the direction of the noise. "Are there bears around here?"

"Aye," he replied. "Black bears but not many. It's more likely Phil encountered a skunk."

Emma laughed again. Although Phil could handle himself very well out in the wild, she wasn't too keen on him going head-to-head with a skunk and bringing the results back to their room. Still smiling, she studied the ghost of Blaine Brown and thought that Marjorie Wood-bine would have been a lucky woman to have such a charming and decent man by her side, and how heartbroken the young woman must have been at his death.

"Is your death what you need my help on?" Emma asked him, getting back on topic. "Do you need me to explain what happened to you so you can pass over to the other side?"

He turned to her, a bit of offense edging his young face at her question. "Oh no, ma'am. I've already been there. So has Nana Abby and the rest of the family." Blaine paused, then added slowly, "At least most of them."

"What do you mean by that?" she asked. "Are some caught here on this side?"

Blaine nodded. "We believe so." His face turned stormy, his jaw set. He looked Emma directly in the eye. "Two children. Can you help us?"

"I can certainly try."

More rumbling and thrashing caused them to look in the direction of the bushes. From overgrowth emerged a ruffled but excited Phil. "Guess what I found in there?" he called to Emma.

"A hedgehog having tea and scones?" she called back.

"Very funny." While he walked in Emma's direction, Phil slapped at his pants to remove the twigs, leaves, and dirt that had stuck to him like Styrofoam packing peanuts.

"He probably found our family graveyard," Blaine told her, his voice still serious. "If he wants to visit it again, tell him to approach it from the house side. It's less overgrown there and he might even find a bit of a path left."

As Phil reached her, Emma held up a hand signaling she was not alone. "How did these children die?" she asked Blaine, returning to the real issue. "From illness?" She knew that in prior centuries a lot of children died from diseases that were now nearly eradicated, or at least had remedies.

"No, ma'am," Blaine told her, the words awl sharp. "We believe they either met with a mortal accident or . . ." he said, his voice trailing off, "or were murdered."

Emma sucked in a sharp quick breath. Phil remained silent, but put a comforting and supporting hand on her shoulder as he waited. He was used to her having conversations that didn't include him. Emma raised a hand and placed it over his, glad he was there.

"Their names are Chester and Clarissa," Blaine continued. "They're twins born to Nana Abby."

Emma remembered something Abigail had said about the time the photo was taken. "Did they go missing around their eighth birthday, shortly after that formal photograph was taken in front of the big house?"

"Yes," Blaine confirmed.

Emma paused to absorb everything she'd been told. "How did you know I was coming to Misty Hollow?" she asked. It was something she had been curious about since she'd arrived.

"I overheard Gino telling his wife and the cook about a guest coming who could talk to ghosts," Blaine explained. "We've been waiting for you."

"That's why you were all on the porch when I arrived."

"Yes, ma'am. Gino has had a few other guests come and go, but you were the only one who noticed us. We were quite excited."

Emma remained silent for a moment, then turned to face Phil. His hand slipped from her shoulder, but she took it up and held it. "Two of their children died, possibly an accident." She paused. "Or even murder. And they haven't crossed over to the other side yet. Blaine and his family want me to look into it."

Phil was quiet for a moment, then gave her hand a squeeze. He turned in the direction Emma had faced while conversing with Blaine. "Mr. Brown," he said, addressing the unseen spirit, "we'll *all* look into it. Emma, Granny, and I. We're a team." He slipped his hand out of Emma's and held it out in the direction he'd aimed his words.

The ghost of Blaine Brown looked down at the living man's hand, made of flesh and bone and blood, as his had once been. He glanced at Emma, who gave him a slight nod of encouragement. Blaine placed his own hazy hand into Phil's warm one and went through the motion of a handshake, neither feeling the physical agreement, but both sensing the bond.

Smiling, Emma turned back to Blaine. "I'll need more details about their disappearance. Let's meet again later today, maybe right after we talk with Gino about his work, or even after dinner when it's quiet."

The ghost nodded. "We're usually on the front porch in the evening. But if we're not, send your Granny for us."

· CHAPTER SEVEN ·

"I WAS about to send a search party out for you two," boomed Gino good-naturedly when they walked into the kitchen. "Marta said you left shortly after sunrise." He was sitting at the big oak table, a mug of hot coffee in front of him, a tablet in his hands. Marta was bustling around the stove. The homey scent of cinnamon, apples, stewing meat, and fresh, strong coffee hung like a warm comfy blanket over the room. Vanessa was nowhere to be seen.

"We've been exploring," Phil told him, with more than a little childlike excitement. "We got into the old farmhouse and looked around, and later I found an old graveyard. From the markers, it seems to be the Brown family plot."

Gino put down his tablet. "Wasn't the old house locked?"

"The back door wasn't shut tight," Phil explained. "A little jiggle and it popped open. But I made sure it was locked tight when we left."

"I've only walked past it," Gino noted. "What did it look like inside?"

"Crammed with boxes and old furniture," Emma told him. She took a deep breath, sucking in the delicious scent of baked goods. "The tables and chairs they use for weddings here are stored in the kitchen."

"It's a sturdy structure," added Phil. "Very well crafted. Not as large as this place by a long shot, but roomy enough."

Marta delivered a basket of fresh baked muffins to the table. "The oatmeal will be right up, along with some eggs."

"We need to wash up," Emma said, "especially Phil. He was rooting around in the bushes looking for the well and graveyard."

"I stumbled upon the graveyard by sheer luck," Phil corrected. "But Emma's right about cleaning up."

"Nonsense," Gino said with a wave of his hand. "We're not formal around here. Just hit the bathroom in the hall or wash up at the kitchen sink. You can shower after you eat."

"The eggs are almost ready," Marta added, still not looking directly at Emma. "And the apple bran muffins are best when hot."

Emma and Phil, both starving, made a quick decision. "I've got dibs on the hall bathroom," Emma said as she made a dash out the door.

A few minutes later, Emma, Phil, and Gino were chatting pleasantly over breakfast. "Marta," Emma said, after inhaling half a muffin, "these muffins are divine. Best I've ever had."

"I'm with you on that," added Phil as he slathered butter on his second half.

"Marta is a whiz at baking," Gino said as he scooped more scrambled eggs onto his plate from a covered serving bowl. "Wait until you see what she can do with rhubarb."

Emma turned to Marta with excitement. "I love rhubarb pie."

For the first time, Marta allowed a tiny smile in Emma's direction. "Unfortunately, it's out of season. But I'll be making an apple pie for tonight's dessert, if that suits you, Mrs. Whitecastle?"

"Another favorite," Emma assured her, happy that she got the housekeeper to melt a little.

Marta turned to Phil. "Mr. Bowers, can I get you some bacon or sausage?"

"No thanks, Marta," Phil told her, wallowing happily in the food on the table. "This is plenty. Any more and I'll have to head back out for that two-mile run we missed this morning."

"Is Vanessa coming down to breakfast?" Emma asked as she poured milk over her oatmeal and sprinkled it with Marta's special granola of toasted nuts, coconut, and dried cranberries.

Gino shrugged. "She said she was earlier when I checked on her, but who knows?" He turned in his chair toward the stove. "Do you know, Marta, if Mrs. Costello changed her mind about breakfast?"

Without looking directly at her employer, Marta said, "Mrs. Costello had me bring a tray up to her about twenty minutes ago."

Gino turned to look out the large window by the

kitchen table. It faced the lake, its surface slightly shimmering under the light breeze. "I'm really sorry, folks, about her unsocial behavior," he said to Phil and Emma without looking at them. "She's not always like this. Vanessa usually loves company."

"Maybe she doesn't feel well," Emma offered as an explanation, remembering what Granny had said.

Gino turned back to them. "She did look pretty pasty when I checked on her this morning, but she said she was fine."

"You don't need to apologize for me, Gino. If apologies are needed, I can do it myself."

They all turned to find Vanessa standing in the doorway between the dining room and the kitchen. Dressed in jeans, boots, a cream turtleneck sweater, and a cranberry designer jacket, she looked ready to leave the house, not join them. And just in case her attire didn't broadcast her intention, the oversized sunglasses perched on her nose sealed the deal, along with the large leather satchel grasped in one hand.

Vanessa adjusted the paisley pashmina draped across her shoulders and flipped her long blond hair back. "I'm going out for a while," she announced to the room. She turned to Emma and Phil. "I am sorry for not being a better hostess, but I'm sure you'll survive."

"Where are you going?" asked Gino, getting up from the table.

"Just out," Vanessa answered.

"That bag is your overnight bag," Gino noted. "Are you just going overnight?"

"The rest of my luggage is by the door."

"We have guests, Vanessa," Gino said, his jaw clenched

as he fought to keep his voice low and even. Emma and Phil glanced at each other before looking down at their half-eaten breakfasts in embarrassment. Marta turned toward the stove and stirred the stew as if she'd heard nothing.

"Your guests," Vanessa said, her words full of defiance. "They're always your guests, Gino. And besides, you'll be spending most of the day with her talking about stupid ghosts for your next stupid book. You won't even notice I'm gone." Vanessa turned sharply on her heel and headed for the front door to punctuate her point.

Gino followed, grabbing her by the arm, stopping her before she had gotten more than a few steps through the dining room. The Costellos moved out of sight so that those left in the kitchen couldn't see them, but they could still hear them.

"You're making a scene, Vanessa," they heard Gino hiss. "All because you're here and not in Europe where you can fawn over some pretentious literary asshole."

"At least he pays attention to me," she hissed back.

"How many times have I begged you to go away with me, just the two of us, but you always have an excuse. Even in Europe you made no time for me, even after I kept my promise to not spend any time there writing." Gino's voice was more of a growl. "Those so-called *stupid* books don't write themselves. I work hard to give you the jet-setting life you want, but it's never enough, is it? You like my fame and my fortune, but you really can't stand being with me, can you, Vanessa?"

"You're not fun anymore, Gino," Vanessa shot back. "You were once, when we were first married, but now you're just some stuffy middle-aged intellectual. Well, you may be happy being stashed away here in homespun hell, but I am not."

The sound of her boots could be heard, sharp and determined on the hardwood floor, as she continued to the front door.

"Are you coming back?" they heard Gino ask, his voice fainter as he followed her. "Or is this it? You've stomped off so often, I can't keep track."

Phil picked up his coffee and got up. He motioned to Emma and she picked up her mug and followed him out the back door to the large deck. A minute later Marta came out the back door with the coffeepot.

"I am so sorry, Mrs. Whitecastle, Mr. Bowers," she said simply as she refilled their mugs.

"You have nothing to apologize for, Marta," Phil told her. "I think we just came at a bad time." He turned to Emma. "Perhaps we should leave, darling. We can take care of that other matter from a nearby hotel or something, can't we?"

Marta was heading back into the kitchen and caught Phil's comment. Before Emma could answer, she turned quickly back to them. "Please don't go," Marta begged softly, her head bowed slightly, her fingers touching her crucifix. "It won't be good for Mr. Costello to be alone."

"He won't be alone, Marta," Emma told her with surprise. "He has you and Leroy. I think we're a distraction in the Costellos' personal issues."

"No," the housekeeper begged softly. "He needs you, good people like you, here." Her eyes, small dark raisins in her doughy face, darted between Emma and Phil in supplication while she fingered her cross. "I can't help him, and Leroy . . ." Her voice drifted off, leaving the sentence incomplete. "This has happened before, her leaving," she whispered to them with one eye on the back door. "He . . . It's no good for him. He gets very depressed. Drinks too much. His work helps. He brought you here to work, yes?" She paused, then quickly made her last plea. "Your daughters are very good, very close friends, like sisters. Mr. Costello is almost like family, yes?" Before they could blink Marta left the coffeepot on the table between their two chairs and scurried back into the kitchen.

"What do you make of that?" Emma asked Phil, her eyes wide with curiosity.

He shrugged and took a drink of his coffee. "I'm not sure, but Marta pulled out the big guns to get us to stay with that comment about Kelly and T."

"She has a good point, Phil. Gino isn't just anyone. And he's done us favors many times without any hesitation, even without knowing us personally."

Phil took another quick drink of his coffee, his eyes fastened on the lake. Morning was in full bloom, the trees surrounding the lake glorious in bronze, red, and rust plumage. The air was crisp and clean like fresh laundry. Overhead, clouds continued to move in. Rain was definitely coming later in the day. Off in the distance, they could hear a boat's motor.

"Stay or go?" Emma asked when Phil said nothing.

Phil remained silent and continued to study the lake while he sipped his coffee mechanically. Emma gave him his space, knowing this was how he was when his brain was fully engaged with a problem. He would quickly assess the details of their quandary, working out and weighing possibilities. Her ex, Grant Whitecastle, was a knee-jerk kind of guy, making decisions, often bad ones, on the fly without considering consequences or all options. When Phil made a decision or gave her his opinion, whether she agreed with him or not, she could trust the process. She sipped her coffee and waited, ignoring the chill that was starting to creep through her running clothes.

She was reaching for the coffeepot to top off her mug when Phil turned to her. "I'm inclined to at least stay today, maybe tomorrow, and see what happens. With Leroy gone and Marta clearly concerned about Gino, I think we should be here for support if he needs it. It will also give us time to see what the Brown family wants." He gestured with his free hand. "On the other hand, we could also offer to leave and see what Gino says. He might be embarrassed by what we witnessed today, though I think he's going to want us to stay. If for no other reason than to help him with his research as originally planned. He might want to bury his problems in his work." He smiled at Emma. "But if you want to go, darling, I'd be all for that, too."

"That's exactly what I was thinking, the part about staying at least today and seeing what develops. We don't want Gino to feel totally abandoned." Emma put down her coffee mug. "Although I wish Marta would stop clinging to her crucifix whenever I'm around. It makes me feel like a demon she's trying to exorcise."

"Well, sweetheart, she knows you talk to spirits and a lot of people do think such things are evil." Phil laughed. "But she can't think you're all bad. She said she'd make sure you had bananas, didn't she? And she did beg us to stay."

"Still," she said, "it makes me very self-conscious." Emma topped off Phil's mug and her own, and settled back in her chair, holding her hot mug between her hands. "But she sure makes great coffee. And granola."

"And muffins," Phil added, raising his mug in salute. "We might want to stay just for the food."

They spent another minute in comfortable silence, then Phil asked, "Do you think Vanessa is gone for good?"

Emma took her turn at studying the lake while she gave the question thought. "I think it's safe to say she won't be returning to this place at all."

"You got that right!" came a voice by the railing.

Emma glanced toward the kitchen door to make sure Marta wasn't nearby or listening. "What can you tell us, Granny?" she whispered as the ghost came into view.

"Vanessa packed up her duds and took off," the ghost reported, "but I think you already know that."

"We were there when she walked out," Emma told her, still keeping her voice down. "Did you find out anything new?"

Phil got up and went to the railing, leaning against it near the place Emma had directed her question. Granny looked him over, then smiled at Emma. "I like the way the cowboy here is always thinking and always has your back."

"Me, too, Granny." Emma said, smiling at Phil.

"When I got back here," Granny reported, "Vanessa had already showered and put on her face." The ghost sniffed. "In my opinion, she wears way too much of that goo. She's more attractive without it."

"What's Granny saying?" Phil asked.

"That Vanessa wears too much makeup," Emma reported.

"That's Granny," Phil said with a low chuckle. "Always on topic."

Granny glared at Phil. "I have a right to my opinion, especially if you want my help."

Phil stared straight ahead at Emma. "My comment didn't go over very well, did it?"

"Do I really have to answer that?" Emma asked him with a grin. She shifted only her eyes to Granny, who was just to the right of where Phil stood, acting as a decoy in the event someone came out of the house. "What happened after that, Granny?"

"She called someone," Granny reported, "but I don't think Vanessa got an answer because she left a message for them to call her back, then hung up right away and got dressed."

"Did they call her back?"

"Someone did a few minutes later," Granny reported. "I'm not sure if it was the same person, but I think it was. The call started all sweet, like the earlier one, but then it turned serious and Vanessa got very upset." Granny paced along the deck as she tried to remember, then came to stand close to Emma.

"But the earlier call," Emma said after considering Granny's words, "was there anything in that call to make you think there were problems?"

"No, none at all," the ghost said. "But in this one Vanessa kept asking when she was going to see him again and I don't think she liked the answer because she started whining about how much she needed to see him and how it was important. The other person must have stuck to their guns, because that's when Vanessa brought up the baby."

"Ah, so she is pregnant," Emma said with a slight nod of her head.

"Yep. And I'm betting it's the dude's on the phone. It was right after that that the call ended. Kind of sounded like it was unresolved." Granny floated back and forth as she pieced together what had happened. "But there's something else," the ghost said. "Right after that call, Vanessa called someone else. This time there was no gooey talk or pleading. She was all business and said they needed to meet."

Suppressing her urge to ask Granny more, Emma shot a look toward the kitchen door. She didn't see any signs of Marta. Getting up, she went to the kitchen door, opened it, and poked her head inside. Marta was sitting at the table peeling apples.

"Marta," Emma said, not going inside. "Mr. Bowers and I will be taking another walk before we clean up, this time down by the lake. Would you please tell Mr. Costello that we'll see him in the library in about an hour and a half to two hours if he feels like working on his research?"

"Certainly," the housekeeper said, barely looking up from her work. "So you're staying, then?"

"For now, yes."

This time Marta did look up and this time she didn't finger her crucifix. Emma attributed that to one hand holding a paring knife and the other a juicy half-peeled apple. "Good, Mrs. Whitecastle. I'm very happy to hear that, and I'm sure Mr. Costello will be, too." She looked relieved.

Emma and Phil left the deck and headed down a narrow walkway across the large lawn toward the lake. They walked hand in hand while Emma brought Phil up to date. Granny floated alongside them.

"Granny," Phil asked as they walked, "do you think Vanessa went off to meet up with the baby's daddy or whoever was on the second call she made?"

Emma reported to Phil after Granny answered. "Granny couldn't hear the other side of the calls and didn't hear of any set plans."

"Do you think there are really two different people here?" Phil asked. "It might be the same person but Vanessa dealing with them in two different ways—all sappy and vulnerable the first time and with anger the second time."

"That's a good possibility," Emma agreed.

They had reached the dock and walked out onto it, coming to a stop near the end where there was a bench. They sat down and Phil put his arm around Emma's shoulders and pulled her close against the chilly air. Granny hovered nearby.

"The Costellos' domestic problems are not why we're here," Phil reminded them. "The less we know or are involved, the better."

"I agree," Emma said, patting Phil's knee. "We'll stay for moral support and to help Gino with the book. But no more prying." She aimed her last comment at Granny.

"Hey, you asked me to spy on her," the ghost pointed out.

"Yes," Emma admitted, "I did ask you to look in on Vanessa, but no more. Okay? As Phil pointed out, this isn't why we're here. We'll mind our own business, help Gino with his book, and be on our way."

"What about the Browns?" Granny asked. "Are we keeping our noses out of that, too?"

"That reminds me, Granny," Emma told her, "we had

a long talk with both Abigail and Blaine and got more information. Basically, many years ago, two of the Brown children went missing, and the family doesn't think the children have crossed over yet. They want me to try and locate them."

"You mean they were murdered?" the ghost asked, her eyes as big as dinner plates.

"They're not sure. Blaine said if they weren't, then they met with a fatal accident. Either way, the family wants to reunite with them on the other side."

A motorboat sped past them on the lake, its occupants giving them friendly waves. Phil waved back. "What other information did Blaine give you?" he asked.

"All I know so far," Emma said to both Phil and Granny, "is that the missing children were eight-year-old twins. Their names were Chester and Clarissa. They are Abigail's children and Blaine's aunt and uncle." She looked at Granny. "I told Blaine that we'll talk again later, maybe after dinner."

Granny put a hand to her mouth a moment and shut her eyes tight. "Oh my," she murmured. "That poor Abigail lost two of her children at such a young age." She opened her eyes and fixed them hard on Emma. "We must help them, Emma."

"We will, Granny," Emma assured the ghost with tenderness. As cranky as Granny could get, she was also very empathetic toward both the living and dead, especially when it came to children. "It won't be easy to track down what happened to those children all those years ago, but we'll do as much as we can. I promise." She smiled at Granny and Granny gave her a small smile back.

"Isn't it unusual for a family to be hanging out together on the other side?" asked Phil. "I mean none of them died at the same time. Some died decades apart."

"Hard to say," Emma told him. "Granny and Jacob found each other after death."

"But we didn't pass all that apart in time," Granny added.

"That's true, Granny," confirmed Emma. "You and your husband died a short time apart, but did you find him on the other side or did you connect again at the homestead?"

The ghost gave it some thought. "It was at the homestead. I don't see him when he disappears from there, only when we meet up in a common place. And Jacob doesn't travel around like I do. He's content to stay put near your house in Julian." Emma had built her home on Granny and Jacob's old homestead in Julian after Phil's family had deeded it back to her. She often saw the ghost of her great-great-great-grandfather sitting peacefully on her big porch.

After Emma relayed Granny's comments, Phil said, "I'll bet it's this place and the old house that pulls the Brown family back together. They were a tight-knit family, no matter which generation they came from. But they all had this place in common."

"I'll bet you're right, Phil," Emma said. "I wonder if there are any of their descendants left in the area. We'll have to ask Gino."

"Couldn't hurt," he agreed. "They might know some family history to tell us that might help." He studied the lake. "But I wonder why the spirits of the children didn't return here to join them."

Granny narrowed her eyes. "Maybe they have unfinished business, like making sure whoever murdered them got caught."

"Could be, Granny," agreed Emma. "Maybe the children are caught here, waiting for justice. Or maybe their spirits are simply confused. We'll have to find out what they were doing the day they disappeared."

Emma stood up and stretched. "I'm ready for a hot shower." She turned to Phil and gave him a mischievous grin. "How about you?"

Phil laughed. "That shower did look large enough for two, didn't it?"

"Barely," she said, holding out a hand to him. "But we'll make it work."

Granny shook her head and started to disappear. "You two are worse than a couple of jackrabbits. And at your age!"

· CHAPTER EIGHT ·

ONCE they were freshly showered and dressed, Emma and Phil made their way back downstairs to the library. Granny had taken off to recharge her energy. They found Gino seated at the big oak desk poring over some papers. On the desk was a laptop. The French doors to the deck were partially open, letting in the autumn air. Gino lifted a haggard face their way when he heard their footsteps and plastered a smile on his face.

"Have a seat and let's get to work," he said with an eagerness that seemed only partially real. He indicated a couple of chairs he'd pulled up to the desk.

"I'll let you two work," Phil said. "I'm going to make myself comfy and read this wonderful book." He held up the book Gino had given him the night before.

In spite of his words, Phil made no move toward another seat and Emma didn't take one of the ones at the desk.

Instead they looked at each other, wondering if they should say something to their host about the morning's activities.

"Is it too chilly with the doors open?" Gino asked.

Emma turned to him. "No, not at all."

"There's a rainstorm moving in later," Gino said. "I thought it would be nice to air the place out a bit before it gets here."

Phil was about to say something, but Gino stopped him. "Let's address the elephant in the room," he said, his eyes settling first on Phil, then Emma. "Or should I say the missing elephant in the room?"

Phil stepped closer to the desk. "Gino, Emma and I don't want to be in the way of your personal life, so if you'd like us to leave, we'd certainly understand under the circumstances."

Gino waved off Phil's concerns with a large hand. "No. No. Please stay. This isn't the first time Vanessa has left in a huff, although it might be the last. As I told you both last night, I've had the feeling she's had one foot out the door awhile now."

Emma exchanged another glance with Phil, wondering if Vanessa told Gino about the baby. "So she won't be coming back today?" she asked.

"Not today for sure," Gino answered. He sounded exhausted though it wasn't even noon yet. "Maybe not ever. Who knows." He put the stack of papers down. "You know, I do need a favor, if you don't mind. I was going to wait until Leroy came back with his car. But since I'm not sure when he'll be back, maybe I should take care of this now and we can tackle this work after lunch."

"What do you need?" Phil asked. "Whatever it is, we'll be happy to help."

"Even with murdering my philandering wife?" Gino asked without hesitation.

"Ah," Phil stammered. Emma stood next to him, speechless.

Gino laughed but there was no joy in the sound. "Don't worry, folks. I may write about crime and murder, but to date I've never even considered such a thing." He stood up. "How do you feel about giving me a lift into Worcester? Vanessa took the SUV we leased and Leroy has the sedan, so I'm stuck. With Leroy and Marta needing occasional wheels, we need two vehicles."

"Sure," Phil said. "Whatever you need, except for that murder thing." The three of them shared a nervous chuckle.

"I called the car rental place earlier and reserved another SUV for tomorrow," Gino told them. He pulled out his cell phone. "I'll call back and see if they have one for today, but I'm pretty sure they do. At this rate, I'm going to be their best customer." He made the call while Emma dashed upstairs to grab their jackets. When she came back down, Phil and Gino were waiting by the door.

"All systems go," Gino said, opening the front door for them. "Maybe we can go over some of my ideas for the book in the car."

As Emma walked out the door, she spied Abigail Brown sitting in one of the rockers on the front porch. Seated next to her was the spirit of a middle-aged man with dark hair and a full beard. Abigail smiled at Emma. "This is my husband Warren. He passed well before me. I told him that you're going to help us." Emma remained silent, but gave the ghosts a nod of understanding.

Phil plugged the address for the car rental agency into the GPS of their rental, a beige, midsized, four-door sedan. Because he was such a large man, Emma insisted that Gino take the passenger's seat while she sat in back. She'd positioned herself behind Phil so she could see Gino while speaking with him.

"According to the GPS," Phil said as he pulled the car out of the drive and onto the road, "it should take about forty minutes or so to get there."

"Sounds about right," said Gino. "It's mostly small roads, no major highways, between here and there."

"What made you pick this area for the book?" Phil asked.

Gino thought about the question, then answered, "I'm not sure, except that I've always liked New England and its history. It's so Americana, Massachusetts being one of the first colonies and all. This is where the country started, right over on the coast at Plymouth Rock." He pointed out the window at the thick woods, interrupted every now and then by a clearing with a home or a small road. "Throughout these woods you can often find evidence of the early settlers in bits of old stone fences or foundations. There are even a few abandoned villages dotting New England."

"Why abandoned?" Emma asked.

"Various reasons," Gino answered. "Back in the 1700s, a bad illness or influenza could decimate a small village. Those that survived often left, afraid the place was cursed. Or maybe a fire broke out and burned the settlement to the ground, or a severe flood washed it away." He turned to look at Emma. "Many crop failures sent farmers looking elsewhere to make a living."

"I could see that," Phil said. "Times were hard back then and villages not very close together."

They rode along a few miles before Emma asked, "So which came first, the story about the serial killer or the location?"

"I had the story in mind first," Gino told her, glancing back at her. "When I thought about the setting, I remembered reading about abandoned villages and homesteads and decided rural Massachusetts would be just the place." He chuckled. "Besides, I hadn't written anything about this area yet."

Emma looked out the window. "It certainly is lovely here; even the more populated areas."

"And very different from either California or Chicago, huh?" asked Gino with a grin.

Phil and Emma nodded in agreement as the road entered the center of a small, active town. "But not that different," Phil noted, pointing out a couple of chain restaurants.

"So tell me," Emma began, "how do you imagine the paranormal coming into your book?"

Gino gave her question solid thought before answering. "Like I said last night, I see it as more of a diversion to keep the killer from being found out. The place where he stashes his victims is rumored to be haunted and he helps fan those rumors to keep people away."

"And as I said last night," Emma told Gino firmly, "most ghosts do not scare people in the fashion usually seen in movies or on TV."

"So, in your opinion," pressed Gino, "they are not scary?"

"I've encountered some that have been quite intimidating, but they can't harm a living person physically. They don't have that power. They are limited in what they can do." When Gino looked at her, puzzled, she added, "For example, say a ghost was in this car and angry enough to want to hit you with a baseball bat."

Gino laughed. "That must be the ghost of Steve Monahan, a kid I knew in college. I heard he died a few years ago. I took his girl away from him and he did come at me with a bat. Fortunately, some other guys got him under control before he could crack my skull open."

Phil glanced over and laughed. "See, Emma must have gotten a bead on something like that."

Gino wasn't buying it. "I doubt it. Steve and I made up eventually, and I'm sure there are others who've wanted to take a bat to me, though he's the only one who actually tried."

"Well, for this example," Emma continued, "let's say the ghost of Steve Monahan was about to take a bat to your head. First of all, a bat is a solid object and spirits are not. Steve would not be able to hold it or even pick it up as a ghost. If he tried, his hands would go right through it. Same thing if he tried to hit you with his fists. They would simply go through you like you were nothing but air. In this case, you'd be solid, but Steve would not be. The most you might feel is a bit of air circulating from his efforts." She thought about what Blaine had said about being able to pull his father back from the edge of the barn roof. "There might be incidences when a ghost can feel or touch a living person, but it would be very rare and then only for an instant. There'd never be enough contact time for a ghost to grab a weapon and wield it or to physically hit someone."

"I've often heard," Gino said, truly interested, "that people claim there is a cold breeze when spirits are around. Is that true and why is that?"

"Spirits need energy in order to manifest," she explained. "Heat is energy. When they are present they absorb the heat, leaving behind cooler air. One ghost present might not make a significant difference, but several definitely can." She paused. "Of course, this is a very simplified explanation."

Gino digested the information. "So ghosts throwing things around a room or moving tables and chairs is malarkey?"

"Pretty much," she answered. "Although I have witnessed ghosts moving in such a quick manner that the air around them moves, creating an air current. It might move paper or curtains, lightweight things like that, but never anything with any serious weight, like a bat."

"Unless the ghost inhabited a live body," added Phil.

Emma nodded. "That's true. Sometimes spirits can overtake a living person and use his or her body to communicate."

"Like with your pal Milo Ravenscroft?" asked Gino. "I've done some reading on his experiences. Interesting guy."

"Yes, he is," responded Phil. "He's also a great guy and married to Emma's best friend."

"I didn't realize that," Gino said. "I thought he was just Emma's mentor." He glanced from Phil back to Emma.

"He is, but that's how he met Tracy," Phil told him.

"What Milo does is called channeling," Emma explained. "Milo can and does channel spirits. He's quite talented in calling them from the other side. I don't have that gift. The ghosts I meet usually come to me or I encounter them somehow by chance. Although I have channeled a few." She took a deep breath and plunged on. "And sometimes, though it's rare, a ghost can inhabit a body and try to influence the host individual to do its bidding."

Fascinated, Gino twisted around so far to look at Emma that his seat belt nearly choked him. "Have you ever seen that yourself?"

"Yes," she answered truthfully, remembering several incidents. "A while back we encountered a vengeful ghost that was manipulating people into killing themselves."

"Damn!" cried Gino.

"Yes, it was quite terrifying, but it's not that easy. A living person is much stronger mentally and emotionally and usually fights off the urges to do wrong without even realizing what is happening to them. But like I said, it's fairly rare to my knowledge, even in Milo's experience."

"There's a premise for you," Phil said to Gino as he made a turn into the parking lot of the car rental agency. "You can have the killer be possessed by a ghost. Maybe the ghost does live at the old farmhouse and is making the killer bring the bodies back as sacrifices." He parked near the front of the rental office and killed the engine.

"Jeez, Phil," Gino said with a shake of his head and a short laugh. "That's pretty creepy and a very good premise. Maybe you should take up writing novels. You obviously have the imagination for it." He got out of the car and Emma got out of the back to make the transition to the front passenger seat.

"We'll wait, Gino," she told him as he held the door open for her to enter. "Just to make sure the rental goes off without a hitch."

"Okay," he said, glancing back over his shoulder at the small office. "As soon as I know everything's a go,

I'll wave to you so you can head back to the house or do some sightseeing. I think I've picked your brain enough until after lunch."

While they waited, Phil said to Emma, "You gave him a good basic tutorial on ghosts."

"Yes, but I don't think it was what he wanted."

"Nonsense, it was clear Gino was very interested in what you were saying."

Emma shrugged, watching the door of the office. "Maybe, but the reality of spirits doesn't have all the creepy bells and whistles I think he was hoping to put into his book." She turned to Phil, amusement clear on her face. "But what was all that about ghosts asking for sacrifices from a murderer?"

"You didn't like it?" he asked with a laugh.

"Not particularly, but it *would* make a great book or movie."

"You don't think it could happen?" Phil looked at her, waiting for her to consider the question.

She thought about that and didn't like what crossed her mind. "On the contrary, if a strong spirit took over a very weak-minded individual, it might."

Phil tapped her knee. "There's Gino, but he's not waving, he's walking over. Maybe they didn't have the rental they promised."

When he got to the car, Gino leaned on the open window ledge on Emma's side. "Hey, I got to thinking. Our breakfast was interrupted and I'm getting hungry. You guys like fried seafood? You know, New England has the best." Before they could answer, he added, "There's a place not far from Misty Hollow that's fantastic. A buddy of mine told me about it. I went there twice last week, it's so good. Why don't we have lunch there and continue this conversation?"

"What about Marta?" Emma asked. "She was making stews for our lunch."

"Don't worry about that." Gino waved off her concern with a hand. "The stew can be reheated for our dinner. Marta will probably be thrilled not to have to cook another meal today. I'll give her a call and let her know. I'll sweeten the pot by giving her the rest of the day off. We can reheat the food ourselves."

Emma turned to Phil, who said to her with a grin before she said anything, "You know how *I* feel about fried seafood, darling."

She twitched her nose at Phil in annoyance before turning back to Gino. "Give us the address and we'll meet you there."

· CHAPTER NINE ·

THE place was called simply Frank's. It sat on the northwest corner of an intersection on the far edge of the village of Whitefield. Whitefield was close to Misty Hollow, but in the opposite direction from Worcester. The building was painted brick red, trimmed in black and white, and was decorated with weathered fishing equipment such as nets, traps, and buoys. It was obvious from looking at it that it had started life as a shack, the original building distinct though attached to various additions made over the years. In the front was a sizeable patio. A large parking lot took up its right-hand side and curved toward the back. It seemed to be the most happening business on the road, with most of the other buildings appearing to be light industry or retail stores catering to rural life.

Even though it wasn't quite noon, the place was busy.

They stepped through the large door and were immediately hit with the warm thick smell of frying oil and fish. The menu was posted on the wall behind the counter in large black letters painted on a long white particleboard that stretched the length of the counter.

"This will be easier," Gino said, handing Emma and Phil paper tri-fold take-out menus he pulled from a holder on the counter. Once they settled on their food, Phil sent Gino and Emma to find seats while he stood in line to place their orders.

"Over here, Phil," Gino called to him when he came out of the order area holding a tray with napkins, thick plastic plates, a ceramic mug, two plastic glasses, and metal utensils. They were seated at a picnic table inside, next to a window.

"Too chilly to sit outside?" Phil asked with surprise.

Emma pointed out the window. "Too wet." Clouds had been clustering when they left the car rental place and now it was raining. It wasn't a hard rain, but it was wet enough to make the few diners at the picnic tables outside dash for the dining room while they crouched over their food to keep it dry.

"I would think it would be lovely to sit on the porch at the house and watch the rain on the lake," Emma said as she distributed the items from the tray.

"It is," Gino told her. "We've had a couple of small rainstorms since we've been here. The last one was in the evening. There's nothing more peaceful than a nice fire, a good book, a glass of brandy, and the sound of rain." He stood up, took the mug, and indicated the beverage dispensers near the trash and condiment counter. "This is a serve yourself place on the drinks."

Emma picked up a fork. "I can't remember the last time I saw real plates and silverware at a place like this."

Gino chuckled. "I said the same thing when I first came here. Frank, the owner, told me he tries to be as green as possible. Said he'd rather hire some kids to wash dishes than fill landfills."

Phil turned to Emma. "Iced tea?" She nodded and Phil took the two tall glasses and followed Gino.

Emma turned her face back to the patio and watched the rain splattering on the now empty tables. Spotting something odd, she did a double take and refocused her attention, not on the rain but through it. A young girl was on the patio, twirling in the rain, her arms outstretched, her young face turned upward. Her long brown hair wasn't getting wet, nor did her sneakered feet stir puddles. She wore jeans and a short-sleeved shirt and was transparent. She was a ghost. Emma's heart sank. The child had died young, maybe when she was only ten or eleven. The ghosts of children always saddened Emma. The Brown children were young when they disappeared. This girl, however, was contemporary, and from her clothing, especially the bright yellow cartoon character on the front of her shirt, Emma guessed she had not died long ago. Emma tapped lightly on the window. The girl didn't hear her, so she tapped again, a little harder. This time the girl stopped spinning and stared at Emma. Emma smiled at her and the girl smiled back and waved.

"Whatcha looking at?" Phil asked, returning with their drinks. Gino wasn't with him.

"Where's Gino?"

"He went to the men's room while they brewed a fresh pot of coffee. Why?"

Emma looked past Phil to make sure Gino wasn't there, then turned back to the window. The child was gone. "The spirit of a little girl was out there just now."

"Not one of the Browns, I take it," Phil said as he took his seat next to her.

Emma shook her head. "No, a modern girl. I wonder how she died. It couldn't have been very long ago judging from her clothing."

"I couldn't swim," a small voice answered.

Emma turned and looked toward the sound. The ghost of the girl was standing at their table, next to Phil. She was a cute little thing with an upturned nose and round cheeks. "You drowned?" Emma asked softly, keeping her voice low.

The girl nodded. "I fell into the pond. My brother ran to get help, but it didn't come in time." She turned her head downward. "We weren't allowed to be there alone, but we sneaked away when Grammy was on the phone."

Emma could only imagine the grief and guilt of the poor grandmother who'd been watching them. "What's your name, sweetheart?"

"Mazie," the child answered. "Mazie Elizabeth."

"Do you remember when you drowned?" Emma asked, her voice barely a whisper.

The child gave it some thought, then shrugged. She had no clue and it didn't surprise Emma. Spirits often lost track of time after they died, and a child more so.

A middle-aged man with thick gray hair and a pronounced belly under his full apron approached their table laden with their food order. He placed large red plastic baskets of various fried fish and seafood, fries, and onion rings, along with small tubs of coleslaw, on the table in front of them. "Is there anything else I can get you folks?"

"This will be great for starters," Phil answered, eager to send the man off so Emma could continue her chat with the ghost. "Thanks."

"If you have room when you're done," the man said, "we have homemade apple pie and apple crisp. The apples come from our own orchard."

Mazie squealed with glee at the sight of the man. "That's my Grandpa Frank."

After Frank left, Emma caught site of Gino. He was talking to some people by the beverage counter. She quickly turned to the child. "Mazie, have you been to the other side yet?"

"You mean with the other dead people?" She asked the question naturally, as if asking about a favorite ice cream. "Yes."

"Sure," Mazie answered. "But sometimes I come here to see Grandpa Frank. And sometimes I visit Grammy, but mostly Mommy and Daddy and Christopher. That's my brother." She scrunched her hazy brows together. "That's okay, isn't it?"

Emma smiled. "Of course it is, sweetheart. Come and visit them as much as you like. It helps them to not be so lonely." Emma paused, still keeping an eye on Gino, who looked to be holding court on the other side of the dining room. Phil had turned so it looked like she was speaking to him instead of into thin air. It was a practice he'd perfected over time.

"Mazie," Emma asked, "have you talked to other people like me? You know, living people who can see you?"

Again the child gave the question serious thought. "A couple of times. There's the lady who came to the pond after I died."

"She lives here in Whitefield?"

Mazie nodded. "Mrs. Monroe. Everyone says she's a witch, but she seems nice to me. She's old but not ugly like witches in stories."

"What did she do when she came to the pond?"

"She told me not to be afraid and that I should go with them."

"Them?" Emma asked, confused. "With Mrs. Monroe?"

Phil had an arm across the back of Emma's chair and slightly tapped her shoulder, signaling her. She looked at him and he jerked his chin in the direction of the beverages. Emma looked up and saw Gino shaking hands with the men he had been speaking with, taking his leave.

Mazie shook her head, not paying attention to Emma or Phil. "No, there were others. Like me. Mrs. Monroe said to go with them, so I did."

Emma went on alert with a possibility. "Were these others children? Like maybe a brother and sister?"

Mazie shook her head at the question. "No, just a couple of grown-ups who were like me. You know, dead already."

"Where does Mrs. Monroe live, Mazie?" Emma said in a rush as Gino started toward them. "Do you know?"

"Sure." The child's face brightened. "She lives in the yellow house on Ash Street, across from the library. The one with the red door. Everyone knows that."

"Thank you, Mazie," Emma whispered quickly. "It was nice to meet you."

Gino reached the table just as Mazie drifted off toward the kitchen and her grandfather. Gino took his seat, placing his cup, which was now full of steaming hot coffee, on the table. "Good. The food's here. But you shouldn't have waited on my account. Fried food isn't good cold."

Phil gave Emma a knowing smile, then said to Gino, "No problem. We kept ourselves amused. And the food just got here. Frank delivered it himself."

"Dig in everyone," Gino said as he picked up a fried clam and popped it into his mouth.

Instead of getting separate meals, Phil had ordered them a family-style feast, doubling up on some of the seafood. They began filling their plastic plates with the food. Emma piled her plate high. Taking her first bite of a large sea scallop, she closed her eyes and softly moaned. She heard chuckling. She opened her eyes and found Gino watching her with amusement. Next to her, Phil was barely containing laughter. He pointed his fork at Emma and said to Gino, "Wait until she really gets going."

Emma finished chewing and wiped her mouth with a paper napkin. "What? You two have never seen a woman enjoy her meal before?"

"Gino," Phil said, "get what you want now of the food, because in ten minutes this table will look like a plague of locusts hit it."

Gino bit into a large onion ring and watched Phil and Emma exchange looks while he chewed. Phil's was one of affection and amusement. Emma looked ready to push Phil off the bench, but then returned to her food, eating two plump clams one after the other. He next compared the plates of his dining companions. Phil's was filled, but Emma's was overflowing.

"I thought you were the one who loved fried seafood, Phil," Gino noted.

"That was merely a ruse," Phil answered. "Emma has a fried food addiction, especially shellfish. We're trying to find a program for her."

Emma, her mouth full, nudged Phil with some force. "Quit talking about me like I'm not here."

He laughed and ignored her. "Notice, Gino, that she didn't touch the coleslaw or the rolls, just the fried food."

In defiance, Emma shoved an entire onion ring into her mouth, quickly followed by another, with a clam chaser.

"Vanessa," Gino noted with interest, "won't touch fried food. She was with me the first time I came to Frank's and she hated it, even though she had a nice piece of grilled halibut. I think the place is too down-to-earth for her." He ate another clam. "So what's your secret, Emma?" he asked after swallowing. "How do you keep so slim if you eat like this? Especially if you're on TV. The camera adds weight."

Emma tried to answer, but her mouth was too full. She kept chewing.

Shaking his head and smiling, Phil answered for her. "Exercise. Lots of it. Plus it's her only food vice. Might even be her only vice, except for me." The men laughed. "Whenever we visit Kelly in Boston," Phil continued, "I have to take Emma to one of these local places so she can get her fix of greasy clams and scallops. No fancy restaurants, just fish shacks like this."

"And onion rings," Emma said, still chewing.

"Oh yeah, can't forget the onion rings." Phil chuckled again. "Gino, I thought this woman was too perfect to be real until I saw her go after my aunt Susan's fried shrimp and corn fritters like a starving field hand." At the mention of the shrimp and fritters, Emma gave an enthusiastic thumbs-up and washed her food down with iced tea.

"Yep," Phil said, giving Emma a wink. "That's when I really fell in love."

"I should be embarrassed," Emma said, laughing at herself as she wiped her mouth, "but I'm not. I only scarf fried fish and seafood down like this a couple times a year."

"And onion rings," Phil reminded her.

"God, yes." She looked Gino in the eye and whispered, "Onion rings are my kryptonite. I can't get them down fast enough. Especially big, fat, beer-battered ones like these." She plucked another onion ring from her plate and held it aloft to study its crispy brown goodness.

"Do onion rings take away your ghostly superpowers?" Gino stuck a scallop with his fork.

"Fortunately not," she said with mock relief. She bit the onion ring in half.

Phil laughed again. "But I pity the ghost that gets between Emma and her fried food."

They had made a serious dent in the feast when Emma stopped for a breather. "Gino, since we came in separate cars, do you mind if Phil and I drive around the village before heading back?" Phil looked at her with surprise, but said nothing.

Gino shrugged. "Not much to see around here, but no problem."

"Are you sure it won't interfere with the research for your book?" she asked. "That is why we're here."

Gino waved off her concerns. "You've already given me a lot to think about, so go, have some fun. We can talk tonight before or after dinner if I think of more questions."

"Will you be okay?" Emma asked. "You know, considering Vanessa."

"I'll be fine," Gino assured them. "As I said, it wasn't totally unexpected and not the first time this has happened." He drained his coffee and left to get a refill.

"What did you have in mind?" Phil asked once Gino was out of earshot.

"There's a woman here in the village by the name of Mrs. Monroe. Mazie told me about her. Seems she's a medium. I'd like to talk to her. She helped Mazie cross over. You never know, she might have come across the spirits of the Brown children." Emma popped the last clam on her plate into her mouth and reached for more out of the communal basket.

"Do you know where to find her?

"According to Mazie, she lives in a yellow house by the town library." She dipped another clam into some tartar sauce and tossed it into her mouth and chewed. "I think she said Ash Street."

Gino returned, his full coffee mug in one hand, his phone in the other. "Seems Leroy's taking his leave, too."

"He quit?" asked Phil with surprise.

"No, nothing that drastic," Gino assured them with a smile. "He said some other people he knows showed up at his friend's today and he wants to take another day off to spend time with them. Since we're not really deep into the writing and research process yet, I told him to take two, if he needed them." Gino took his seat. "Seems everyone is taking time off from me."

"What do you mean?" asked Phil.

"When I called Marta to tell her we wouldn't be back for lunch and that she could have the rest of the day off, she asked if she could take the rental car when I returned to go to Connecticut. Said she'd always wanted to visit there." He took a long pull of coffee. "Since Vanessa isn't around and Marta's work mostly concerns Vanessa, I gave her tomorrow off, too."

Remembering how concerned Marta was about Gino being alone, the news surprised Emma.

Frank approached the table. "Mr. Costello," he said, "some friends of mine are here and would like to meet you, if it's no trouble."

"Frank," Gino said with his signature heartiness, "I told you to call me Gino. And of course I'll meet your friends."

"They are over there," Frank said, pointing to two middle-aged women standing nervously by the doorway to the kitchen. "They'd like you to sign a couple of books if that's okay."

Gino waved them over and they approached. They each clutched a copy of Gino's latest novel. "Would you please sign our books, Mr. Costello?" The shorter of the two women asked. "Sign it to Sheila."

"I'd love to, Sheila." Gino held out a hand for one of the books. "Do either of you have a pen?"

"I do," Emma answered and produced one from her purse. She handed it to Gino, who quickly scrawled his autograph and a short message to Sheila in one of the books and handed it back to her. He held out his hand for the book held by the taller woman, but she wasn't inter-ested in him. She was staring at Emma. Sheila nudged her and the woman came out of her trance and handed

Gino the book. "My name's Mary Jane." He signed it and handed it back to her with a smile.

Mary Jane thanked him and hugged the book to her chest. She turned her eyes back on Emma. "Are you Emma Whitecastle, the ghost lady on TV?"

Emma smiled. "Yes, I am."

"Sheila," the woman said to her companion. "This is Emma Whitecastle. You know, the lady with that show on ghosts and other weird stuff."

Sheila stopped studying Gino's signature and looked up, peering at Emma through thick glasses. "Oh my! It is!" She grabbed one of the unused napkins and thrust it at Emma. "Can we have your autograph, too?"

Emma gave both women a warm smile. "Of course, but how about I sign one of these promo cards my station gives me to hand out?" Emma slipped a hand into a side pocket of her purse and came out with a couple of four-by-six cards. On one side was a lovely headshot of Emma. On the other side was information about *The Whitecastle Report*, her TV show.

"Oh, Mary Jane," the shorter woman gushed. "Cecilia is going to be so sorry she didn't come, too." She turned to Emma. "Cecilia's our sister. A friend of ours called to tell us that she saw Mr. Costello having lunch here today, but Cecilia said she was too tired to come down to see him."

"Guess she's not a fan," Gino said with a crooked grin. "It happens."

"She's not much into reading about crime," Shelia said, "but she loves Mrs. Whitecastle. Never misses her show."

Emma pulled another card out. "Here, I'll sign this to Cecilia and you can take it to her. How about that?"

"Wow," said Mary Jane, taking the signed card. "She's

going to flip out, and she's going to be very upset that she didn't come with us. Thank you so much." Sheila and Mary Jane turned expectantly to Phil.

"Don't look at me," Phil told them. "I'm a nobody. Just Emma's boy toy." Everyone laughed.

"Are you here to see Fran Monroe?" Shelia asked Emma.

"Do you know Mrs. Monroe?" Emma asked, her interest on high alert.

"Everyone does," Sheila answered. "She's the town witch."

"Sheila!" Mary Jane dug an elbow into her sister's side. "Don't go saying that. It's not nice. Besides, she's more like Emma here, just not famous." Mary Jane looked at Emma. "Is that why you're here in Whitefield, to see Fran?"

"Actually, ladies," Gino interjected, "Emma is here helping me research a new book."

"How exciting!" the two sisters said almost in unison.

Frank came out of the kitchen and started clearing off the empty baskets and plates. "Okay, you two, quit bothering Mr. Costello. We'd like him to come back."

"Frank, this is Emma Whitecastle," Sheila said with enthusiasm. "She has a TV show about ghosts. You have two famous people here today."

Frank, his hands full, jerked his big head toward the door. "And I'd like them both to come back, so off with you." Reluctantly, the two sisters waved and made their way out the door, holding tight to their signed books and cards.

When the sisters and Frank were gone, the three of them sat nursing their drinks. Lunchtime was in full swing and the place was beginning to get busy. The commotion with the sisters had caused people to stare at their table with curiosity, but no one else approached them.

"We should go and free up this table," Phil suggested.

Emma started to get up, but Gino didn't move. "So," he said, looking from Emma to Phil, "who's this Fran Monroe?"

Emma and Phil exchanged glances, silently communicating, weighing possibilities and explanations, while Gino watched with interest.

"Just from your expressions, I'm thinking this is going to be good." Gino drained his coffee mug and set it on the table. Swinging his long legs over the bench, he got to his feet. "Let's talk about it outside."

· CHAPTER TEN ·

MARTA Peele appeared very happy to see all three of them back from their excursion, especially Gino with the new rental vehicle. Before she left, Emma asked Marta to give her a rundown of what was ready for their supper later.

They'd told Gino they would fill him in back at the house, where there was privacy. He and Phil were waiting for Emma in the den. They were just as eager to get Mrs. Peele out of the house as she was to be on her way.

The housekeeper showed Emma the two stews, one with meat and the other vegetarian, in the refrigerator and gave her instructions on heating them both.

"Please do not microwave them," Marta said. "It's much better to bring them to the right temperature slowly on the stove, otherwise the meat gets tough and the vegetables overcooked."

"Don't worry, Marta," Emma assured her, "I'll take care with the food."

"And there's apple pie over on the counter."

"I do believe her pie is just as good as mine," came a voice from near the pie. "I watched her make it and she definitely has the knack."

Emma didn't dare look in Granny's direction. Instead, she kept focused on Marta. "It smells delicious, Marta." Emma noted the woman was now clutching her crucifix. "Do you know anyone in Connecticut?"

Marta seemed nervous as she answered. "I have an old friend who lives just outside Hartford. I'll be staying with her. I gave Mr. Costello her number in case you need to reach me. He said I could take a day or two."

"She called her friend while you guys were out," Granny said, floating closer. "Her name's Gertrude and it doesn't sound like she's doing very well. Poor thing."

Emma took note of Granny's words, but smiled at Marta. "Is that why you were so determined that Mr. Bowers and I stay now that Mrs. Costello is gone, so that Mr. Costello wouldn't be alone if you went to see your friend?"

"Yes," she admitted, lowering her voice but still clutching the crucifix. "I knew Mrs. Costello might leave. I've gotten to know the signs. She'd promised me a day off to visit Gertrude later in the week. Gertrude has a bad heart and I wanted to see her while I was in the area, but I would never leave Mr. Costello alone, so I thought that with you folks here this might be a good time to take the trip. Also the girls might come this weekend and I wouldn't want to miss them." She paused, adding, "I won't be gone long."

Emma started to place a hand on Marta's shoulder, but the woman backed up a step and rubbed her crucifix as if starting a fire with two sticks. She was out of her uniform and dressed for travel in black slacks and a white shirt worn under a gray cardigan. "Don't worry, Marta," Emma told her, withdrawing her hand, "we'll be fine until you return. And I promise we'll take good care of Mr. Costello."

The usually dour housekeeper perked up and offered a small smile. For the first time since their arrival, Marta looked Emma directly in the eye. The contact wasn't long, but it was long enough for Emma to see fear in her eyes.

"Marta, I can see that something else is bothering you." The housekeeper didn't say anything, but looked away, so Emma added, "Why do you keep rubbing your crucifix when I'm around? Are you afraid of me?"

Emma half expected Marta to bolt. To grab her overnight bag and boogie out the front door with determination, as Vanessa had earlier but for a different reason. Instead, Marta let her hand drop from her crucifix. She folded her arms in front of her and slowly brought her eyes back up to Emma's. They were sad, as well as tinged with fear. "It's not you, Mrs. Whitecastle. At least not directly. I can tell you are a very nice lady." Marta lowered her voice. "Much nicer than Mrs. Costello."

"She's got that right," Granny quipped. "It's not even a contest."

Emma suppressed a smile. "Then what is it?"

"It's . . . it's . . ." she stammered. "It's the spirits around you and in this house I fear."

That took Emma back. "The spirits? You can see them?"

"I knew it," Granny said, slamming her right fist into her left palm. "She's always a little squirrely with me around."

Marta's hand went to the crucifix again as she shook her head side to side. "Oh no, Mrs. Whitecastle, but I can feel them. I could from the moment I stepped into this house. Even before you and Mr. Bowers arrived I felt it, but it's much stronger now that you're here. Even now, right this minute. I . . . I know that you're supposed to be able to speak to them. Please tell them to go away before I return from seeing Gertrude. Can you do that?"

Emma smiled at the woman. "Marta, you're right, there are spirits in this house. I've met them and spoken with them. But they are very friendly and won't hurt you or anyone else in the house. You have my word on that."

Marta leaned forward and whispered, "Even the one that's in the kitchen right now? It was here earlier, when I was making the pie, and it doesn't seem friendly at all."

Granny put her hands on her hips. "Is she calling me unfriendly?"

Emma laughed lightly. "The spirit that is here now with us is the ghost of my great-great-great-grandmother. Her name is Ish Reynolds, but everyone called her Granny Apples because she was known for her apple pies. She said she watched you make yours."

"She's *your* ghost?" Marta asked. "One you keep with you?"

"Humpf," groused Granny. "That makes me sound like a pet, like Archie."

"She's a ghost that travels with me a great deal." Emma paused, then tried again to reassure the frightened housekeeper. "Really, Marta, Granny or the other spirits that visit this house will never hurt you." Seeing Marta relax a bit, Emma asked, "How long have you been able to sense spirits?"

Marta buttoned and unbuttoned the middle button on her cardigan, the nervous action replacing rubbing the crucifix. "It started when I was a little girl in Germany. Then it stopped. It didn't start up again until the past year or so."

Emma thought about the time line. It coincided with Kelly and Tanisha becoming friends. "Have you ever felt a spirit hanging around Kelly or Tanisha when they visit Chicago?"

Marta seemed very thoughtful for a moment. "Yes, I have, a few times. At first, I thought I was going crazy. But then realized with Kelly being your daughter and all, it might just be real."

"That's Granny," Emma explained. "She loves the girls, just like you do, and keeps a close eye on them."

Granny still wasn't pleased. "Now you're making me sound like a guard dog."

"And you're sure this Granny or the other spirits won't hurt me?"

"Never," Emma assured her. "The ghosts you feel in this house are the spirits of the Brown family. They owned Misty Hollow many years ago and seem very nice." Emma was pleased to see the fear start to fade in Marta's eyes even more. "Now go, Marta. Be with your friend and don't you worry about Mr. Costello."

"What happened to you?" Phil asked when Emma finally joined them in the den.

"Marta and I were having a little girl chat," Emma explained. "The friend she's going to visit is quite ill. I was assuring her we'd be fine while she's gone."

Gino had been sitting on one of the large sofas. He got to his feet. "Is she gone yet?"

"She's just leaving now," Emma told him.

"I want to see her off." Gino excused himself and left the room.

"Just girl talk?" Phil raised a suspicious brow at Emma as she took a seat next to him on the other sofa.

"It seems Marta Peele can sense spirits. She can't see or hear them, but she often knows when they are around. That's why all the crucifix rubbing."

"So it's not you specifically?"

Emma shook her head. "She's known about the Browns, or at least about their presence, from the moment she got here. I assured her that the spirits were friendly and wouldn't hurt her. She's also been sensing Granny since our arrival. I think our talk helped quite a bit."

Phil leaned over and planted a kiss on Emma's cheek. "Good job, Emma."

Emma turned her head and planted her own quick kiss on him, but on his mouth. "I have a suggestion. Let's take Gino with us when we visit Mrs. Monroe."

Phil looked surprised. "Really?"

She nodded. "Yes. Marta is very concerned about him being alone, for one thing, and I think it might be good for him to learn more about spirits."

Phil rubbed his chin with a thumb, thinking over her suggestion. "Is the second reason for his books or to help him understand Tanisha better?"

"Both."

"Then sure," Phil agreed. "Let him tag along if he wants. You can ask him when you explain who this Fran Monroe is and why you want to meet her."

When Gino returned from saying good-bye to Marta, Emma filled him in on her visit with Mazie at the restaurant and on Fran Monroe. He'd taken his prior place on the sofa across from Emma and Phil and had leaned back, one arm draped across the top of the sofa, one long leg crossed over one knee, and listened. For a long time he didn't say anything. When Emma was done, Gino got up and went to the desk. On it was a laptop. He opened it and fired it up. Emma and Phil gave each other looks, questioning if they should say more, like about the Browns. Emma hadn't gotten to that part of the story yet.

"Are you checking out Emma's story?" Phil finally asked, his voice edged with defensiveness. He got up and went to the desk.

"Of course," answered Gino as he navigated the Internet. "Wouldn't you?" He glanced up at Phil. "I'm not saying Emma's lying, Phil, but I'm a bit of a skeptic about this stuff. A good writer always checks his facts."

Emma joined the men at the desk. She placed a hand on Phil's shoulder. "As I recall, Phil, you came right out and called me a liar when we first met."

Phil gave her a sheepish glance. "Guilty as charged."

Gino started pecking out information on the keyboard. "If this Mazie drowned, there would have been a news story about it."

"Mazie is an unusual name," Phil noted, "but it's too bad we don't know her last name."

Gino stopped typing and raised the index finger of his right hand into the air. "Ah, but I think we do." He stopped to dig through his recent memory, then shot them a grin. "When I first met Frank he told me his last name is Russo. What can I say, we *paesans* stick together." He put his fingers back on the keyboard. "I also met his son that day. His name is Chris and he's Frank's only kid, as I recall."

"That would make him Mazie's father by default," Emma pointed out. "And Mazie did tell me that her brother's name was Christopher."

Gino was excited. "So Mazie's last name would also be Russo." He typed some more, then clicked on a promising link. "Bingo! There it is."

Emma reached out and tapped the photo of a young girl that popped up on the screen. "That's her. That's Mazie."

The article reported on the tragic death of a ten-year-old girl named Mazie Russo who drowned at a place called Little Neck Pond earlier in the year. "Very sad," Gino said, his voice low. "I can't imagine losing T even now, let alone when she was just a half-pint." The room was blanketed with a thick silence as all three parents considered the horror.

"My brother Paulie was killed by a car when he was just eleven," Emma told Gino. "My parents are still not over it. And never will be."

Gino cleared his throat. "So this woman you want to go see, what's her name again?"

"Monroe," Emma told him. "Fran Monroe. Probably short for Frances. She lives in Whitefield, across from the library according to Mazie."

Gino typed *Fran Monroe Whitefield* into the search engine. Up popped a few references. Gino tapped the screen with a finger. "You're right, her full name is Frances. It says in this news clipping that she was once the town librarian. She retired a few years ago after serving for forty years."

"Is there a photo?" Phil asked.

"Not with this article." Gino navigated back to the search results and tried another link. "Bingo!" he called out again.

"What's with all the bingos?" asked Granny, coming into view on the other side of the desk. "You guys playing the game?"

Over Gino's head, Emma gave Granny a slight shake of her head before turning her attention back to the photo of Fran Monroe. The photo showed a short, stocky woman with cropped gray hair accepting an award in the shape of a crystal book. Gino's fingers flew over the keyboard as he put in more search information.

"Gee, Gino," Phil said with a chuckle, "you type faster than my secretary. If this writing thing doesn't work out for you, I'll give you a job."

"For years," Gino said with a hearty laugh, "I hunted and pecked my way through books. Finally, I smartened up and took a typing class. Best thing I ever did." His fingers paused, hovering over the keyboard in perfect typing posture. He lifted his head and looked across the room, out the glass doors toward the lake, his mind momentarily somewhere else. "It was actually Janelle, Tanisha's mother, who suggested I take the class. It used to drive her nuts watching me index-finger my way through a manuscript." He smiled to himself and turned his attention back to his laptop. "She said I should either learn to type properly or dictate my work. I tried the dictation, but it just wasn't comfortable for me, so I took the typing class." He stopped typing again. "I've never told Tanisha that."

"You should," encouraged Emma, giving Gino a pat on his shoulder.

Gino went back to checking out another article on Fran Monroe. "So you're curious about this woman?" Gino asked.

"I'm hoping she can help us," Emma told him.

"With my book idea?" Gino asked. "Or do you want to know more about the young girl who died?"

Emma and Phil exchanged glances, then Phil spoke for them both. "Neither actually."

"Oh?" Gino stopped reading the article and looked at Emma with curiosity. "Then for your show?"

"Just tell him the truth and get it over with," Granny groused. "The man's got to learn more about ghosts for T's sake, if for no other reason. Besides, I'm tired of being your dirty little secret."

Emma scowled at Granny and decided to jump feet first into the deep end of the pool. "You're hardly that, Granny. Didn't I tell Marta about you?" Phil shot her a surprised look that quickly softened into support.

Gino, who had gone back to reading the laptop screen, stopped and stared at Emma as if her mind had slipped its track.

Emma, expecting such a reaction, turned to face Gino head-on, her arms crossed in front of her. Granny floated over and stood next to Emma in support, although only Emma knew it. Still, she was happy to have the ghost by her side. Phil took a step back to watch the whole scene play out like live theater.

"Gino," Emma began, "I was speaking to Granny, the

spirit in the room with us right now. She's my great-great-great-grandmother and almost constant companion."

Gino didn't say anything for a long time. Then he turned his eyes back to the glass doors and the lake. Once again lost in his thoughts.

Phil broke the silence. "You okay, Gino?"

Gino didn't say anything or look at any of them. He got up from the desk and slipped past everyone, making a slow zombie walk toward the doors that led to the deck. He didn't go out, but stood in front of them, still staring at the lake. Outside, a light rain was still falling.

Granny leaned over toward Emma. "Did the news strike him deaf and dumb?" By way of answering, Emma shrugged.

Phil walked over to the wet bar and fixed a scotch, neat without ice. He took it over to Gino. "Would you like this?"

Without taking his eyes off the landscape, Gino held out his hand. Phil placed the heavy, short glass into it and didn't let go until he was sure Gino had a grip on it. Automatically, the author brought the scotch up to his lips and took a long drink, still not taking his eyes off the outdoors. After his second sip, he turned to them.

"You say this ghost's name is Granny?" he asked Emma.

"Yep, that's me," answered the ghost.

"Yes," answered Emma. "Her real name is Ish Reynolds, but everyone calls her Granny."

"Including my daughter?" asked Gino.

Phil and Emma again exchanged looks, each understanding that Gino wasn't in shock, but combing his memory.

"Busted!" announced Granny.

Gino started to take another drink, then thought better of it. "Vanessa once told me she thought she heard T talking to someone named Granny during one of her visits. Vanessa assumed it was T's grandmother who passed away about seven years ago. But T always called my mother Grandma, not Granny. I thought she was addressing her great-grandmother, the one I told you about, but she called her Nonnie. Granny and Nonnie could sound alike if you're not paying close attention, so I dismissed it because T and Nonnie were close and I didn't think it unusual for her to speak to her dead great-grandmother. After all, people talk to their dead loved ones all the time." Gino ran his free hand through his hair. "For a long time after she died, I talked to Janelle like that. It made me feel closer to her. Then during another one of T's visits, I passed her room and overheard her talking. She clearly said *Granny*. I stuck my head into her room and asked who she was talking to and T said she was just reading something aloud." Gino paused. "After that, I never heard her say the name again."

"Yeah," said Granny, "I remember that day. It was a very close call and T hated lying to her father like that."

"There really is a Granny," Phil said. "Bowled me over the first time I realized it was true." He held out his hand for the glass. "Would you like another drink?"

Gino handed him the glass. "No, but thanks. I think I'd like a clear head for this." He walked back to Emma. "So this Granny ghost is here right now and you told Marta about it but not me?"

"I told Marta just a few minutes ago," Emma explained. "She sensed something odd in the house and was afraid. I told her she had nothing to worry about."

Gino pointed a thick finger at Emma. "Is that why Marta was rubbing her crucifix like Aladdin's lamp whenever you were around?"

"You picked up on that, too, huh?" asked Phil with amusement.

Gino laughed. "Hard not to."

"Yes, that's why," confirmed Emma. "I introduced her to Granny and she seemed somewhat comforted. At least enough to leave her cross alone."

"We bonded over pie," Granny added with a satisfied grin.

Gino paced back and forth in front of the cold fireplace. Every now and then he'd stop and start to say something, but changed his mind and went back to pacing. Finally, he stopped long enough to ask, "So this Granny ghost travels to Chicago when T visits?"

"It's more like Granny pops in to check on her," Phil explained. "She pops in on Kelly, too. She's become very close to the girls. It doesn't matter where they are, Granny can find them."

After a few seconds, Gino let loose with a deep laugh. "As a father, I find that rather comforting. It's kind of like having a GPS tracker on your kid. That I could get used to, even though T is an adult." When he stopped laughing, he turned to Phil and stared at him. "So you can see and talk to ghosts, too? Am I in the minority here?"

Phil shook his head. "Not a lick. But the more I hang around Emma, the more I can sense them. Kind of like Marta can, although I'm not afraid of them."

Gino scratched his head in bewilderment. "So this Granny ghost wants to meet Fran Monroe? Or are you interested more in Frank's poor little granddaughter?"

"Again, neither," answered Emma. She went over to the coffee table and sat on the sofa in front of the large photo album. She opened it, then looked up at Gino. "I want to show you something."

Gino took a seat next to Emma on the sofa. Phil took a seat across from them. Emma opened the album to the photo of the big farmhouse with the Brown family posed in front on the steps. "This is the Brown family. The people who owned this house originally," Emma noted.

"Yes," agreed Gino. "It says so right there in the caption. This was taken around 1880."

Emma pointed to a boy and girl sitting side by side on the steps. "This is Chester and Clarissa Brown. They're twins and were eight years old when this photo was taken."

Gino, who had been looking at the photo, cut his eyes sharply in Emma's direction. "How in the hell do you know that?"

Granny hovered next to Phil. "Boy, this is gonna be fun."

"Because this person," Emma said, pointing to a young Abigail, "who is the mother of the twins, told me, just this morning. Her name is Abigail. Chester and Clarissa disappeared shortly after this photo was taken and were never seen again."

Emma brought her eyes up to Gino's. "The Brown family wants me to try and find out what happened to them. And reunite them all, if possible."

Gino leaned back heavily against the sofa and scrubbed his face with his hands. "Oh boy," squeaked out from behind his thick fingers.

"You okay, Gino?" asked Phil. "I know this is a lot to

absorb, but it's the truth. The Brown family was on the porch waiting for Emma yesterday when we arrived. She's been in contact with them off and on since."

Gino lowered his hands and stared at Phil, then moved his disbelieving eyes to Emma, where they locked. "You've been here less than twenty-four hours and you're telling me the ghosts of the people who built this house have hired you as some sort of PI?"

"Hired *us*," stressed Granny, even though only Emma could hear her.

"I know it sounds screwy, Gino," Phil told him, "but, believe me, you get used to it."

"Ha!" Gino snorted. "I'm not so sure about that." He stabbed an index finger at the photo, making a dull thumping sound. "These kids have been missing over a hundred years. How do you propose to find them now?"

Emma took a deep breath, held it a few seconds, and released it. "Well, that's why I want to meet Fran Monroe. She's a local medium and might know something. Maybe she's encountered the spirits of these children somewhere."

Gino stood up and started for the hallway. When Phil and Emma didn't follow, he turned back to them. "What are you waiting for? We've got a ghost hunter to meet." He glanced around the room, his eyes roving but not settling anywhere in particular. "You, too, Granny ghost."

Emma pointed at a spot across from her. "It's just Granny, Gino, and she's right there next to Phil."

Gino looked at the spot Emma indicated. "Then come on, Granny, or do ghosts need a special invitation or incantation of some kind?"

Granny jerked a thumb in Gino's direction. "I like this guy, Emma. He's got moxie. Just like his daughter."

As they were slipping into their jackets by the front door, Gino lightly smacked his head with a hand. "I just realized that with Marta taking the new car, I'm without wheels again until either she or Leroy returns. I guess you're driving."

· CHAPTER ELEVEN ·

ONCE again Phil drove and Emma was in the back. Granny hadn't come with them, saying she'd catch up later. They weren't able to get Fran Monroe's exact address off the web, but they did have the address for the Whitefield Library on Ash Street. Phil plugged it into the GPS and they took off for town along a tree-lined country road dotted with houses and fields. The rain was coming down in fits and starts as they traveled the quiet roads.

"Mazie told me it's a yellow house with a red door, across from the library," Emma said as they again entered the small, quaint town of Whitefield.

Traffic was heavier and people were on the sidewalks, hoods and umbrellas up against the rain, bustling about their business. Shops and restaurants were open. They passed a school with a sign identifying it as Whitefield

Elementary School. The parking lot in front of the main building was full, but the playground was empty, the kids inside keeping warm and dry. Sadness filled Emma, knowing that it was probably Mazie's school. They moved along with traffic for a few blocks, following the GPS until it directed them to turn left onto Ash Street.

"Can't this Granny go ahead of us and see if this woman is home first?" Gino asked.

"It doesn't work like that," Emma told him. "Spirits have to have an emotional connection with a place, thing, or person before they have a strong enough bond to make contact on will. Granny can pop in on any of us or our homes, because she has that connection. The Brown family goes between the two farmhouses because those locations are important to them. Their emotional connection is to Misty Hollow more than to the people who stay there."

"Will Granny be able to get a bead on me now?" he asked.

"Possibly," Emma answered. "She might already have a connection to you considering she's visited Tanisha at your home, although she's never mentioned anything."

Gino laughed. "Is that a good thing?"

Phil joined him in the chuckle. "It's a mixed blessing, believe me."

"True," Emma agreed with a smile. "But Granny will be the first to tell you she's no snitch. Her words, not mine. I often try to pump her about the girls and their activities and she stonewalls me, saying what happens in Boston, stays in Boston."

"A hundred-plus-year-old ghost says that?" Gino looked skeptical.

"She says a lot of odd things," Phil answered. "She loves TV and picks up a lot of phrases and slang from it, both modern and stuff from vintage movies, especially crime movies."

Emma shook her head with amusement. "It's true. Maddening sometimes, but true. But I know Granny would come straight to me if Tanisha or Kelly were ever in trouble."

"That's comforting." Gino glanced in the backseat but only saw Emma. "Hey, Granny, you can keep an eye on my daughter any day."

"She's not here right now," Emma told him. "She'll catch up to us later."

"So you're on board with all of this?" Phil asked him. "You know, about the ghosts and all?"

Gino shrugged, his jacket collar bunching up around his ears. On his head was a dark gray tweed cap. Phil had covered his dome against the chill with his baseball cap. "Not sure," Gino said honestly, "but as a writer I like to keep an open mind. Not to mention, except for this ghost malarkey, I trust you two and so does T. Who knows? There might even be a book in all this. I've gotten ideas from odder places."

"Malarkey?" Granny snapped, popping in. "Where does this bozo get off calling spirits *malarkey*? He's the one who makes stuff up and gets paid for it. He's a professional liar." Emma snorted.

"Let me guess," Phil said glancing in the rearview mirror at Emma, "Granny's here now and objecting to Gino's use of the word *malarkey*?"

"You got it," Emma confirmed.

Gino glanced at Emma. "Seriously? I ticked off a ghost just now?" Emma repeated what Granny said and everyone in the vehicle laughed out loud, except for Granny, who still had her nose out of joint.

"That will give you an idea of what we put up with day in and day out," Phil said to Gino.

"Granny's a pistol, that's for sure," added Emma.

"Humph!" groused Granny. "I don't need to sit here and listen to this nonsense. I'll catch up to you there."

"I'm guessing Granny just left again," Phil said.

"How do you know?" asked Gino.

Emma turned toward Gino. "As we discussed earlier, you may feel a slight change in the air temperature when a spirit comes or goes. It's generally cooler when they are around."

Gino chuckled. "From the moment we stepped foot in the farmhouse, Vanessa was cold. Maybe that's why."

Phil pulled over, parking behind a small sedan. "Here's the library and there's a yellow house almost directly across the street."

Emma unbuckled her seat belt, but before either she or Phil could open their doors, Gino stopped them. "Is it possible we could send this Granny ghost to check up on Vanessa?" Before Emma could answer, he quickly tacked on, "Not to spy on her, but to make sure she's okay. She hasn't been feeling that well lately and I'm concerned."

Emma didn't dare glance at Phil. Gino was very observant, and any eye contact might alert him that they knew something they shouldn't, or that he didn't. "I'm not sure Granny has had enough contact with Vanessa to zero in on her whereabouts," Emma said, hoping to deflect the request. "She's not with us 24/7 and even we've hardly seen Vanessa."

"Besides," Phil added. "Granny is stubborn as an old mule. She'd only do it if she wanted to do it."

"I heard that," a disembodied voice called out.

The yellow house was small and built in the saltbox style so common in New England. It was painted a cheerful canary yellow with black shutters and white trim. The three of them left the car and crossed the wet street after waiting for a couple of cars to pass by. The rain had stopped, but the thick dark clouds overhead warned that it could be starting up again at any second. They hustled up to the front porch of the house and stood in front of a red lacquered door with a large brass doorknocker in the shape of a lion's head.

"Since we've been talking about ghosts," remarked Gino, touching the knocker lightly with an index finger, "I half expect this doorknocker to take on a face like in *A Christmas Carol*." He gave off a mock shiver.

Phil laughed as he pressed the doorbell to the right side of the door. He turned to Emma with a grin. "That's what we get for hanging out with writers."

As soon as Phil pressed the bell a loud scrambling and barking came from the other side of the door, but no footsteps. Phil pressed it again. There was still no response, except for more barking, heavy and rich, like a seasoned baritone. "From that bark," Phil said, "I'm guessing that the beast on the other side of this door is some kind of hunting hound."

"Hold your horses. Hold your horses," came a muffled voice. It didn't come from inside the house, but from outside to the right, followed by footsteps. Soon someone came into view from around the corner of the house. The figure was short and stumpy and dressed in a dark brown oversized jacket with big front pockets and a large hood pulled down low. Except for the tall rubber boots in bright pink with purple and yellow polka dots, the person could have been taken for a large forest toadstool. All three of them turned and stared at the approaching figure while the barking swelled to a frenzy.

"Howard!" the figure yelled at the door. The barking stopped on a dime, followed by a low whine. "It's okay, boy, they're friends."

When the hood was dropped back, the three of them saw a hearty but elderly woman with short-cropped silver hair, rosy lined cheeks, and small blue eyes that twinkled in her round face. "About time you got here," she said to them in a clipped voice. "I've been waiting for you."

"Are you Fran Monroe?" Emma asked.

A small smile crept across the woman's face. "That's who you're looking for, isn't it, Emma Whitecastle?"

The three of them stared at the woman a few seconds before Emma asked, "Mazie told you I was coming?"

"Not exactly," Fran answered, still maintaining the smile. "She told me she met a woman at Frank's place who could see and talk to her. She said the woman's name was Emma and described you as very pretty with short blond hair. From there it wasn't difficult to figure out who you were, especially since I keep up on famous mediums." The woman laughed. "Of course, there could be other mediums named Emma, but I took a chance that I had you pegged." The dog inside whined again.

"Come on," Fran said to them as she flipped her hood back up and stepped off the porch. "Let's get inside where it's warm and dry and we can make proper introductions. Besides, Howard's going to have a fit if we stay out here.

We'll go in through the back so we don't muddy the front hall."

Without another word they followed Fran Monroe off the porch and around the side of the house from where she'd come. In the back was an impressive garden bordered by woods and an enclosed porch. She led them up the stairs and through a glass storm door onto the back porch. It was large and furnished with sturdy chairs and a table. Following Fran into the house, they found themselves in a small room with a bench and a coatrack on the wall from which hung a couple of sweaters and jackets. Along the edge were rubber mats with a small assortment of sturdy shoes. Taking a seat on the bench, Fran started pulling off her boots, placing them on one of the rubber mats. "I hope you don't mind," she told them, "but could you take off your wet shoes? You can leave them here in the mud room." On the other side of another door, the dog whined impatiently. She shrugged off her jacket and hung it on a coat peg.

"Of course," Emma answered. She sat down on the bench and started pulling off her ankle boots and coat. The men followed suit, removing their shoes, coats, and hats. Soon they were all inside a large cozy kitchen in their stocking feet, being eagerly greeted by a large basset hound.

"That's Howard," Fran told them, indicating the dog. "He's a bit miffed that I went outside to refill the bird and squirrel feeders without him, but with him being built so low to the ground, when it's wet outside he gets his entire undercarriage muddy."

Phil bent down and rubbed the dog's ears and head with enthusiasm. "I love basset hounds. I had one as a kid. His name was Poindexter." The dog's tail wagged happily as he made a new friend.

"Howard is our fourth hound," Fran told them. "I love the goofy critters. Howard's twelve. We had to put his sister Betty down about six months ago. Always difficult, but you have to do what's best for them." She pointed through a wide-framed arch. "The parlor's right through there. How about you folks go in and get comfortable and I'll put together some hot refreshments. Does hot chocolate sound good?"

"Sounds marvelous," answered Emma for all of them. "May I help you?"

"I'll make it," said a soft voice from the doorway. They turned to see an African-American woman about Fran's age, with salt-and-pepper hair dressed in shoulder-length braids held back with a large clip. Like Fran, she was dressed in jeans and a thick sweater. She was taller than Fran and not as thickly built. "You go in and sit with your company, Fran."

Fran smiled at the woman. "I thought you were taking a nap?"

"With all Howard's commotion?" the woman said with a laugh as she entered the kitchen.

Fran put an arm around the woman's waist. "Guess we should make proper introductions. This is Heddy Hanover, my wife, and of course you know I'm Fran Monroe." She turned slightly to Heddy. "Sweetheart, this is Emma Whitecastle, the famous medium."

"Ah," said Heddy, "the one Mazie told you about."

"The same." Fran turned to Gino. "And if my old eyes are correct, this gentleman is none other than Gino Costello, the novelist."

"Did Mazie tell you about him, too?" asked Emma.

"No," Fran said with a chuckle, "but word's gotten around that Gino here has leased Misty Hollow for a bit. Which is very interesting considering Misty Hollow is haunted. It also explains a lot about your presence, Emma."

Before they got any further, Emma put a hand on Phil's arm. "And this basset hound aficionado is Phil Bowers, my fiancé."

"Now you all scoot into the parlor while I make the hot chocolate," Heddy said to them, shooing them off like a bunch of unruly children.

"You're in luck," Fran said, once they were in the parlor seated on overstuffed sofas and chairs. The room was large and cozy, filled with mementos, photos, and books, with lots of spaces for curling up to read or to take a nap. "Heddy makes much better hot chocolate than I do. It's a special recipe she picked up in Mexico when she was teaching down there."

Phil's eyes lit up. "Mexican hot chocolate? Thick, with lots of spices?" Fran nodded. "I live in San Diego most of the time," Phil continued, "and there's a little Mexican restaurant by my office that makes the authentic stuff. It's heaven."

"So Heddy is a teacher?" asked Emma.

"Retired," answered Fran. "I retired from the library about the same time. We met about fifteen years ago at a library conference but didn't move in together until we both retired. We got married last year." Fran beamed. "Now we do a lot of volunteer work with various children's groups in the area."

"That's lovely," Emma said with a smile. "Did you know Mazie before she died?"

Fran nodded sadly. "I did. She never missed our Saturday morning story time at the library. That's one of the programs Heddy and I handle. We do story time for several small libraries in the area."

"Can Heddy see ghosts, too?" asked Phil.

"No, just me," Fran answered, "but she's gotten quite adept at sensing their presence."

"Same with Phil here," Emma told her.

Fran glanced at Howard, who was on his back by the fireplace, exposing his belly to Granny. "Speaking of which, there's one here now entertaining Howard. Did she hitch a ride with you folks? Because I don't recognize her."

"Yes," Emma said, "that's Granny, my great-great-great grandmother." Emma turned to Granny. "Granny, this is Fran. She can see and hear you."

"So I gather." Granny waved to Fran. "My pleasure."

"Tell me about Mazie," Emma said to Fran. "She said you came to her after she died."

Fran took a deep breath. "A few days after I heard that poor Mazie drowned, I went down to the pond. Something was nagging at me, like unfinished business, so I went down there and sure enough, there the poor child was, or at least her spirit, not quite sure of what to do next. I helped her cross over." Fran's downturned mouth turned up slightly at the edges. "Now she visits me and her family from time to time." The sadness returned again. "She was such a sweet child. Bright as a new penny. So very tragic."

Heddy came in holding a silver tray with five mugs of steaming, thick hot chocolate that gave off the homey scent of cinnamon and nutmeg. She put the tray down on the coffee table and handed each of them a heavy, color-ful mug, then took a seat next to Fran.

"So," Fran said after they'd all taken several sips of their delicious hot chocolate and praised Heddy for the same, "how are the Browns of Misty Hollow? Are you teaming up to do a book about them?"

• CHAPTER TWELVE •

E MMA held her warm mug with her right hand and cupped the bottom of it with her left. She glanced at Gino and Phil in turn, but before she could say anything, Gino answered. "I asked Phil and Emma to help me research a crime novel with a ghostly side plot. Our daughters are best buds, so they agreed to help me with the research. None of us knew anything about the history of Misty Hollow before now."

Heddy stared at Gino a long time before finally saying, "But you yourself don't believe in spirits, do you, Gino?" He chuckled nervously and shifted in his seat. He'd taken a large armchair next to the sofa Phil and Emma occupied. "I don't have the gift that Emma and Fran share," Heddy continued, "but I can tell a nonbeliever when I see one." She said it with a sly smile.

"Let's just say," Gino said with a wink in her direction,

"that I'm here with an open mind and a powerful curiosity."

"That's a start," Heddy said. "When we lose our curiosity, our mind dies, open or closed."

Emma brought Fran and Heddy up-to-date on the Browns and their request. When she finished, Fran said with wide-eyed wonder, "Wow, Emma, you are the real deal. I've been to Misty Hollow many times, but I've only been able to see and speak to Blaine, and that hasn't always been the best connection. I grew up here and the haunting of that property has always been local legend, especially the old farmhouse."

"I've only seen and spoken to Blaine and Abigail myself," Emma told her. "The other spirits just appear like hazy outlines."

"Yes, that's kind of what I see of them, too," Fran confirmed. "They're like shadows that you catch out of the corner of your eye as they pass."

"So you're from here?" Phil asked Fran.

"Not originally," Fran said. "But my family moved here from Vermont when I was only five so it's like I was born in the area."

"Did Blaine tell you about the missing children?" Emma asked before taking another sip of her delicious chocolate, feeling its warmth down to her toes.

"Yes, he did," Fran said.

She set her mug down on a nearby small table and got up, going to a short bookcase crammed with old books. Bending down, she ran a finger across the faded spines of the books until she located the one she wanted. She plucked it from the shelf and retook her seat.

"The missing Brown children have been part of the

local color as long as I can remember. Every child grow-ing up here in the last hundred years is sure they've seen Chester and Clarissa Brown. At Halloween, groups of teens go into the woods trying to conjure them up. Of course, they are all sure they do." She winked at Emma. "Some parents use Chester and Clarissa as cautionary tales for their children. You know, things like don't talk to strangers or you might end up like the Brown twins."

"Or," added Heddy, "be good or the Brown twins will get you."

"I don't like that one bit," Granny said with a scowl. "I don't like scaring children with boogeymen, especially spirits. We're generally a friendly bunch."

Fran turned to Granny, who was still next to Howard, much to the delight of the old dog. "I totally agree, Granny. All the ones I've met have been nice enough, even the cranky ones, and people shouldn't use fear to control their children."

She paged through the old book on her lap. "This is the history of Whitefield and it has a few paragraphs about the Browns and about Misty Hollow being haunted." She handed the book across to Emma.

"Have you ever tried to find the twins?" Emma asked. Her eyes scanned the text Fran pointed out. It reported that many people have seen the children over the decades since their disappearance.

Fran nodded and stretched her short legs out in front of her. "I didn't come into my medium gifts until about twenty or so years ago. I think they were always there, but I wasn't sure what they were or how to use them until then. Once I realized what I had, I did try to search for them in the woods where people claimed they saw them."

"Fran has seen other spirits though," Heddy said with pride.

"That I did," Fran confirmed. "Several over the years, but none were the missing Brown children."

"So Blaine asked you to help find them, too?" Phil asked.

"Over the years," Fran explained, "I'd looked for them on my own, more out of curiosity, but found nothing. I would walk in the woods by the old farmhouse off and on and even stumbled upon the old well and graveyard, but again nothing. Then one day I made contact with the young man I came to know as Blaine Brown. I asked him if the children had ever made it over to the other side and he told me they hadn't and asked me to find them. I kept looking but have never been able to find them." She seemed sad admitting to the last part.

"What about that well?" Phil asked. "I saw it this morning, along with the old graveyard. It's all locked up, but maybe they fell down it."

Fran shook her head. "I have a copy of an old newspaper from that time and there's an account on how they lowered someone with a lantern down into the well after the children disappeared and found nothing." She sighed and hugged her mug to her thick torso. "I honestly don't think Chester and Clarissa are anywhere near the town or the farm."

"Do you know of any other mediums who have tried to contact them?" Emma asked.

"After the Brown family sold the property, it became a bed-and-breakfast," Fran said. "It was cute and the owners did well. Sometimes they even used a haunted theme to sell rooms or staged ghost-sighting weekends." She scoffed, like a bulldog clearing its throat. "People from out of town flocked to those, and again people claimed they saw the children, but it was all in their minds. If the guests sensed any spirits at all, it was other members of the Brown family, but they always claimed it was the kids."

Emma turned the information around in her head, then turned to Gino, who had been sipping his chocolate while soaking up the conversation. "Gino, if this were one of your whodunits, how would you proceed on a cold case?"

Gino flashed his grin around the room. "I thought you'd never ask."

Everyone laughed, including Granny. "I can see where T gets her snappy sense of humor," the ghost said.

"Are there accounts by the family of where and when the children were last seen?" Gino asked.

Fran nodded. "Yes, I have a bound edition of copies of the local newspaper from back then. It covers nearly ten years or so. The paper was just one page long and came out weekly, but there are some stories about the Browns in it."

"We start there and look at everything in those papers," Gino told them with enthusiasm. "You never know when something might provide a clue."

"And Emma can question Blaine and Abigail more about it," Phil added. "Especially Abigail since she was there at that time."

Granny moved in closer to the group. "Now we're cooking with gas."

Emma turned to Fran and Heddy. "I'd like you ladies to help, too, since you know the area and the history."

"That's Fran's department," Heddy said. "I haven't been here that long and I'm not a history buff."

Fran beamed with excitement. "I'd love to work with you, Emma." She reached over and clutched Heddy's hand. "How exciting is this, sweetheart? I'm actually going to work with Emma Whitecastle!"

Heddy smiled at her then looked at Emma. "She hasn't said so, but Fran's a huge fan and never misses your show."

Fran blushed and giggled. "And maybe I can learn more about spirits from you, Emma."

Granny drifted over to Fran. "Emma's a great mentor, but she gets a bit uppity and bossy at times. Just ignore it. I do."

Fran broke out into loud laughter while Emma narrowed her eyes at Granny.

Gino, totally lost by the exchange, sent a raised eyebrow in Phil's direction. Phil leaned toward him. "You'll get used to that. It's like being at a party where only a couple of people speak your language, so you have to wait until someone translates. But I'm guessing Granny just said something sassy and unflattering about Emma. Maybe later, after a drink or two, we can get Emma to tell us about it."

· CHAPTER THIRTEEN ·

"ANY word yet from Vanessa?" Emma asked Gino as she watched him looking at messages on his phone. He'd been checking quite often, his brow furrowed with worry each time.

He shook his head. "Not a word." He put the phone on the table. "But she always makes me cool my heels for a day or so before she deigns to answer my messages. It doesn't seem to occur to her that I might worry."

They had just finished dinner and were enjoying some brandy. Emma had heated up the stews Marta had made earlier, and they had eaten it from big bowls in front of the fire, along with slices of crusty bread. Soon Fran would be joining them to see if they could contact the Browns about more information on Chester and Clarissa. Granny had just come in to report that at least Blaine would be popping in later.

Emma watched Granny, wondering if she should ask the ghost to try to contact Vanessa Costello just to make sure she was okay. Granny seemed to like Gino, so Emma didn't think she'd mind.

"What are you looking at?" Granny asked, noticing Emma studying her.

Instead of responding, Emma stacked the empty stew bowls and utensils on the tray she'd used to carry them earlier and rose to take them into the kitchen.

"Let me help you, darling," Phil said, putting his glass down on the table.

"Yes," added Gino starting to get up. "You got the grub on the table, let us guys clean up. After all, you are my guests."

"No," Emma protested, "you both sit still. There's only a few dishes. I'll pop them in the dishwasher and put the food away. It won't take but a few minutes." As she walked out of the room, she caught Granny's eyes, indicating for her to follow.

"I have a favor to ask you, Granny," Emma said as she rinsed the dishes and placed them in the dishwasher.

"I'm all ears," the ghost said.

"Gino is worried sick about Vanessa. Do you think you could try to locate her? Not to spy," she quickly added, "but to report back if she's okay or not." Emma dished the remaining beef and vegetable stews into separate lidded containers and put them in the refrigerator. Marta had made enough of both to last them two more meals. They would have Marta's pie when Fran arrived.

"I don't know if I can get a bead on her," Granny answered, "but I'd be happy to try. I can see how concerned he is, not that I think she's worth it."

"Be nice, Granny," Emma lightly scolded. She set the stew pots in the sink and added dish soap to soak them.

Granny sniffed with displeasure. "I just don't trust the woman and she treats Gino awful. No wonder T doesn't like her."

"That's really none of our business. I just want to give Gino some peace of mind."

"Yeah, it would be good for him to go to bed tonight knowing she's safe."

Granny had just popped out when the doorbell rang. Emma called to the men that she'd answer it, thinking it would be Fran.

"I see it's raining again," Emma said as she took Fran's wet coat and hung it on the coat tree by the front door.

"Steady but not hard," Fran answered, as she took off her boots and set them next to three other pairs lined up in the foyer.

"You don't have to do that, if you don't want," Emma told her.

"It's a good New England habit in bad weather," Fran replied with a grin. "And it makes us keep our socks darned. At least that's what my grandmother always said."

Fran stepped deeper into the foyer of the large house. "This is so nice."

"You've never been here before?"

"Not since it was a B&B, and then only twice." She glanced into the formal living room and across the hall into the dining room. "I attended one of the ghost nights out of curiosity and the other time a friend and her husband from out of town stayed here and I visited them. I know the property better than the house, having walked all over it and the woods around it while looking for the

Brown children. One of the best locations in the entire county."

"Phil and I are quite smitten with it ourselves. It's a huge house. We're thinking it might be fun to rent for a family vacation."

Emma showed Fran into the den. Both men got up when the women entered and shook hands with Fran. "Where's Heddy?" Gino asked.

"She tutors every Monday night at a local school. She's quite active in the adult reading program." Fran said the words with great pride.

"I am very impressed with how active and dedicated you ladies are to education at all levels," Phil told her. "My aunt Susan has volunteered for years with a program for challenged children in our area. You would hit it off famously."

"I agree," Emma added with a smile. "Maybe you'd like to visit us for a weekend in Julian. That's where Phil grew up and where Granny is from."

"Julian, California?" Fran asked, her face bright with excitement. "Heddy and I wanted to visit it when we were in San Diego a few years back on vacation, but we ran out of time."

"Then before we leave," Emma said, "let's exchange e-mails and telephone numbers and talk about a date for a visit. I might even talk Milo and Tracy into coming down at the same time."

Fran's eyes got wider. "Milo? You mean Milo Ravenscroft? I remember reading somewhere that you two were close."

Again, Emma nodded. "Milo mentored me when I first started speaking with spirits."

"And he's married to Emma's best friend," Gino added. When Emma glanced over at him in surprise, he tacked on with a wink, "You see, I pay attention."

Phil laughed. "We could make a party of it. You come, too, Gino, and maybe the girls. We have plenty of room for everyone between Emma's house and mine."

"Okay," Fran said, fanning herself with her hand, "now I'm all aflutter with anticipation."

"Speaking of the girls," Gino said, holding his phone aloft. "I just got a text from T. They will be here on Thursday night for the weekend." He continued looking at his phone, studying it.

"I'm so glad," Emma said, her words full of happiness at the thought of seeing Kelly and Tanisha. "And Marta will be back by then. She wouldn't want to miss them."

"Is that Mrs. Costello?" Fran asked.

"Marta is Gino's housekeeper," Emma explained. "She's currently visiting a friend in Connecticut and is quite fond of our daughters."

"I'm afraid my wife isn't here right now," Gino told Fran as he pocketed his phone. "Would you like a drink, Fran? We're having brandy, but we also have wine, beer, and scotch."

"A brandy would be nice on a cold wet night like this," Fran told him. "Thank you."

"Come take a seat, Fran," Emma said, showing her to a seat next to where Gino had been sitting. "I think this would be a good place. We can sit two on a side."

She picked up the photo album from the table and opened it to the page with the Brown family in front of the big farmhouse, where they were currently gathered. "This is a history of Misty Hollow," she explained to

Fran. "This is a photo of the Browns right before the two children went missing."

Fran immediately pointed to Chester and Clarissa. "Here they are." When the others looked at her with surprise, she explained, "I've seen this photo before in old historical records. In one that talks about their disappearance and the haunting of this house, the children are circled to identify them." She flipped through the photos that showed the various stages of renovation of the house and property. "What a great album to have on hand for guests, but there's no mention here of the place being haunted. The last owner really tried to capitalized on that. I guess the current one doesn't want to or doesn't believe it."

"He certainly never mentioned it to me," Gino said. "And neither did my friend who recommended this place. He and his family stayed here a week last year."

"Could be they aren't sensitive to spirits," Emma noted as she moved two stocky white candles from a side table to the coffee table. Phil lit them while she dimmed the overhead lights and made herself comfortable next to Phil. She noticed that Fran had closed the album but left it on her lap, her hands laid on top of it.

"So séances really do use candles to beckon the dead?" Gino asked as he handed Fran her drink. "I always thought that was just an embellishment for the movies. Do we hold hands, too?"

"Ghosts will come with or without candles, Gino," Emma told him, "but it does set the atmosphere. Plus, the darkness might help Fran and I see them if they are a bit shy." Emma gave him a small amused smile. "But no holding of hands or chanting, I promise."

Emma settled back against the sofa and made herself

comfortable. Phil did the same. Across from them Fran calmly sipped her drink while keeping one hand on the album. Only Gino seemed antsy. "So this is it?" he asked, still standing. "We just wait and hope they show up?"

"Pretty much," Emma told him. "Just relax and let's have a nice visit."

Gino took another sip of his drink and rolled his shoulders to relax. "Okay."

"Fran," Phil asked, "are there any of the Brown clan still in the area?"

Fran gave it some thought while she sipped her drink. "There are Browns in the area. It's a common last name, after all, but I don't think any of them are direct descendants of these Browns. As I recall, the last members of the Brown family to own Misty Hollow were Alice and Robert Brown. They were quite elderly and their children had left the area. When Robert passed away, the kids convinced Alice to sell the place and move closer to them. I believe it was someplace in North Carolina." Fran stroked the album. "Such a shame that no one in that family appreciated the history of this property enough to hold on to it."

Emma looked at Fran. "The first time I held that album I got a distinct vibration from it. Are you feeling anything?"

Fran shook her head. "No, but I have gotten such sensations from other items connected to spirits. I was hoping I would with this."

"Vibrations from the dead?" Gino went to the bar and brought the brandy bottle back. He refilled his glass and held the bottle up in question. The other three shook their heads, turning down the offer. "I don't know whether to be amused, scared, or fascinated," Gino said with a laugh. "Maybe all three." He put the bottle down on the table and took a sip from his glass before settling on the sofa next to Fran.

Phil looked at Fran. "I was going to ask the Browns about this, Fran, but since we have time to kill, so to speak, let me ask you. I was going over those old newspapers you gave us and noted that the Brown children weren't the only people to go missing around that time." Gino put down his drink and perked up, paying close attention.

Phil got up and went to a big high-back reading chair. It was the same chair Vanessa had been seated in the night before. On a small table next to it was the bound volume of old newspapers Fran had given them. He fetched the book and returned to his seat next to Emma.

"Phil's had his nose in that book ever since we got home from your place," Emma noted to Fran. "He only stopped for dinner."

"It's fascinating reading," Phil said, putting on his glasses. "The stories really give you a sense of life in this area at that time. There are farm reports, weather reports, birth and death notices—it's a time capsule for that period."

"But other children went missing then?" Gino asked, his eyes bright with curiosity.

Phil nodded and reached for a lamp next to his end of the sofa. He glanced at Emma. "Is it okay if I turn this on, darling?"

"Sure, go ahead." Emma was just as eager as the others to see where Phil was going with the information.

After snapping on the light, Phil opened the book to one of several places he'd marked with slips of paper. "It starts here, about two years before Chester and Clarissa disappeared. A girl went missing from another town. There are a couple of follow-up stories, but it doesn't look like she was ever found, or if she was, the paper didn't write about it."

He flipped through a few more of the pages. "Here's a story a few months later about a missing boy from Passer Heights." He looked at Fran. "I looked for that on a map, but didn't find it. Do you know where that is?"

"Was," Fran clarified. "It was a small village about ten or twelve miles from here. It struggled to exist until a major fire destroyed it around 1900."

"Gino," Emma said, "you were telling us about villages that disappeared for one reason or another. Passer Heights sounds like that kind of place."

"He's right," Fran confirmed. "It happened a lot, especially in the 1700s through the mid-1800s. These were mostly small settlements that never took hold or that people gave up on and moved from after some sort of catastrophe. After the fire, Passer Heights was never rebuilt, and years later the area was annexed by another small town. Passer Heights is now the name of the housing development that sits on the site of that old village." Fran pointed out the French doors. "Even the making of that lake took a settlement."

They all turned, but could see nothing in the dark except for the lit outline of the dock and a few low-level lights lining the paths to it and the guesthouse.

"That lake is man-made?" asked Phil.

Fran shook her head. "Not really, but originally there were two lakes, a small one and a large one, almost side-by-side, separated by a strip of land. This end was the original larger lake. Farther up was the smaller lake. On the land that separated them was a small village known as Job's Arm. It was originally settled around the time of the American Revolution by a man named Job Armstrong."

"Didn't that village have flooding problems in bad weather?" asked Gino.

"Yes," Fran answered, "except the middle of the land was elevated. When there was flooding it became like a small skinny island, which according to historical accounts, old Job liked just fine. He was supposedly a bit of a crabby recluse and tyrant. He and several generations of his family lived on that land until sometime in the 1800s. After Job died, the family started leaving Job's Arm, nearly abandoning it. Eventually the strip of land was blasted down and leveled off well below the water line so the two lakes could become one large lake."

"I'm surprised that's not mentioned in the album," Emma said.

Fran shrugged. "It happened up toward the other end of the lake, so maybe didn't figure into the history of this place. Most people from around here don't even know that once there were two lakes, let alone a village called Job's Arm." She turned to Phil. "Were there other missing people?"

"Yes, as a matter of fact," Phil said, putting his reading glasses back on. "Starting two years before the Brown children went missing, there seems to be several accounts of people disappearing, mostly young women and children, from various parts of the area. None are very close together in time, and they might not have anything to do with each other, but I found it interesting nonetheless."

"Maybe a serial killer?" suggested Gino.

"The thing is," said Fran, "news back then wasn't immediate like it is now. There were no telephones. Mostly folks got news from people who traveled through the area. By the time a story of a missing woman or child found its way into the paper, it might have been several months old, unless someone looking for the missing person immediately hopped on a horse and went from village to village making inquiries." She took a sip of her drink. "Also, sadly, it wasn't that uncommon for wives and older children, or servants, to run away from bad or abusive situations. Life was hard back then and people were hard. Job Armstrong wasn't alone in that."

"They didn't run away," said a voice from near the fireplace. Fran and Emma turned in unison to see Blaine Brown come into view just as the candles flickered, then steadied themselves.

· CHAPTER FOURTEEN ·

"I'M guessing we're not alone," said Phil to Gino as he put the bound book of old newspapers down on the table. Gino turned in the direction Fran and Emma were looking, but saw nothing.

"Blaine Brown just arrived," Emma told them. She turned to Blaine. "Thank you for coming, Blaine. I believe you know Fran Monroe already."

"Nice to see you again, Blaine."

"Fran," Blaine said tipping his head slightly. "Maybe together you can find Chester and Clarissa." The words came out in fits and starts, like a bad cell connection, until he came clearly into view. "My family would be grateful."

"Ask him about other missing people," Phil said to Emma.

Gino got up and retreated to another high-back chair a few feet away, taking his brandy with him. "Don't mind me, folks, but I think I can observe better from here. You know, a wide-angle view of everyone. I don't want to miss a thing."

Phil laughed. "You think you have a new book idea here, don't you?"

Gino raised his glass. "I'd be a fool if I didn't."

"Well, I'll be," Fran said with excitement, pressing her hands down on the album on her lap. "The book is definitely talking to me now."

"Blaine," Emma began, "there are questions we'd like to ask Abigail. Is she coming tonight?"

"I think she's already here," Fran said. When Emma looked at her, Fran jerked her chin over toward the door. Emma turned and saw the outline of Abigail come into view. "Well, I'll be," Fran said again quietly. "This is a first for me. Thank you, Emma."

After Emma made the introductions and let Phil and Gino know what was happening, the spirit of Abigail Brown drifted closer to them.

"Abigail," Emma began, smiling at the image of the old woman, "thank you for coming. We have a few questions to ask you that might help us find Chester and Clarissa."

"I'm here to help," the spirit said just as Emma noticed the flames on the candles dancing and hazy images start to appear. "We're all here to help."

"Oh my," said Fran with wonder as she turned her head this way and that as the room filled with shadowy forms.

"What's going on?" asked Gino.

"It seems," answered Fran in a hushed voice, "that we have a Brown family convention going on here. The room is filled with spirits, but only Abigail and Blaine are clearly visible and are speaking."

Gino took another swig of his brandy.

"Ask about other missing people, Emma," Phil prodded.

"Abigail," Emma began, "around the time the children went missing, did you hear of other people disappearing? Maybe some other children who were never found?"

The ghost of the elderly woman thought about the question, then answered, "From time to time you did hear about a young wife who left her man and went back to her people, or a young man who left to find his fortune."

"Are you sure that's what happened to them?" Emma asked.

"You were never quite sure, of course," Abigail said. "Not in all instances. Sometimes the young man would return, sometimes not."

"What about children specifically?" asked Fran. "There'd be no reason for them to take off on their own."

"Sometimes young boys ran off," Abigail said. "Especially if they were being mistreated. There was that time young Albert Kenmore went missing right after his mother passed. His father was an awful, awful man. Some folks even believed he killed the boy, but then someone ran into Albert a few months later working for a blacksmith near Worcester."

"What about the time those girls went missing?" said a fuzzy image by the bar. The voice was male but that was all Fran and Emma could tell about the spirit.

Abigail raised her head and looked in the direction of the voice. "Yes, that's right." She turned her attention back to Emma. "There was a time when two little girls went missing. It was about a year before Chester and Clarissa disappeared. They weren't sisters and it didn't happen exactly at the same time, but about a month apart. One lived two villages over and the other was a girl from town, right here in Whitefield."

After Emma relayed the information, Phil said with excitement, "I remember reading about that." Picking up the bound newspapers, he thumbed to pages he'd marked. "One was Penelope Worthington and the other"—he paused while he found the next marked page—"was Helen Foster."

Abigail nodded. "The Worthington girl was from Whitefield. Her father ran the general store." Emma confirmed Abigail's recollection of the names with Phil.

"Penelope was a wild thing," Abigail said, "and almost a woman. She behaved quite unseemly, much to her parents' shame. She probably ran off with some young man. At least that's what everyone, including her parents thought."

"Another thing," Phil noted. "All these people went missing in the summer. Even allowing for a lag in news time, that's pretty consistent."

"That makes sense, doesn't it?" asked Gino. "If they were leaving the area, they wouldn't travel in bad weather. Although that doesn't explain the missing young children."

"True on both counts," said Phil. "But according to these reports none of the disappearances happened in spring or even fall when the weather hadn't turned nasty and cold yet." He turned toward the fireplace. "Abigail," he began, but Emma caught his eye and motioned to the left of his gaze, in the direction Abigail was hovering. He turned toward the ghost. "Abigail, was there anything special that happened every summer in the towns and villages around here?"

A murmuring filled the room that only Fran and Emma could hear. "The others are considering your question, Phil," Emma explained.

Gino cleared his throat and rubbed his arms. "It's getting cold in here. Just how many ghosts are in the room?"

"Not sure," Fran answered. "Blaine and Abigail are still the only ones who are visible. The others are more like shadows, but we can hear some of them." Fran looked around the room, trying to make out individual images. "But I'm guessing maybe six to eight."

Phil glanced over at Gino and grinned. "Welcome to my world." Gino ran a hand over his head a couple of times, but said nothing. He settled back in his chair again to watch.

After the spirits finished talking over Phil's question, Blaine turned to the living and said, "They say there was always just one big celebration in the summer. It was a summer fair and dance in the town square. It was held on July fourth in honor of Independence Day. The whole town and people from neighboring farms and villages came. It was the same when I was alive." Emma took on the role of translating to Gino and Phil.

"That fair and dance is still going on today," Fran noted, smiling at the collection of hazy figures.

"The year the twins went missing," Phil asked, "was it after the Fourth of July or before? The newspaper account says it was shortly after."

"It was that same day," Abigail answered before the others could confer. "I remember it clearly. We'd all gone to town for the dance, but we never saw Chester and Clarissa after that. I thought they were spending the night with their cousins in this house and everyone who lived here thought they'd come home with us. No one noticed they were gone until the next night when I walked over here to fetch them home."

While Emma filled in the men, Fran flipped through the book on her lap. "Emma told me that this photo of the big house with all of the family was taken shortly before the children disappeared."

"Yes," Abigail confirmed. "On their eighth birthday a few weeks before. The traveling picture man took it."

"Who is the traveling picture man?" Emma asked.

"He's a man who passed through every year and took pictures of new babies and newlyweds and such," Abigail replied. She laid a hand on the side of her face. "I can't remember his name."

One of the other spirits floated forward, coming slightly into view but not completely. He appeared tall and muscular with a beard. Emma recognized him as Warren Brown, Abigail's husband. "His name was French," Warren said. "I believe it was Beau French."

Abigail pointed at the speaking spirit. "That's right, Warren. I remember now. It was Mr. French." She shook her finger in the air as more information came to her. "He was a widower, I believe. He traveled around on his buggy passing through year after year. He'd rent a couple of rooms at the small hotel in town and stay a few weeks taking his pictures. That year my father-in-law asked him to come out and take one in front of the new house. We all put on our Sunday best for it. It was such a beautiful day."

"What are they saying?" Gino asked with impatience, but Phil held up a hand, signaling for him to wait for Emma.

Fran got up from the sofa and crossed over to Abigail with the album still in her hands. She showed it to the ghost. "Did Beau French take this photo?"

Abigail looked it over. "Yes, he did. That's the one." She smiled and tried to touch it but her hands went through the book. "I'm so happy it survived all these years." She pointed to a youngish woman standing on the steps just behind the seated twins. "Oh my, that's me. Look at how young I was." The other ghosts in the room all gathered around Abigail and the book, murmuring amongst themselves as they looked it over.

Fran flipped pages until she found the other photo, the one of the old house. "Mr. French took that one, too," said Warren. "I remember that day. He took a bunch of them of the other house, the kids, and the barn. I remember him saying that he liked taking pictures of people doing everyday chores and especially of children playing." Emma and Fran exchanged glances.

"It says here," Emma noted as she got up and joined the group around the album, "that this photo was taken sometime in the 1870s and the other, the formal photo in front of the new house, was done in the 1880s, but the children in both photos look like the same children. In fact, Chester and Clarissa seem to be in both of them. Do you remember how long passed between these two photos?"

Again, there was murmuring between the collection of spirits. Finally, Warren spoke, "None at all, except maybe a few days. As I recollect, these photos were both taken the year this house was completed, which was in the spring of 1881." Emma looked at Abigail and Warren. Both were fading. Abigail looked worn out.

"Did the children like Mr. French?" Fran asked.

"They all seemed kind of shy around him," Abigail said, her voice low and breathy as she lost energy. "I don't think they liked having their pictures taken. Especially the ones where they had to sit still."

Blaine stepped forward. "Emma, do you know what happened to Chester and Clarissa?"

Emma shook her head. "Not exactly, Blaine, but now at least we have some more information to go on." She looked around at the gathering of spirits. "Before you go, tell me, do any of you remember where Mr. French lived and where he went after he left Whitefield?"

"He was from Worcester," Warren said. "I remember that."

"Yes," Abigail agreed. "I remember that, too. I don't remember his exact itinerary, but I know it included Passer Heights and the villages of Balser and Hampshire. I had people in Hampshire and Passer Heights and he would take their photos also. I remember because we would use Mr. French to pass along letters and small packages."

"Wait a minute," Warren said. Stepping away from the group of spirits, he paced the room, coming more into focus. Emma looked down at the big family portrait, running a finger across the rows until she found Warren in the group. He was dressed in a stiff suit in the photo and his hair and beard were neatly trimmed and dark as night. He must have been in his midthirties when his children went missing. Studying his spirit, it looked like he'd died in his fifties.

"Wasn't that summer the last one French came through here?" Warren asked the group of spirits. Again, murmuring, like bees on a summer day, filled the room. Another spirit, a female Emma couldn't make out, spoke up from the crowd. "I think you're correct, Uncle Warren. I don't recall him coming back through these parts again."

"But didn't Mr. French help us look for the children?" asked Abigail.

"That he did, Abigail," Warren agreed. "He helped us search until he had to leave for the next town. Then I don't think we ever saw him again."

"How long did you search for the children?" Emma asked.

"Months and months," Warren said. "Some of our boys rode into neighboring towns and put the word out."

"And when was the last time you remember actually seeing them?" Fran asked.

The ghosts were quiet, then the unidentified woman spirit said, "At the dance. They were playing with some of the other children. That's the last I saw them." More murmuring could be heard as the group of spirits agreed that it was at the dance.

"Peculiar thing, I'm now thinking," Warren said as he ran a hand through his thick beard, "that we never saw Beau French again after that summer."

"Are you saying," began Blaine, "that Beau French might have had something to do with the twins going missing?"

"That's exactly what I'm thinking," Warren said to his family. He turned to Fran and Emma. "That's where all your questions are heading, is it not, ladies?"

"I'm afraid it's crossing our minds as a possibility,"

admitted Emma. More muttering from the crowd of ghosts as they all considered the possibility.

"But why would Mr. French want to hurt Chester and Clarissa?" Abigail asked, her voice growing reedy and thin as her image faded.

"There are a lot of sick and evil people in the world, Abigail," Fran explained in a sad, slow tone. "It happens to the children in our time, so why not in yours?"

CHAPTER FIFTEEN

"A FAMILIAR traveling salesperson would be good cover for a murderer and predator," noted Gino as soon as Emma and Fran brought the men up-to-date. He got up and went to his laptop on the desk. The Brown clan had left and once again warmth filled the room.

"Exactly," Phil agreed. "The children would know him and the adults would trust him."

"Abigail said a lot of the children were shy around French," Emma noted, "but young children are often shy around strangers."

"Young ones are also quite perceptive," added Fran. "They often get gut feelings about people without knowing why, much as animals do."

Phil picked up the bound newspapers. "Boy, I wish this was scanned and searchable. It would make it much faster to find out about other missing kids."

"But even if we do decide that Beau French was preying on the area's children," Emma pointed out, "it doesn't help us locate the spirits of Chester and Clarissa, which is what the Browns want and need for closure."

Fran sat back down on the sofa and put the album on the table. "Do you think," she said after taking a long pull on her brandy, "that they will stick around after they're united with the spirits of the twins?"

Emma shrugged. She'd sat back down, too, and was also nursing her drink. "I don't know. They might, deciding their mission is accomplished. But maybe some will linger because of their affection for Misty Hollow."

"Ha!" said Gino, slapping the desktop with the palm of his right hand. "Beau French is on the Internet."

"You're kidding?" said Phil. Getting up, he went to look over Gino's shoulder.

"Right there," Gino said, pointing at a spot on the screen. "His name popped up under serial killers on this Wikipedia page."

"He was a known serial killer?" asked Emma with surprise. She and Fran turned to face the men.

"Now we're cooking," came a voice near the bar.

Fran and Emma turned quickly at the familiar sound to see Granny coming into view. "Granny's back," Emma announced to the men.

"I've been here all along," Granny said coming closer, "but I've been hanging back and watching. That was all pretty interesting." She and Emma exchanged looks, and Granny shrugged. "Sorry, Emma. I couldn't find Vanessa."

"That's okay, Granny," Emma told her with a small smile. "I know you tried."

"Who is Vanessa?" asked Fran. "Another member of the Brown family?" The men turned and watched them with interest.

Instead of looking at Fran, Emma looked Gino straight in the eye. "I sent Granny to see if she could find Vanessa, but she couldn't. I'm sorry and so is she."

"I just couldn't get a bead on her," the ghost said with genuine sadness.

Gino looked at Fran as he answered her question. "Vanessa is my wife. She stormed out of here this morning after we had a fight." He turned to Emma. "You and Granny can stop looking. I know where Vanessa is, at least for the moment. About the time I got the text from T, I noticed one from my bank that had come in earlier. I have that service where they text me whenever a major purchase is made on my credit card. Seems Vanessa checked into the Plaza Hotel in New York earlier today."

"I'm very sorry, Gino," Fran told him with sympathy.

Gino took a deep breath, his powerful chest expanding with the effort. "I'm actually glad she wasn't here for this, or my assistant Leroy for that matter. Vanessa would have been scared to death and Leroy would have made a mockery out of it."

"And you?" Phil asked.

Gino expelled a tiny, rough laugh. "I'm not sure what to think, but here it is right on the Internet." He jabbed again at the screen. "It says that Beau French was a traveling photographer. He was hanged in 1884 for murdering two little boys in New York, and was suspected of killing other children who had gone missing in the area."

"New York," Fran repeated to no one in particular.

"I'll bet it got too hot for him here with the Browns nosing around day and night," Granny said, "so he moved on and decided not to return."

"Granny thinks French might have moved to New York because things were getting too complicated around here," Emma told the men. "I think she has a good point."

"I do, too," agreed Gino. "Back then, communication wasn't instant like it is now. It might take months or even years for investigations or concerns about someone to catch up to him, even if the Brown family put a lot of time and effort into it. New York isn't that far away to us, but back then it was a major distance."

"And French could take his occupation with him," Phil pointed out. "No one would think twice about an itinerant photographer showing up in town. He could support himself wherever he went."

"Saying for argument's sake," Gino began, "this Beau French did abduct and kill the Brown children, where would he have stashed their bodies?" He looked from Emma to Fran. "If we find the bodies, will the children be reunited in the hereafter with their families?"

"Hard to say," Emma answered honestly, "but often that happens."

"French could have disposed of the bodies almost anywhere," Phil pointed out. "There is quite a bit of undeveloped property and acres of woods in the area even now, probably more then."

"And if he was an experienced killer," noted Gino, "I doubt he hid them anywhere near Misty Hollow. We could be looking for a needle in a haystack."

Gino found his discarded glass and retrieved the brandy bottle. "Would any of you care for another drink?"

"What the hell," Phil said, picking up his own glass for a refill. "It's not like we're driving anywhere tonight." Both women turned the offer down.

"We have pie," Emma announced. "Marta made pie today before she left," she told Fran. "Would you like some with coffee?"

"Thank you, Emma," Fran said, "but if you all don't mind, I think I'm going to head for home. It's been quite an emotionally charged night, for which I want to thank you. I've never been part of something like this and I can't wait to tell Heddy about it." She walked over to Emma and the two women exchanged warm hugs.

"Can I keep the book of newspapers?" Phil asked. "I'd like to keep looking through them, at least through 1884."

"Of course, Phil," Fran said. "Be my guest. One last question though." She looked at Emma. "Where do we go from here to find those children?"

Emma had been wondering the same thing. "I was thinking that maybe tomorrow we should hike around the area where the family last saw them."

"You mean the town square?" asked Fran.

"Yes, and fan out from there," suggested Emma. "The area isn't that large, is it?"

Fran closed her eyes in thought. "Not really. It's about five miles from here to the town of Whitefield. But fanning out would mean covering quite a bit of territory."

"I doubt French would have disposed of the children near town," Gino offered after refilling Phil's glass. "If he had, they probably would have been found during the initial search."

After considering the puzzle, Phil added, "And I'm sure the town has expanded a great deal since then, so if he buried them near the village, wouldn't they have been found during excavation for the new roads and buildings built over time?"

"That's an excellent point, Phil," Gino said, clinking his glass against Phil's. "I'll make a crime writer out of you yet."

"I have a really good map of the town at home," Fran said. "As well as some historical ones. How about we meet tomorrow, go over them, and decide where to look? Now that we know where the children were last seen, we might have a better shot at finding them. All these years, I've been focusing my search around Misty Hollow and the surrounding woods.

"There's a donut shop right across from the town square," Fran said. "How about we meet there around nine thirty? That will give the commuters enough time to get their coffee and donuts and clear out before we get there."

"That good for you, Granny?" Emma asked.

"Sure, except for that donut part," the feisty ghost answered. "It doesn't seem right that I can smell them and not taste them."

"Granny's good to go," Emma told everyone with a sly wink at Fran.

As Fran headed for the door, she said, "This storm is supposed to clear out by morning, but it's going to be muddy and wet where we'll be tramping around. If you have boots, I suggest you wear them."

Emma and Phil exchanged looks of worry, which Gino caught. "Don't worry, guys," he told them. "There's this great place I discovered just on the edge of town my first few days here that has fishing and hunting equipment, including cheap boots and gear."

"That must be Fish, Field and Farm," Fran said with a big smile. "I was going to suggest it myself. And it opens at eight a.m."

"That's the place," Gino said with a grin. "It's real close to Frank's restaurant. Much to Vanessa's dismay, I came home from there with a couple of plaid flannel shirts and some rubber boots. I also got Marta some birdseed. She'd noticed the first day here that the feeders just outside the kitchen window and along the back porch were empty and she couldn't find any seed. I think she said there's even a few feeders down by the guesthouse."

There was a vibration and Gino glanced at his phone. "It's Leroy," he said after looking at it. "He said he'll be back in the morning." He turned to Fran. "That's my assistant." He started writing a reply. "I'll let him know we'll be gone most of the morning so not to rush back."

· CHAPTER SIXTEEN ·

EMMA and Phil were running the loop they had not taken the day before, starting down the drive and onto the paved road for the first leg, instead of down the road toward the old house. The rainstorm had passed through the night before, leaving the area soaked but fresh. The air was crisp and clean as they jogged side by side, burning off the calories from the fried food the day before and sparking their energy for the busy day ahead. When they left the house, they'd not seen Gino but had heard him running the shower in his bathroom. They left him a note in the kitchen that they had gone for a run.

"I think the road that circles back by the old house is coming up," Phil said after they'd gone about a mile. "Do you want to take it or run farther on the paved road?"

"Let's take it back to the house," Emma said. "We're

going to get plenty of exercise today tramping around the woods and I want to see if any of the Browns are about."

They ran several more yards until an opening in the tree line exposed a driveway on the right. Continuing their pace, they turned down it. The drive wasn't paved but covered in a sturdy packed surface of dirt and gravel dotted with occasional small puddles. The narrow road was lined on both sides by trees and shrubs.

"Are you sure this is the right way?" Emma asked.

"Pretty sure," Phil said as they put one foot in front of the other. In spite of the chill, both of their faces were starting to shine with perspiration. "It was the only drive on this side of the main street," he continued. "They probably don't use it very often so don't bother paving it. The road from the big house to the old one is much larger and paved." He glanced down at the road. "Although it looks like someone has used this one recently from these tire tracks in the wet dirt." He stopped and squatted, examining the tracks. "In fact, there's more than one set here."

They'd gone about another half mile when Phil pointed ahead. "See, there's the house just up ahead."

A few more steps and Emma pulled up short and stopped. Phil took a few more steps before stopping himself and turning around. "What's the matter, darling?"

"I'm starting to feel the spirits, Phil, and they're disturbed."

"Are they saying anything?" he asked with concern.

She shook her head. "No, but there's a negative vibration in the air." She closed the short distance between herself and Phil. "We need to see what's there," she whispered, "but be quiet about it."

Together they moved forward, keeping close to the trees and moving in single file. Phil went first, with Emma close behind him. "Let me know," he whispered back at her, "if anything changes, ghost-wise."

They approached the house quietly. "Anything?" Phil asked. She shook her head.

"You gotta come quick," Granny said, popping up and scaring Emma.

"What's going on, Granny?" Emma asked, a hand over her heart to calm its machine-gun beating.

"Someone's dead," the ghost said. "Someone new! In the kitchen!"

"Granny says there's a body in the kitchen," Emma said to Phil as she started running for the house.

"Emma, wait," he shouted as he took off after her. When he caught her, he grabbed her arm and pulled her to a stop. "You don't know what's going on in there. If there is a body and it's a murder, the killer might still be around."

"But maybe whoever it is isn't dead but just hurt," she countered. "It's not like Granny can check for a pulse." She yanked her arm from him.

"Trust me, Emma," Granny said, "I know death when I see it."

Emma looked at Granny a moment, then at Phil, and conceded. "Is there anyone else in there, Granny?" Emma asked. The ghost shook her head and started for the house.

"Granny said no one else is there," Emma told Phil. Together, they quickly made their way to the old farmhouse.

A gray SUV was parked by the back door. The two of them listened, but heard nothing. Phil peeked in through one of the kitchen windows. "Granny's right, Emma," Phil told her. "Call nine-one-one."

Phil started to grab the back doorknob, then hesitated.

"What are you waiting for?" Emma asked as she yanked her phone from the pocket of her running jacket and dialed the emergency number.

"I don't want to smudge any prints that might be there," he said.

"Good thinking," Granny said, tapping the side of her head with a fingertip.

Remembering how flimsy the lock was, Phil leaned down and gave the door several hard pushes near the knob with his shoulder. It popped open as easy as a paper lunch bag.

"The cowboy's got skills," Granny said with pride.

Phil entered first, followed by Emma, who was on the phone with the emergency dispatcher giving the location of the farmhouse. On the floor in a pool of blood was a man dressed in jeans and a short black leather jacket. His head was facing the door. It looked like he'd been shot in the back a couple of times as he was leaving. Phil stepped carefully around the body and crouched down next to him. He pressed fingers against the man's neck. Emma held her breath and waited. A few seconds later, he looked up at Emma and shook his head. Emma told the operator that the man was dead.

While they waited for the police, Emma called Gino and told him what had happened. Then she called Fran and told her so she wouldn't be waiting for them at the donut shop. Gino and the police made it to the old farmhouse about the same time, Gino on foot.

"What in the hell is going on?" Gino asked, rushing

up to the front of the house where Phil and Emma were sitting on the porch steps, waiting.

"We don't know," Phil answered.

A local police officer got out of his vehicle and approached them. "Are you the folks who called nine-one-one?" he asked. The officer introduced himself as Officer John Cadbury. He was slim and very young, probably only in his early twenties.

"Like the candy," Emma noted automatically. It had just popped out.

"Yes, ma'am," Officer Cadbury responded without an expression, "but no relation."

"Yes, we called," Phil answered, getting to his feet. "There's a dead man in the kitchen of this old house. I'm Phil Bowers, an attorney from San Diego, and this is my fiancée, Emma Whitecastle, and our friend Gino Costello. We're staying with Gino at Misty Hollow. We were out jogging this morning when we noticed a strange vehicle parked here so we checked it out and found the guy."

"It looks like he was shot in the back," Emma added, remaining on the steps.

The officer looked at Gino. "You Gino Costello, the murder-mystery guy?"

"Yes," Gino answered. "I'm leasing Misty Hollow for a few weeks."

The officer nodded. "Heard you were in town." He turned back to Phil. "You want to show me what you found, Mr. Bowers?"

"Of course. We'll have to go around the back. The front door's locked. But don't worry, we didn't touch anything," Phil quickly added, "except for me checking to see if he was alive. I also popped the back door lock using my shoulder against the door."

Gino started to follow, then glanced back with concern at Emma.

"Go," she told him. "I'll be fine here. I'm sure more police will be coming."

After they left, Emma pulled the sleeves of her jacket down over her hands and wrapped her arms around herself. Cold was starting to creep into her bit by bit, like a cat stalking a mouse. She started to shiver. They were supposed to be looking for long-dead children, not finding fresh bodies. Her mind roared into overdrive considering the possibilities. Maybe that's why the door had been unlocked yesterday when they were here. Maybe people were using the old farmhouse as some sort of a meeting place and this meeting went sour. Drugs and serious crimes certainly weren't limited to urban areas. And local people might know that the old house was used only for storage.

Granny floated into view. "You okay, Emma? You look kind of pasty."

"I'm okay, Granny. I just wasn't expecting this."

"Who was?" the ghost shot back.

Emma looked around, trying to focus on the area around the porch. She didn't see any spirits but Granny. "Have you seen anyone from the Brown family, Granny? Maybe they saw what happened here."

"I haven't, but I think they're around. It feels kind of odd, you know what I mean? Like the energy of this place has been disturbed."

"Yes, I do know what you mean. I felt something off just before Phil and I got here." Emma closed her eyes, but except for the off-kilter feeling, she couldn't get a bead on the Browns. She opened her eyes. Granny looked concerned. "I'm okay, Granny. Really. Why don't you go see what the men are doing? I know you want to." She gave Granny a tiny smile.

"Nah," Granny said. "I'll stay here with you. They're just gabbing and going over Phil's story and waiting for other cops. When the coroner or forensics people get here, then you're on your own."

"Did you see the spirit of the dead man at all, Granny?"

"Not so much as a whisker. He might have already crossed or is confused. You know how newbie spirits are."

A deeper shiver went through Emma. She hugged herself tighter and closed her eyes again. "I'm freezing, Granny. Are you sure the Browns aren't here? Like all around me?"

Granny hesitated, her attention caught by something. "Someone is, Emma, but it's not one of the Browns as far as I can tell. He's right behind you. Maybe it's the dead guy."

Emma jumped to her feet and spun around. On the porch was the hazy outline of a tall man with thick, dark wavy hair. Emma didn't see the face of the man lying dead on the kitchen floor, but she did notice his clothing. Like the corpse inside, the ghost was wearing jeans and a nice leather jacket. Under the jacket was a Henley jersey with three buttons open at the neckline.

"What's your name?" Emma asked him, but he didn't answer. As Granny suggested, he seemed confused, and kept holding his hands up and looking at them, noticing their transparency. He had a rugged face, lean and slightly lined around his eyes, like he'd spent a lot of time in the sun while alive. He appeared to be in his mid to late thirties.

"Who did you meet here?" she asked, hoping to get him talking. "Who did this to you?"

Finally, the ghost looked up at Emma. "Can you see me?"

"Yes," she answered, "I can."

"Am I alive or dead?" he asked. "I saw someone in the house that looked like me, but here I am."

"Buddy," Granny said, floating closer, "you're dead as a doornail, like me."

"Granny," Emma scolded in a low voice. "Be nice. Can't you see he's in shock?"

"So?" snapped Granny. "What's it gonna do, kill him? The sooner he understands his predicament, the sooner he can help us figure out what happened." Emma had to admit that Granny had a good point.

The spirit wavered for a moment, as if he was going to faint, then righted himself. "But I can't be. I can't."

"But you are," Emma confirmed, much more gently than Granny had broken the news. "And you need to cross over to the other side. But before you go, can you tell me your name?"

"Um . . . I'm . . . I'm not sure," the spirit floundered, and ran a hazy hand through his equally hazy hair. He floated off the porch and turned around, looking at the house. "Why am I here? I can't remember anything."

"Oh boy," Granny quipped. "It looks like death gave him amnesia."

"You probably came here to see someone," Emma prompted, getting off the porch and moving closer to him. "Who did you come here to meet?"

Before the ghost could concentrate any further, the sound of heavy tires and moving vehicles could be heard. They were coming from the direction of the big house. In seconds another Whitefield police SUV pulled into the driveway, followed by an ambulance.

The new ghost's eyes widened at the site of the authorities and he took off into the nearby woods.

"Follow him, Granny," Emma said. "Try to find out what happened to him."

"On it, Chief."

From the police vehicle stepped a man in his forties in uniform. Two people, a man and a woman, both on the young side, got out of the ambulance. The cop approached Emma. "I'm Sergeant Colby Johnson. Where is everyone?"

"You have to go around to the back. The body's in the kitchen," Emma told him.

"And who are you?" he asked, giving her the once-over with an experienced eye. He was a bit heftier than Cadbury, with a slight paunch spilling over his thick belt.

"Emma Whitecastle, one of the people who found the body."

"Officer Cadbury back there?"

She nodded. "He's talking to my fiancé. We were together when we found the body. I made the call to nine-one-one." Her teeth started chattering.

Johnson went back to his car, returning with a small blanket. He handed it to Emma. She gratefully accepted it and immediately wrapped it around herself.

"One of you check her for shock," he said to the EMTs. "The other come with me around back to see what's going on."

The woman EMT stayed with Emma and started checking her vitals. "I'm fine," Emma protested. "We were jogging and I got cold from being all sweaty." It was the truth, but only partially. The newly minted ghost had chilled her to the bone.

"It's just a precaution," the woman told her as she worked. She was Asian with long, dark straight hair pulled back into a ponytail. Her name tag said *A. Chen*.

Once she was pronounced okay, Emma, still wrapped in the warm blanket, walked around the back to see for herself what was happening. Phil was giving his statement to Cadbury, while Johnson, wearing gloves, was going through the gray SUV. Gino was watching everything with interest, observing and filing each bit of information away in his mental filing cabinet. Emma went over to him. "Anything new, like an ID?" she asked.

"Nothing that I've heard," Gino reported. "They did call the medical examiner's office. Someone's on their way from Worcester."

They heard another car approach and soon another officer arrived. This one was African-American and carried a camera. He started taking photos of the crime scene and the surrounding area, inside and outside of the house.

Johnson approached them. "You feeling better, Mrs. Whitecastle?"

"Yes, thank you, Sergeant. I was chilled to the bone." She started to remove the blanket, but he stopped her.

"Keep it until you leave. We still need to get your statement before we can let you go."

Cadbury walked up to them. "I'm ready to take your statement, Mrs. Whitecastle."

Johnson gave her a peculiar look, then said, "Hmmm, Whitecastle? As in the burgers?"

"Yes," she answered, "but no relation." She caught the slightest trace of a smile start across Cadbury's face before it disappeared.

CHAPTER SEVENTEEN

"WELL, that certainly put a crimp in our day's plans, didn't it?" Gino noted as he put a bowl of steaming scrambled eggs down on the kitchen table.

While Emma and Phil took quick showers, taking advantage of the many bathrooms in the house to get it done faster, Gino had gotten breakfast going. He'd made scrambled eggs and bacon and had warmed up Marta's muffins from the day before.

"Sorry there's no oatmeal today, Emma," Gino told her. "Mine would be inedible. But I do know my way around a basic egg breakfast."

"No apologies, Gino," Emma said as she scooped a small portion of eggs onto her plate and grabbed a warm muffin. "This is fine. I'm not sure I have much of an appetite after this morning."

Phil brought the coffee carafe over and filled each of

their mugs. "This coffee should perk you up, Emma." As he filled her mug, he kissed the top of her freshly shampooed head, taking a deep appreciative sniff that never got old to him. He put the carafe down on the table, took a seat next to her, and started filling a plate.

They fell upon their food in silence, all of them having a better appetite than they'd expected. When the food was all gone, Emma grabbed a banana from the fruit bowl on the table. "So who do you think William Otis was?" she asked as she started peeling it.

William Otis was the dead guy. The police found his name on his vehicle registration and confirmed it against the driver's license found in his wallet in his jeans. He lived in Portland, Maine. After taking all their statements, Sergeant Johnson had let them go, but asked that they stay close to their phones for a few days.

Both men shrugged at her question and sipped their coffee while thinking. "Could be anyone," Phil said, answering first. "Johnson said he wasn't robbed. Looks more like a meeting that went bad. Possibly drugs or something like that."

"Yeah," Gino agreed. "They're dusting the place to see if his fingerprints show up. They want to see if maybe he's been there before. If he was local, he might even be one of the guys who moves equipment around for the owner. But with a Maine address, who knows."

Gino's phone rang. He looked down at it. "Speaking of the owner of Misty Hollow, there he is now. I expected him to be calling once the police reached him." He picked up his phone and walked out of the room to take the call.

Phil and Emma cleaned up the breakfast dishes then

rinsed off their muddy running shoes and set them on the back deck to dry. When they were done with their short chores, Phil retrieved their jackets from the hall and they took their coffee out to the back as they had the morning before.

"Gino's in the library, still on the phone," Phil reported. "But it sounds like he's talking to Vanessa, not the owner of this place."

Emma hugged her mug tightly between her hands and stared out at the lake, which was peaceful today after last night's storm. "I'm glad she called, no matter what the news. At least he knows she's okay."

Granny materialized near the railing. "Sorry, Emma, but that dead guy got away from me. He crossed over before I could interrogate him. And I can't find even a disembodied wisp of any of the Brown clan."

"William Otis, Granny," Emma said to the spirit. "That was his name, and that's about all we know. And don't worry. I'm sure the Browns will eventually show up."

Emma turned to Phil, not bothering to whisper now that Gino knew about Granny. "Granny says that Otis crossed over."

"Does that mean we can't talk to him?" he asked with concern.

"Pretty much," Emma answered, "unless he crosses back to this side for some reason and returns here. She's also trying to find the Browns to see if they know anything about what happened at the house, but they aren't communicating right now."

They were silently considering the lost opportunity when Gino came out from the kitchen.

"Here," Emma said, handing him a fresh mug of hot coffee. "We made another pot and brought a clean mug out for you."

He took the steaming mug and thanked her, but his face looked more haggard than before he took the call. He turned and looked out at the lake, ignoring his coffee.

"Boy," Granny said after looking him over, "Gino looks like he's ridden a few hundred miles of hard road today."

"Everything okay?" Phil asked. "With the owner of Misty Hollow, that is."

"Huh?" Gino shook himself out of his stupor and turned back to his guests. "Oh yeah, that." He leaned against the railing and took a drink of coffee before continuing. "The police called him. He doesn't have a clue who William Otis was or why someone from Maine might be in the old farmhouse, let alone dead in its kitchen." He took a sip of his coffee. "He lives near D.C., but has a local guy who takes care of this place, like a handyman. His name's Malcolm. I've seen him twice. The first day we arrived and another time when he cut the lawn. He's with the police now." Gino took another sip of coffee. "The owner also wanted to know if I still wanted to stay for the rest of my lease. He said he understands if I want to leave." Gino chuckled softly. "It amuses me that he thinks a murder would scare off the likes of me."

"So you're staying as originally planned?" Emma asked.

"Actually, I've decided to stay longer," he announced. "With Vanessa gone, I can stay as long as I want. I told the owner to plan on me renting the place at least through

Thanksgiving, possibly through the end of the year, if he and his family don't need it for Christmas. He said it was okay and to let him know, but that Leroy should move into the house since Malcolm will be closing up the guest cottage soon for the winter. I don't think Leroy will mind. He can take the suite you're in. He likes that room. Marta should be okay with it, too, since she doesn't have any family. I'll hire the people who clean it for the owner to help Marta out. If he wants to see his friends, Leroy can go back and forth to Chicago once in a while." He smiled for the first time. "Who knows, maybe T will decide to spend Thanksgiving here with her old man and visit more often since it's just a short drive from her place."

He turned back toward the lake and sipped his coffee. "I like this place. Really like it. I think I can bang out a book here in no time, especially without all the distractions of Chicago."

"Wow, this is a change of events, isn't it?" said Granny.

"And what if Vanessa comes back?" Emma asked.

Gino sighed deeply, his shoulders raising and lowering. "She's not coming back." He turned around. "I got another notice from my bank. Vanessa bought a one-way ticket to Rome. She's leaving me for him."

"Him?" Phil asked.

"I'll bet it's that guy on the phone," said Granny. "The one that put her in the family way."

"Raphael Brindisi," Gino answered. "They began an affair about a year ago when we crossed paths at an international book conference. I thought it would burn itself out, like her other indiscretions, but it didn't. They've been meeting not-so-secretly since then. I didn't really want to go to Italy when he invited us, but I did want to see for myself if I had a chance of holding on to her. But it was clear I'd already lost."

"Do you think he knows she's pregnant?" Granny asked Emma. In answer, Emma gave a little shrug.

"Have you spoken to her?" Emma asked Gino.

"Yeah, just now. After I got the notice about the plane ticket, I texted her, letting her know I knew about the ticket and that it was okay, that maybe it was time for us to part ways since she's so unhappy. I assured her I wouldn't fight it or get nasty." He looked like he was about to cry, but took several deep breaths and kept himself together. "She called me and told me she's pregnant."

"And there it is," announced Granny.

"And it's not yours?" Phil asked.

Gino shook his head. "I had a vasectomy right before Vanessa and I got married. She said she never wanted kids, but apparently Raphael does."

Just then Leroy Larkin walked into view from the side of the house. He was going down the path toward the guesthouse, his backpack slung over one shoulder, and hadn't seen them.

"Leroy," Gino called out. "You're back."

Leroy looked startled at hearing his name and turned, his face changing to a wide smile upon seeing them lined up on the back porch. He changed his course and came up the back steps to greet them. "Kind of chilly to be out here, isn't it?"

"Nothing like fresh air and a view of nature," Gino said, waving the hand holding his mug in the direction of the lake.

"Would you like some coffee, Leroy?" Emma asked.

"No, thank you, I'm good," Leroy answered. "I thought

you guys were going to be gone this morning. There was only one car in the driveway when I pulled in."

"A lot has gone on in the short time you've been away, my lad," Gino announced.

"Ain't that the truth," quipped Granny. "It's been a regular telenovela around here." Emma shot Granny a stern look. "What?" snapped the ghost. "It's not like anyone but you can hear me."

"Let's see," Gino began. "First of all, Vanessa left me."

Leroy's face didn't display any emotion. "Vanessa does this with regularity, Gino. She's probably holed up in some luxury penthouse wearing down the numbers on your credit card. She'll be back. She always comes back."

"No, buddy, not this time," Gino told him. "She's leaving me for Raphael Brindisi."

"That poser?" Leroy asked with clear contempt.

"Yep, that poser," Gino confirmed. "But wait, there's more," he said, holding up a finger and sounding like a TV pitchman. "It seems this place is haunted, and finally"— he paused and held up another finger—"sometime in the last twenty-four hours someone was murdered at the old farmhouse."

This time Leroy slumped against the post next to the steps. "Murdered?"

"Yep and for real," Gino confirmed, "not from the pages of any book."

"Oh my God," Leroy said under his breath. "Who was it?"

"Some guy named William Otis," Phil told him. "The police are over there now. Emma and I found him during our morning jog."

"Wow!" Leroy shook his head. "I go away for two nights and all hell breaks loose."

"And more news, but more pleasant, at least for me," Gino said, this time with a small smile. "I've decided to lease this place at least through Thanksgiving, maybe longer. I think it will be a good place for me to work. I'm actually onto something a little different for my next book, thanks to Emma and Phil." Gino paused and took another drink of his coffee. "Leroy, how does a book about a serial killer from the 1800s strike you?"

"A period piece?" Leroy asked with even more surprise. "Like Anne Perry? You've never done one of those."

"No time like the present to try new things," Gino countered with a grin. "It would take more research, but I think it could be very interesting. We might have stumbled upon a serial killer right here at Misty Hollow."

Leroy started to roll his large wide-set eyes with great exaggeration before catching himself and plastering a more compliant look on his face. "Did you folks hold a séance or something?"

Granny drifted over to Emma. "I can see this guy's not a believer."

"More like something," Gino said, his excitement turning quickly to annoyance. "Why don't you get settled in and we can talk about it later. By the way, Marta will be gone for a few days. A friend of hers in Connecticut is quite ill and she's gone to be with her. That's where the other car is. So we'll be fending for ourselves."

Leroy gave his employer a long, almost feline look. "I'm sure we can make a few beds and heat some soup in her absence, Gino, especially with Vanessa gone." Emma noted that Leroy had dropped the more formal

Mrs. Costello now that Vanessa was out of the picture. "Let me drop off my gear and I'll be back," Leroy said, heading back down the steps.

He was at the bottom and starting down the path when Gino stopped him. "You know, Leroy, if you want to get working now you can start researching on your own. Look up everything you can on itinerant photographers in early 1800s New England—how they worked, equipment, processing of photos—stuff like that. And especially see what you can find on someone named Beau French. He was a real photographer hanged in 1884."

"Beau French. Photographer. 1884," Leroy said, making mental notes. "Got it. Would you mind if I worked from the cottage," he asked, "considering you have guests?"

"Not at all, Leroy," Gino told him. "We can circle back around at dinnertime to discuss your findings."

In silence the three living people and one ghost watched Leroy go down the path to the guesthouse.

"I take it Leroy doesn't care for your wife or for ghosts," Phil said to Gino, breaking the silence.

"I'm not sure he cares for anyone, really," Gino said, still watching Leroy. "Although they don't like each other, he and Vanessa were bound by their common disdain for me, although Leroy tries hard to hide his."

"Then why do you keep him on?" Phil asked. "I'd bet a ton of applicants would line up for a chance to work with you."

Gino laughed slightly. "Because he's a fantastic assistant. None better on research. And I've had some pretty bad ones over the years." Gino sighed deeply, a man caught between a rock and a hard place. "It's not really disdain on Leroy's part, more like jealousy, and not just of me, but of most published authors. Leroy's public persona is all smiles and rah-rah, but behind the scenes he can be pretty dark. I guess that comes with being a frustrated writer. I should know. I was once one myself." Gino turned his attention back to his guests. "He's written several novels but none have been picked up by a publisher or even an agent. I think when he got this job he thought I might be able to grease the wheels for him. I've tried, but no one I know, including my own agent, has been keen on Leroy's writing. He even tried self-publishing but that was a disaster sales-wise."

"He's really that bad?" asked Phil.

Gino shrugged. "No, not really. His writing mechanics are solid as a steel skyscraper. Even better than mine, truth be told. But writing is so much more than knowing where to put a comma or how to structure a sentence. He just hasn't found his voice."

"You're saying his writing has no heart?" Phil said.

"Yeah, that's it. That's exactly it," Gino said. "You can teach a writer mechanics and grammar, but you can't teach voice. You can't teach someone to leave their guts on the page. Until Leroy learns to do that, his writing will be mediocre and there's plenty of that out there." Gino look toward the guesthouse. "He and I have talked about that many times, but he just doesn't get it."

"Voice, schmoice. Are we going to sit around all day on our backsides?" asked Granny, tapping her foot with impatience. "We should be out looking for the Brown twins. We can't help that Otis guy, but we can help those children."

"Granny's right," Emma said. The two men turned to her, Phil expectantly and Gino with surprise. "She just said we shouldn't be hanging around doing nothing when we could be out looking for Chester and Clarissa."

Gino nodded. "True. No sense hanging around. Do you think Fran will still be up for it?"

Emma pulled her phone out of her pocket and called Fran. In minutes the search and the meeting at the donut shop were both back on, delayed but not forgotten.

"Now we're back on track," Granny said as she started to fade. "I'll catch up to you later. I've got something to do."

CHAPTER EIGHTEEN

THE donut shop was actually a charming locally owned bakery, not a chain as they had expected. When they entered, they were surrounded by the fragrance of baked goods mingled with the rich scent of coffee beans. Though warm and inviting, with colorful walls and soft music, the place was pretty empty. It wasn't quite lunchtime and too late for breakfast. Over by the front window, a young man worked away at a laptop while sprawled in an old leather chair. Behind the counter, a middle-aged woman with short red hair was stacking freshly baked cookies in the counter display. Fran and Heddy were waiting for them at a large round table in the corner. On the table they'd spread out maps.

"You folks want coffee?" Gino said before sitting down. "I'm buying."

"We already have tea," Heddy answered, indicating large cups in front of them.

"I'll take some hot chocolate, no whipped cream," said Emma. "Thank you."

"Decaf for me," said Phil.

After Phil and Emma sat down, Fran asked, with concern and in a low voice, "Hasn't Gino heard from his wife yet? He looks so haggard."

Emma nodded. "Yes. She's fine and he's relieved but exhausted. It's been a rough morning for him."

"For all of you," exclaimed Fran. "Finding that body and all. Any news on that?"

"Nothing," Phil said. "But Sergeant Johnson asked us to stay close in case he has any more questions."

"Ah, yes," said Fran with a smile. "That would be Colby Johnson. He grew up in Whitefield. Only left for college, then came back to marry his high school sweetheart. Good man. Has a lovely family. His wife brought their children to the library almost every Saturday until they got too old. After that they often came on their own to check out books."

Emma studied Fran Monroe. She was a walking, talking encyclopedia of local information, both people and places, but when she spoke of people and things in the town, there was not a sliver of gossip or maliciousness in her tone. She looked from Fran to Heddy and saw how vital and in love the two women were, even in their advanced age. She linked her arm through Phil's and gave him a warm smile. Hopefully, Gino would one day find what they all enjoyed, or even close to it.

"And what did I do to deserve that smile and a snuggle?" Phil asked, mischief dancing in his eyes.

"It's just for being you," she said and laughed.

"Uh-huh," Heddy said, watching them. "So when are you two tying the knot?"

"We're not sure," Emma told them. "But we've talked about next summer after my daughter graduates from college." She glanced at Phil. "Honestly, we'd love to simply elope, but my family and Phil's would have a fit."

"Ha!" said Phil. "That's an understatement. You'd think we were in our twenties the way they're all acting. Even my sons want us to have a big wedding. Not fancy, but big."

Heddy squeezed Fran's hand. "We got married at the cutest little chapel in Vermont, then stayed at a friend's cabin in the mountains for a week after. It was heaven."

"Here you go," announced Gino. He was balancing three large cups on a carryout container. After the drinks were distributed, he took a seat.

"Okay, let's begin," Fran announced. "This is a map of Whitefield back in the 1800s. See here." She pointed to the center of the map. "That's the town square, which is right outside that window." Phil, Emma, and Gino all turned and looked at the tidy square across the street. In the middle was a white gazebo.

"This shop would be located right here," Fran continued, "had it been around back then." She pointed to a corner across from the square with the non-writing end of her pen. "When Abigail and the twins were around, the general store was in this spot." She moved the pen down the road until it drifted off the page. "This is the road to Misty Hollow. The same road you took in here today. As you can see, the town was fairly small back then but thriving and a hub of activity serving many of the smaller villages in the area."

Fran pulled another map from under the other and placed it on top. It was a modern map, a bit larger than the first. "This is the town of Whitefield today. As you can see, it has expanded a great deal. See this circle in the middle? Early this morning, I traced the boundaries of the old town over the current map to give us a perspective of what was here when the Browns were alive. As we discussed last night, if French killed the children, he probably would not have stashed the bodies within the town limits, this smaller circle." She indicated a larger circle on the outskirts of the first one. "This indicates the area where there has been a lot of new development close to the town center over the last century. If he hid the bodies in this area, I think they might have been discovered. Not for certain, but probably. That leaves the rest of the area."

She pulled out the old map again and pointed to an area near the end of the square opposite the bakery. "This is where the hotel was where French would have stayed, according to Abigail. It was the only hotel back then." She switched maps and pointed to an intersection just within the first circle. "And this is where that hotel would have been today, but it's now a small office building." She moved her pointer along a road. "Along with Misty Hollow, this road branches off here and there to reach various points on the lake. This one here goes to the area that was once the site of Job's Arm. On some of these roads I've jotted down some notes. See? Here's the road that leads to the Passer Heights development. Here are the roads that would go to Hampshire, Worcester, et cetera. Of course everyone mostly hops on and off the interstate now to get to these places.

"This is great, Fran," Gino said with enthusiasm. "Very informative."

Fran seemed pleased with the praise. "Heddy and I had a few copies of the current map made at the copy shop before coming here, so you can each have one." She gave everyone their own copy with the drawn circles.

"So how are we going to divide up the search parties?" asked Heddy.

Emma looked at the map, hoping to get some sort of vibes from it, but she got nothing. "I think we should have two search parties, with me and Fran split between them. This many years later, we're not looking for a grave but for the spirits themselves, providing they are lingering near their graves or the place where they died. If they're not, this all may be wasted time, but I know of no other way to look for them." They all murmured agreement.

Gino laughed. "You and Fran will be like human metal detectors, but in this case looking for ghosts instead of lost rings in the sand."

"Something like that," Fran agreed with a grin.

"Why don't I go with Fran and Heddy?" Phil suggested. "And Emma and Gino head in another direction."

"Yes," admitted Emma. "I think that would be a great idea." She looked at the two women. "Did you bring Howard? Animals are great at noticing spirits."

"We sure did," Fran said with a smile, "even though it's quite wet out. He's out in the car right now. He's very sensitive to ghosts, and loves trekking through the woods."

Phil studied the map, then said, "Why don't Emma and Gino take the part south of the midsection of town, just below Main Street, and we'll take the area above.

We can start at the far edges of the outside circle and expand outward."

"One thing to remember," noted Gino. "Back then travel took a lot longer than it does now. Even if he was driving a buggy, French would not have gone far unless he stored the bodies somewhere, then drove them out of town when he left and dumped them somewhere between Whitefield and his next stop." He paused. "But I doubt he did that because it was summer and those bodies would have started smelling by the time he left town."

"That's right," Fran said, "and didn't Abigail say that French stuck around to help with the search?"

"Right. So we really only have a few miles to expand out from the edge of town," added Phil, "because he wouldn't have gone far."

"Just remember," said Heddy, "a lot of that area is still wooded without paths."

Gino grinned at Emma and Phil. "Now aren't you glad I made us stop at that Fish, Field, and whatever to buy rubber boots?"

In response, Emma stuck out her long legs and clicked her heels together, making a dull thudding sound. On her feet were army green rubber boots that came halfway up her calves. Phil and Gino were each wearing a similar pair.

"They're not as cute as yours, Fran," Emma said with a smile while admiring her recent purchase, "but they'll be useful enough back home."

CHAPTER NINETEEN

G INO Costello waded through the woods like a bear
searching for food. Emma was annoyed by the noise,
as it distracted her from concentrating on any spirits that
might be about, but she was also amused. For all his
man's-man appearance, it was clear that Gino spent little
time outdoors. She was sure Phil wasn't having the same
issue. Heddy and Fran clearly knew their way around
nature. Emma had worked in noisy circumstances before
and knew how to handle them. She stood still, closed her
eyes, and took several deep breaths, closing out the sound
of twigs and branches being disturbed and resetting her
sensitivities to what couldn't be seen or heard. After a
few moments, her inner senses had taken over her outer
senses and she became aware of the smallest movements
and air currents around them.

Gino had come to a stop beside her. "You got something?"

"Not yet," she said. "I was just concentrating on the lesser sounds hiding under the surface ones."

"Guess I'm making quite a bit of noise. Sorry about that." Gino chuckled between catching his breath. "I would have made a lousy Indian scout."

Emma smiled at him. Gino was such a good-hearted man, but sadness ran deep in him and not just because of Vanessa. She could see it in his eyes, in the back, hidden from public view, and sensed it in his scent. Gino's personal grief ran in the background, like malware on a computer. She wondered if this was why he had trouble in relationships, especially with his daughter and his wives. She knew deep grief could cause intimacy issues. She'd seen it with her mother. It had taken more than a decade before she fully returned emotionally to her family after Paulie's death. Maybe Janelle's death had put up a wall inside Gino. Phil had told her that Gino had become twice as prolific in his writing in the past ten or so years. He'd buried himself in his work after burying T's mother.

"We'll have to get you out hiking more," she told him with a pat to his shoulder. "Phil will have you used to it in no time, like he did me. I was used to running before we met, but trekking through the brush and over obstacles is a whole different skill set."

She consulted the map. They'd been walking in a crisscross path through the area assigned to them just outside the larger circle for more than an hour. Their journey had taken them through woods and small meadows, and back and forth across a small stream a few times. Their boots were muddy and their jeans wet from brushing shrubs and trees heavy from the rain the night before. They'd seen a few houses built in clearings, with long drives that lead back to streets, but not many. Damp below the waist, above they were warm from the exertion, and both had long since taken off their light jackets and tied them around their waists.

They'd parked Phil and Emma's rental car in a pullout on the edge of the wooded area and Gino had suggested they use the GPS feature on his phone's map app to make sure they could find their way back to the car. He was consulting it now while Emma took a drink from the bottle of water she carried. Before leaving the bakery, Phil had purchased several bottles of water for each of them for the search, and Heddy had handed out small bags of apples she'd brought from home.

"As the crow flies," Gino said, looking at his phone, "we've only gone about two miles. But with all the zig-zagging it's probably been more like four or five." They compared his map against the one Fran had given them.

"We're almost to the road that bisects this section of woods," she noted. "Maybe we should go back and move the car to here." Emma pointed to a spot on the other side of the highway. "And tackle that side."

"Sounds good," Gino agreed. "We've about covered this section anyway." He looked up. "Did you get any vibes from anything?"

"Not a one," she said with frustration. "Not a single ghost, let alone the Brown children. Let's check in with the others and see how they're doing."

"What about me?" asked a voice coming from near a tree.

"Hi, Granny," said Emma as the ghost materialized. "Where've you been?"

"I've been working, that's where," Granny said with a jerk of her head. "I've been trying to talk to the Browns, but they are making themselves scarce. I think the murder in their house spooked them. Funny, ghosts being 'fraidy cats."

"Not really," Emma told her. "They've gotten used to their way of life straddling here and the other side and don't like strangers, especially with all the comings and goings now at the old house with the police investigation."

Emma glanced over at Gino. He was sitting on a fallen log and drinking water from his bottle, watching Emma converse with thin air. His eyes were bright and attentive as he absorbed it like a sponge and scribbled notes in his brain for access later.

"This is all gonna end up in one of his books," Granny said, eyeing Gino. "You just watch." In response, Emma smiled and nodded to Granny.

"I take it you guys haven't found anything?" Granny asked.

"Nothing yet," Emma reported, "but we're about to move to another section and try there."

"Do you really think those kids are still here locally?"

"Yes, I do. We all do," Emma answered.

"Unless you need me to stay with you," Granny said, "I'd like to go back to the house."

Emma studied her. "What's up, Granny? You look concerned."

"I'm not sure," the spunky ghost explained. "It's just a gut feeling I have. I don't trust that Leroy guy. He seems kind of squirrely to me."

Emma glanced at Gino, who was now reading messages on his phone. She lowered her voice. "I saw you follow him down to the guesthouse, Granny. Is that why?"

Granny nodded. "Yeah, but so far he's just played with his phone and worked on his computer. He made a few calls but I don't think anyone answered. Oh, and he made himself something to eat up at the big house. In addition to being squirrely, he's also pretty messy. I think he's gotten too used to Marta cleaning up after him."

"Sounds like he's doing what Gino asked him to do—research," Emma told her, still keeping her voice barely above a whisper. "Why don't you keep trying to reach Blaine or Abigail? And do pop back to the old house. Who knows, maybe William Otis will return."

Granny snapped a salute at Emma and left.

Emma pulled out her own phone and called Phil. Like them, that group had nothing to report except for Howard flushing out a couple of rabbits. They agreed to report back in another hour.

The walk back to the car didn't take long. Along the way, Emma pulled out one of Heddy's apples she'd stashed in her jacket pocket and quickly ate it down to the core. Finished, she tossed it to the ground.

"Litterbug," Gino said with a smile.

Emma laughed and wiped her mouth with the back of her hand. "That's not litter. That core is good eats for the critters out here."

"Frankly, I'd rather a steak or juicy burger about now."

Emma grinned at him. "Or how about fried clams and scallops?"

"And onion rings."

"Definitely onion rings," Emma agreed.

Gino let loose with one of his hearty laughs. "When we're done here, let's head to Frank's. If the others don't want to come, it'll be just you and me."

"It's a date," she said giving him a high five.

When they reached the car, Gino gobbled down one of his apples, which he'd left behind, and tossed the core into the brush.

"So tell me, Gino," Emma said to him after she finished another apple. "How are you feeling today about ghosts and spirits and such? Are you starting to believe or are you still just along for the ride?"

He pondered the question while drinking some water. "Still thinking about it all," he said after putting the cap back on the bottle. "And still along for the ride. But you can bet I'm taking a lot of mental notes."

They took a few moments to lean against the car and study the beautiful and lively nature around them. Wind rustled the trees and unseen birds chirped happily. A squirrel dashed across the clearing in front of the car, quickly followed by another. Several cars drove by on the road, but traffic was light.

"One thing is for sure," Gino said. "You've either given me a whole lot of evidence toward believing in the spirit world, or this is some fantastic and complicated endeavor to screw with my mind." He cocked his head and gave her a questioning grin. "Did Vanessa hire you to do that?"

"You got me," Emma responded, her hands up in the air in surrender. "It's really some big conspiracy to hijack your mind and sell it to aliens. But it was T's idea, not Vanessa's." They both laughed and got into the car.

"You're all right, Emma Whitecastle," he said as she started up the engine and waited for a few cars to go by before pulling onto the paved highway. "I may not be one hundred percent on board with this whole ghost thing, but I am one hundred percent on board with you."

"Why thank you," she said, amused.

"No, I mean it. I knew from what T has said about you that you and Phil were good people, but you specifically surprised me."

"By presenting evidence about the existence of ghosts?" she asked. Instead of pulling onto the now open road, she turned to look at Gino.

"That, too," he admitted. "But I knew you'd been married to Grant Whitecastle and he's a big celebrity and spawn of Hollywood royalty. Hell, his father was the legendary director George Whitecastle." He glanced out the windshield and back at her. "And with you having your own TV gig, I guess I expected you to be more showbiz and less down-to-earth. It's been a refreshing surprise, and Phil's a great guy. He's more rancher than lawyer."

"Phil is great, no doubt about that. I'm a very lucky woman." She flashed a happy smile at Gino. "As for the showbiz thing, I never really felt like I fit into Grant's world, so it wasn't that difficult to leave it behind when we divorced, and my show is nothing like a big network show. If it was, I might not have agreed to do it. I think of it as more educational than entertainment."

Gino laughed.

"What are you laughing at?" she asked.

"I just keep thinking about those women at Frank's and how excited they were about meeting you, and how Fran went all gaga when first in your presence. You are a star, Emma, whether you want to admit it or not."

She looked both ways down the highway again. Seeing

it open, she pulled the car onto the road and headed toward the other half of their assigned area. "Maybe in some circles, but I assure you it's with a tiny *s* not a capital *S*."

He laughed again. "You and Janelle would have liked each other very much. I'm sure of it. And you and my first wife would have gotten along great, too. In fact, the three of you would have had your own coffee klatch, you're so much alike—smart, beautiful, and unpretentious."

"Why did you and your first wife split, if you don't mind my asking?"

Gino was quiet. "Barbara died. Ovarian cancer." He said the words quick and sharp, like the jab of a needle to a vein.

"I'm so sorry, Gino," Emma said, glancing quickly at him. "I always thought you'd been divorced three times. Didn't you say something about with Vanessa you'd be a four-time loser?"

"Vanessa will make the third divorce, but I still feel like a four-time loser at love. Five if you count my relationship with Janelle, even though we never married. Funny thing is, my ex-wives are all alike, and the two women I loved and lost to the Grim Reaper are also very much alike. Maybe I go for the shallow beauties thinking I can hold on to them better." He paused, then added, "And don't go thinking ill of Vanessa. She was right yesterday. I'm not fun anymore. When we first married, it was all parties and travel with exciting people. Then I settled back into my writing, which is very solitary, and she was left to fend for herself and felt abandoned. It was the same complaint from the other ex-wives. Barbara and Janelle both understood the sullen, obsessive, and hermitlike behavior of a writer on deadline, and handled it well." He looked at Emma. "Here I am dumping my truckload of regrets onto you, Emma. I'm so sorry."

"Don't be, Gino. That's what friends are for. I'm here to listen as much as you need me to."

Soon they passed the road that had split their territory. Gino glanced at the map and pointed straight ahead. "Here's the place. I think I can see another turnout up ahead on the left."

Emma spotted it and made a left-hand turn, parking the car close to the edge of the woods. She gave Gino a small smile of encouragement. "Does T know yet about Vanessa?"

He shook his head. "Not yet. I thought I'd tell her when she gets here Thursday. Maybe take a little father-daughter walk." He sighed. "I'm not sure how she's going to take it. She and Vanessa don't like each other at all, but no father wants to flash his failures in front of his children."

Emma thought about Grant. He wasn't a bad father to Kelly, but he wasn't very sensitive to her feelings or concerned about what kind of role model he presented. She gave Gino high marks for being concerned about that. "Does T know about your first wife?"

He shook his head. "No, she just knows that before I met her mother I was married a couple of times. And of course she's heard the wild stories about me in my younger days."

"You should tell her about Barbara someday. You know how you said Leroy needs to leave his guts on the page? Maybe you need to show your daughter your guts and the pain that goes with them."

Gino didn't look so sure. He opened his car door and

started to climb out. "I'll take that under advisement." He stopped, then tacked on, "And I mean that seriously. It wasn't a glib comment."

The remaining part of their assigned area on the map wasn't as thickly wooded as the first section, and they made good time crisscrossing the land, taking it slow enough for Emma to pay attention to any spirits but fast enough to cover it in a reasonable amount of time.

"We're not all that far from Misty Hollow," Emma said looking at the map. "It's a few miles off in that direction." She pointed through the woods, then went back to studying the map. "The lake is in our section of the map. It looks like it runs horizontally along this piece of land. According to this, the location of Job's Arm should be almost straight ahead about a mile or two."

This area was sprinkled with more houses than the last section they'd searched, but still not thickly populated. Wooded areas separated most of the houses, affording them privacy. They encountered a few more disheveled stone fences, their boulders long fallen over and covered with moss.

"These probably indicate property lines from a hundred or more years ago," Gino noted after they climbed over one long one instead of going around.

"Yes, and notice how the trees here are younger than those outside of the fence area," Emma pointed out. "Phil told me that usually indicates that the side with the younger trees was probably once cleared."

"'Twas my home," said a weak voice. "And you're trespassing."

Emma looked around, but saw nothing. She held up a hand to Gino to indicate she'd heard something. She looked again, her eyes narrowed this time as they slowly scanned the area looking for any telltale signs of a spirit. On the third pass she saw him. The hazy spirit of a bent old man in rough homemade clothing was perched on one of the fallen stones not more than three feet away.

Emma approached him with caution so as not to scare him off. "Good day, sir. My name is Emma and this is Gino. To whom am I speaking?"

The bent over spirit eyed her up and down. "Name's Dodd. Alexander Dodd," the ghost said in a warbled but stern voice. "You're on Dodd property and you don't belong here." He narrowed his eyes and looked Emma up and down. "You're a right pretty thing, but you still don't belong."

"We're looking for someone, Mr. Dodd," Emma explained. "Might my friend and I cross your property to do so?" Gino stayed where he was, looking on with his usual observant eye.

"That fella can't see me, can he?" asked Alexander Dodd, pointing at Gino.

"No, Mr. Dodd, he cannot," answered Emma. "He can't hear you either." Emma looked around but saw no other spirits. "When did you live here Mr. Dodd?"

The ghost gave the question some thought. "My woman and I settled here in the early 1800s, right after we married. Had a small place right here. Built this stone wall with my bare hands."

Emma considered the age of the ghost at the time of his death and asked, "Did you know the Brown family from over at Misty Hollow?"

"The Browns? You mean Caleb Brown and his family?" Dodd asked.

Emma nodded. "Yes."

Dodd thought about it before answering. "Yes, I knew Caleb. He had a right good house on that farm of his but was always talking about building another, grander place for his family. Not sure if he ever did it or if it was all bluster."

Emma and Gino exchanged glances. His was curious, wanting to know what was going on. Hers was one of thought. If the big house hadn't been built yet by Caleb Brown, then Alexander Dodd hadn't been alive when the Brown twins went missing. He might not even have been alive when they were born.

"Mr. Dodd," Emma said, "have you seen any children around here in the years you've been keeping watch over your property?"

"I've seen lots of children," he answered, scoffing. "Plenty of nice houses around here now with several little ones in each. They're always running around my property, climbing on my wall."

"But how about children like yourself?" she pressed.

"You mean dead young 'uns, don't you?"

"Yes, I mean the spirits of dead children."

The ghost scratched his chin while he gave it thought. "There have been a few passed through from time to time, but fortunately not many." He started to fade as he used up his energy talking.

Emma started to get excited. "How about a boy and girl about the same age, dressed in clothing from your time?"

Again the ghost gave it thought, driving Emma crazy as each precious second passed and his form dissolved. "Yah, I seen them."

"Can you tell me where they are?" Emma asked. "I'd very much like to meet them. Their family is looking for them."

Again the ghost paused, his form barely hanging on.

"Please, Mr. Dodd," Emma begged. "Please tell me before you go." But he was gone.

Excited but disappointed, Emma told Gino everything Alexander Dodd had told her.

"So they are around?" Gino said, matching her excitement.

"Not just around, but likely they are around here or not very far from here," she explained. "Let's tell the others. We should be checking in anyway."

Emma pulled out her phone to call Phil. While she was on the phone with him, Gino received a call on his phone. He walked several paces away to take his call.

· CHAPTER TWENTY ·

WHEN Emma finished conferring with the other search party, she found Gino sitting on one of the taller boulders. His phone was in his hand, forgotten, as he stared into space. Immediately, she became alarmed.

"Gino, what is it?" she asked, placing a comforting hand on his shoulder. "What's wrong? Is it Tanisha? Vanessa?"

It took him several seconds before he was even aware she was there. "Nothing like that. Nothing tragic, at least I don't think so. That was Neil, my agent." He turned to look up at her and she was relieved to see his face displayed surprise and curiosity, not grief or shock. Behind his eyes she saw his active mind working to process and analyze whatever his agent had told him. "He said he saw Vanessa yesterday in New York."

"But you knew she was there," Emma noted. "Was she with Brindisi?"

Gino shook his head slowly back and forth. "No, she was with Leroy."

Emma took a step back in surprise. "Leroy? Is he sure?" She suddenly remembered Granny's feeling about the man, and was glad she was keeping an eye on him.

"Yes. He saw them at the Plaza in the bar. He thought maybe I was in New York, too, even though he didn't see me with them. He said he started to approach but saw they were having a heated discussion, so left without saying anything. He said he's been wondering if he should call me or not. I told him I was glad he did."

"So he doesn't know that Vanessa left you?"

"He does now." Gino took a deep breath, held it, then let it out slowly. "I'm more curious about why Leroy lied to me about his whereabouts and why they were meeting behind my back." He got to his feet, his jaw clenched. Surprise was being replaced by anger. "I'm sorry to disrupt this search party, but I think I need to go back to the house and have a chat with my *loyal* assistant."

"Of course," Emma said, wondering if she should say something to Gino about Granny's gut feeling. She decided against it for now. It wouldn't help Gino unless Granny learned something. If anything, it might make Gino more perturbed, and he was doing fine on that by himself.

"We're calling off the search for the day anyway," she told him. "We're thinking that since we have a lead on the twins being in this area somewhere, we'll come back tomorrow bright and early. We can cover more area faster if we concentrate our efforts here."

"Sounds like a plan," he answered automatically.

"Please, Gino," she said with concern. "Don't feel obligated to come along. It sounds like you have a lot on your plate without running around the countryside."

"We'll see how everything goes." Gino consulted the GPS on his phone. "The car is this way," he said, and started marching in that direction. Emma caught up to him and they walked back to the car in silence.

Once they were on the road heading back to Misty Hollow, Emma said with caution, "The others are on their way to Misty Hollow, too, to drop off Phil. He and I will head out for a while, to give you and Leroy some privacy."

"No," Gino said, surprising her. He was staring out the windshield. "I'd like you and Phil to be there, to keep tabs on me so I don't blow my top." He turned to her. "Please."

Emma nodded her agreement. It was probably better that she and Phil be there for that reason and, as she admitted to herself privately, she really wanted to hear what Leroy had to say. Granny was right, she was just as nosy as the old ghost.

"Maybe," Emma suggested, "Vanessa called Leroy to tell him she left you and he drove to New York to try and talk her out of it."

"That's a three to four hour drive one way," Gino noted. "And when Leroy came in this morning, he acted like he didn't know about Vanessa. Remember?"

Emma nodded again. "I'd forgotten that." She worked the details of that morning's conversation over in her head, then asked, "Do you suspect that Leroy never went to Boston to see his friend?"

"It's sure a good possibility." He continued staring out

the window, then abruptly turned to Emma. "Would you mind pulling over for a minute."

Without a word, Emma pulled to the side of the road, even though they weren't far from Misty Hollow. She watched while Gino made a call. Seconds later, they heard a short honk from a vehicle and a white compact SUV pulled up behind them. It was Phil with Fran and Heddy. Emma got out of the car and went back to talk to them.

"Anything the matter, Emma?" Phil asked from the backseat. "Is the car okay?"

"The car is fine," she told them. "Something has come up with Gino."

"About his wife?" asked Fran, who was driving.

"Yes," Emma answered.

"I hope she's okay," added Heddy.

"She's fine," Emma quickly assured them. "But he needed to make a quick call before he got back to the house, that's all." They looked at her with curiosity, but all had the good manners not to press further.

"Phil," Emma said, "why don't you come with us from here? No sense Fran and Heddy driving all the way to the house."

"Good idea," Phil said, opening the back door and climbing out.

"Are we still on for tomorrow morning?" asked Fran.

"Yes, of course," Emma answered. "We may be without Gino, but the four of us can continue. I'll call you to set a time and place to meet."

With a wave, the ladies did a U-turn and headed back toward town. Once they were gone, Phil asked, "What's really going on?" Emma filled him in while they gave Gino privacy to make his call.

"Do you think," Phil said after churning the information around in his head, "that maybe Leroy and Vanessa are having an affair?"

"I wondered that myself," Emma said. "It wouldn't be the first time a couple pretended to dislike each other to cover their feelings. But Vanessa did buy a ticket to Italy today, so it looks like the affair was with Brindisi."

"Hey, you guys," Gino called from the car. He'd opened his door and was standing half in, half out. "How do you feel about running me back to the car rental place?"

"Are you going to rent another car?" asked Phil once they were on their way back to Worcester. "You know you're free to use ours until Marta gets back."

"Maybe, but one thing at a time," Gino said, looking straight ahead. "When Vanessa called this morning she told me she'd left the original leased SUV at the airport. I called the rental place right after I spoke with her and they assured me that they would find it and check it back in for me. When I said I wasn't sure in which parking lot she'd dumped it, they told me not to worry because they could track all their vehicles." He turned and looked at Emma and Phil in turn, letting the information sink in.

"So," said Emma, putting the pieces together, "if they could track that vehicle, they could track the one Leroy was using."

"That's right," Gino confirmed with a wide grin. "I just have to look at this like I would one of my books and act like a detective."

"Smart thinking, Gino," said Phil from the back.

"I just called the rental place," Gino told them, "and they told me I had to come in and talk to them. They wouldn't do any of it over the phone." He shrugged. "Who knows, they might not even do it then since the rental agreement is back with the car, but maybe I can schmooze them."

As before, Emma and Phil stayed behind in the car while Gino went inside. This time it took him much longer, but eventually he emerged, grinning and waving a wad of paper as he approached.

"This place must make me hungry," he announced as he slid into the passenger's seat. "How about lunch?" He looked at Phil. "I kind of promised Emma more fried seafood." Phil gave him a thumbs-up and Emma headed the car back to Whitefield.

"You're in a good mood," Phil said once they were on their way back to Frank's restaurant. "Leroy must have passed the sniff test."

"On the contrary," Gino said, shaking the papers in his hand, "he stinks to high heaven, but I'm like one of those hounds you love, Phil. I'm happiest when I'm on the scent of something juicy."

"So the rental place didn't have a problem giving you that information?" asked Emma.

"It was the same young guy at the counter as yesterday. He was reluctant at first and wanted to wait until he could check with his supervisor, who was out." Gino chuckled and shot a wink at Emma. "Isn't it amazing how a Ben Franklin or two can grease the wheels of bureaucracy?"

Seated once more at Frank's, but this time at a table on the outside patio, Gino went through the printout the rental agency had provided. It was chilly out and everyone was bundled in their jackets, but they stayed outside since most of the other diners were inside. "I asked the rental guy to pull the records on all of the vehicles leased under my name. Vanessa's car is already back with the agency and they gave me a receipt for it." He put that paperwork aside, popped a plump fried clam into his mouth, and moved to the next printout with the methodical movements of a man on a mission. "The SUV I leased yesterday, the one Marta took, is right where it should be. It traveled from here to Connecticut and has hardly moved since."

Emma washed down an onion ring with some iced tea. "Glad to hear that. I'd hate to think all your household is under suspicion."

"Me, too." Gino glanced up. "By the way, I called Marta and told her to take another day off if she wanted it. I didn't tell her what was going on, just that we didn't need her right now so to enjoy being with her friend. I don't want her in the middle of all this drama."

"Good call," noted Phil. "By the way, how does she get along with Leroy?"

Gino shrugged. "Okay, I guess. She doesn't seem to mind him but she doesn't go out of her way for him either. It's more like she ignores him." He paused, then asked, "Should I text T and tell her and Kelly to hold off coming?"

Emma shook her head. "Unless you have a plausible explanation, that will send up all kinds of red flags to the girls. They just might drive down tonight to see what's going on."

"I tend to agree with Emma," Phil said. "Today's Tuesday and they aren't arriving until Thursday. Hopefully, this Leroy and Otis business will be cleared up by then. If not, then we can tell them to hold off coming until maybe Friday or Saturday."

Gino moved the paperwork for Marta's vehicle aside. "Now for the interesting stuff," he announced with the glee of a child finding buried treasure. He gulped some coffee from his mug before continuing. "This is the printout for the car Leroy was using. I glanced at it at the agency but haven't studied it thoroughly."

Emma and Phil ate their lunch on autopilot while they waited with anticipation. Gino ran a finger down the vehicle's history, then jabbed hard at one of the entries. "It says here he never went north toward Boston. He went instead to New York. Straight to New York the night he left."

"Does that say exactly where?" asked Phil.

"Not an address," Gino said, "but the general location. It looks like the car was parked somewhere in the city and left there until last night. It was probably left at a public garage while he did whatever he did. The garage isn't near the Plaza Hotel but it isn't that far either. Once he parked it, he could take a cab or the subway or even walk wherever he needed to go."

"So he spent two nights in New York?" asked Emma.

"It looks like he only spent one night," Gino noted, reading more of the report. "Last night he drove back up north and stayed somewhere just south of here on Highway 84." He looked up. "Could one of you check this intersection on your phone?"

After putting on his reading glasses, Phil whipped out his smart phone and pulled up the map app. "Not much there except for a couple of gas stations, a diner, and a motel. It looks like one of those service turnoffs for travelers. It seems to be only about a thirty minute drive from here."

"But that's not very far away," noted Emma looking at Phil's phone. "Why would Leroy stop there when he could have come here, where he already had a nice place to sleep? Was it the middle of the night when he stopped? Maybe he didn't want to bother any of us coming in late."

"I don't think so, Emma," Gino told her. "But here's the really interesting part. It says here the car stopped there last night from six until about nine thirty, then it drove up here to Whitefield." He studied the information again. "In fact, it looks like it came to Misty Hollow." Everyone looked around the table with surprise. Gino held up a finger. "Then it went back to the place on 84 around midnight and stayed there until later this morning, when it traveled back to Misty Hollow again. That was about the time we saw Leroy."

Again, everyone looked around the table, hoping to find answers in their companions' faces. Gino spoke first. "So, who's going to say what's on all our minds?"

Again, eyes darted about, then Phil said, "Okay, I'll say it. It looks like Leroy might have had something to do with Otis's murder."

"He could have come back to Misty Hollow to get something, then went back to the motel to spend the rest of the night," Emma said. "But why? The guesthouse is private. He wouldn't have disturbed any of us coming in late, and ten isn't that late."

"He could have had a rendezvous at the motel," suggested Phil, "and came back to get something he forgot. But we were all still up until around eleven. We stayed in the library talking about our meeting with the Browns after Fran left. You'd think we'd have heard the seen Leroy out the back windows."

"Unless the storm last night masked his arrival and departure," noted Gino. "Later in the night, right after Fran left, it got quite nasty. Remember?"

"You know," Phil said slowly as he dangled a fried scallop from his fork, "there were two sets of tire tracks at the old farmhouse this morning. And they looked fairly fresh to me. One probably belonged to Otis's vehicle and the other might have belonged to the car Leroy was driving." He popped the scallop into his mouth and chewed slowly while he continued to think.

Emma pushed aside her plate. "There is still the matter of Leroy's meeting with Vanessa. Do you think the two are related somehow?"

"One thing is for sure," Phil said, twirling his fork around in the coleslaw on his plate. "We need to let Sergeant Johnson know about this. Did you tell him that Leroy was out of the area when he questioned you, Gino?"

Gino nodded. "Yes. Johnson asked me about everyone staying at the house. I told him Marta was in Connecticut and Leroy was up near Boston." He paused. "But I want to get to Leroy before the cops do. I have some questions I want answered now, not later."

"Hold on a minute," Phil said as he poked at the screen on his phone. "Did any of us bother to look up William Otis in all the hoopla this morning?" He looked from Emma to Gino. Both shook their heads.

Phil kept poking at his screen until he hit information that caught his eye. "Here's something interesting," he announced. "Seems Otis is an author of crime fiction." He looked over the top of his glasses at Gino. "Are you sure you've never heard of him?"

"Positive," Gino said. "He may be new on the scene. Dozens of new authors are hitting the streets every day."

Phil did more searching. "It looks like he just has one book titled *Broken Asphalt* and it's not out yet. It says here that it was recently sold to a major publisher for a *very nice advance*." Phil read more. "According to Otis's website, *Broken Asphalt* 'is the gripping story of a disgraced alcoholic cop who hits bottom after killing a family in a drunk driving accident.'"

Gino immediately got up and started piling their dirty dishes on the tray they'd used. "Let's hit the road. I'm going to get answers if I have to kill that little S.O.B."

"What's up?" Emma asked with surprise. Gino had been angry before, but now his face was flushed with rage.

"That's the premise of one of my unfinished manuscripts," Gino answered with fire in his eyes. He stopped fussing with the trash and looked out across the street, staring at nothing in particular. "It's the book I was working on when Janelle died. Different title, but same premise. It was almost done but I shoved it aside because I couldn't work on it without thinking of her."

Emma took over the cleaning up and took the tray to the trash area, dumping the garbage and leaving the tray with its reusable items on top of a nearby counter. When she got back to the table Gino was sitting down, his head supported by one hand. A strangled sound came from his throat—half anguish, half anger. "Janelle was killed by a drunk driver—an off-duty cop. It was just too close to home to work on the book so I stuck it in a drawer and forgot about it."

"Don't lots of books have similar premises?" asked

Emma, trying to comfort Gino, even though common sense told her there was probably a connection.

Gino raised his face to hers. "So you really think," he said, his voice laced with heavy sarcasm, "that it's a coincidence that the author who had a book coming out with the same storyline as one of my old manuscripts winds up dead less than a half mile from where I'm staying, and my assistant might be involved?"

"No," Emma admitted, cutting him some slack on his tone. "I don't think it's a coincidence. Frankly, I don't know what to think."

"How long has Leroy been with you?" asked Phil. "Did he know about this unfinished book?"

"He's been with me about four years," Gino told them. "I don't recall ever telling him about that book, but he might have come across it in my office. I keep it locked in a file cabinet with other incomplete manuscripts and ideas, but he has a key to that cabinet."

"What about digital copies?" Phil asked.

Gino shook his head. "They were on disks, but I deleted them. I just didn't have the heart to destroy the original printed draft."

"If Leroy did steal it," Emma said, thinking it through, "he could have had the manuscript scanned, then replaced it without you ever knowing. But why would Otis have it?"

"The thing is," Phil said as he ran the information through his legal brain, "if he took the manuscript and didn't put it back and there are no other copies, digital or in print, it could be hard to prove that it was your original idea without a confession from Leroy. Are you sure you never mentioned it to anyone, not even your agent?"

Gino shook his head. "It was a book I was working on

outside of my contracted books. Every now and then I noodle around on a plot that catches my fancy. Most of the time it goes nowhere after a few chapters," he explained. "It's like a writing exercise. And sometimes, like with this book, it develops into something with solid potential, so I finish it and my agent submits it to my publisher. It's like a bonus book. The book I just gave you, the one being released shortly, was developed out of one of those side manuscripts."

After a few seconds, Gino pulled himself together with renewed energy and focus, pulled out his phone, and placed a call. "Neil," he said when the call was answered. "It's Gino. Can you find out everything possible about a newbie author named William Otis?" He paused. "Yeah, that's right, William Otis. I think he has a new book coming out called *Broken Asphalt*. Find out who his agent and publisher are and when the book was bought." He listened, then shouted into the phone, "Are you kidding me?" The few diners near them on the patio turned to stare, then went back to eating.

Gino listened to Neil a long time, then said in a lower tone, "Well, you might want to put your lawyers on standby, Neil. William Otis is dead, murdered last night, and somehow it may be connected to Leroy Larkin. And *Broken Asphalt* may have been stolen. From me." Gino pulled the phone away from his ear and Emma and Phil could hear Gino's agent shouting on the other end.

When the tirade ended, Gino put the phone back to his ear. "No, Neil, I'm not blaming you. You had no idea. I never showed you this book." Another long pause. "Just sit tight for now, Neil. I'm sure the truth will be out soon enough. The police are investigating Otis's death, but don't be surprised if they come calling, asking about him and that book."

When Gino ended the call, Phil said, "I'm guessing that your agent was also representing William Otis?"

"You got it. Neil said he met Otis at a writers' conference and he pitched him the book. Neil loved it, took Otis on as a client, and sold the book pretty quickly. He said Leroy's name never came up in all his talks with Otis about the book."

"I'm sure he's afraid you're going to sue the crap out of him," Phil noted.

"Yeah," Gino admitted, "I'm afraid he is. We've been together almost my entire career and I've never known Neil to be dishonest. Unless I learn otherwise, I'm going to assume it went down as he said it did. Neil reps a lot of well-known authors. He has too much to lose and is too smart to try something like this. But if he is involved"—Gino struck the table with his fist—"he has every right to be afraid, because I will bury him right along with Leroy Larkin."

Gino stood up and took several rejuvenating breaths of the cool clean air. "Now come on, let's get back to Misty Hollow. I want to talk to Leroy before I hand him over to the police."

They were almost to the house when Granny popped into the backseat of the car. "You need to tell Gino something for me," she said to Emma.

She turned to look at Granny. "What's the matter, Granny?" At the same time she saw Phil glance at her in the rearview mirror. Gino noticed nothing, still lost in his outrage.

"Something weird is going on," the ghost said with agitation.

"Did you find something out about William Otis from the Browns?"

"No, not him. It's about that Leroy. After spending a little time at the old house, I popped over to the big house to see if any of the Browns were hanging out on the porch. I didn't see them, but I did see something else."

"Like what, Granny?" Emma said with impatience.

"It looks like Leroy is getting ready to bolt just like Vanessa."

Emma looked directly at Gino. "Granny says Leroy is about to take off."

CHAPTER TWENTY-ONE

THE car had barely come to a stop in the circular driveway when Gino jumped out. The rental car used by Leroy was still there.

"He was right here throwing his bags into the car," Granny said.

"Wait," Emma yelled at Gino, remembering Otis. "He may have a gun!"

Without any indication that he'd heard her warning or not, Gino charged ahead. Instead of heading up the stairs to the house, he trotted around the side to the path that led to the back. From there he headed directly to the guesthouse. Phil hopped out and started for the main house. Emma shouted to him to wait, too, but neither man was listening.

"Go with Phil," Emma called to Granny as she took off after Gino. She handily caught up to him with her long athletic legs and they landed at the front door of the guesthouse about the same time, Gino out of breath and Emma barely breathing hard.

Gino wasted no time grabbing the doorknob and found it locked. Without bothering with a second try, he raised his right leg and kicked the door next to the knob. The lock gave easily. With a mighty push, Emma shoved the larger Gino to the side of the doorway to cover, then joined him. Quickly Gino's brain understood what she was doing and yanked her behind him. They braced themselves for a confrontation, lethal or otherwise. None came. With caution, they entered.

The guesthouse was one very large room with a bathroom across from the main door. There was a small kitchenette with a mini-fridge, a two-burner stove, and a microwave separated from an L-shaped combination seating and sleeping area by a built-in counter with two stools. A queen-size bed was tucked into the alcove made by the short part of the *L*. It was made up but the quilt on the top was rumpled. A love seat, small coffee table, and small upholstered chair filled the seating area. The longest wall had a series of windows and another door, all facing the lake. The door led to a small deck with two painted rockers that matched those at the big house. Although built much later, the guesthouse had been decorated with the same charming antique wallpaper and trim as the main house.

Emma dashed into the bathroom and came out a second later. "Not a toiletry in sight," she announced.

"Looks like Granny was right about him taking off," Gino said. "There's not a piece of clothing or personal effect anywhere. Leroy must be up at the house."

Gino started to head out the door, but Emma grabbed his arm and repeated her warning. "If he killed Otis, then he has a gun."

Gino shook off her hand. "Then let's move it. Phil's up there."

A cold hand of fear grasped her heart and squeezed. She knew Phil could take care of himself, but his bare hands had little force against a gun. She and Gino took off, back up the path to the house and up the steps to the back deck. Way ahead of the out-of-shape Gino, Emma took them two at a time. Finding the French doors unlocked, she burst through them.

"Phil!" she called, quickly looking around the room. It was empty. From upstairs there was the sound of a scuffle and things breaking. "They're upstairs," she yelled to Gino as she grabbed the fireplace poker. She bounded out of the room to the foyer and the staircase.

"Emma, come quick," shouted Granny, popping up at the head of the stairs. "He's got a gun, just as you said."

When Emma reached the top, she was disoriented, not sure from which direction the sound of the fight was coming. From below she heard Gino's heavy steps and turned to see him starting up the stairs, his face flushed and damp with sweat.

Granny saw Emma's confusion. "Gino's room," she shouted at Emma, then disappeared

Just as Emma took off toward that wing, a gunshot vibrated through the house. Emma froze, a strangled cry coming from between her tight lips. Then the house was still. She grasped the poker firmly with two hands and motioned to Gino, who was also frozen, to call for help. Slowly she moved forward, keeping to the middle of the patterned carpet runner that covered the midsection of the hallway, but even then the old floorboards faintly squeaked under her feet.

"I know you're out there," called Leroy. "If you want Phil to live, you'll stay where you are."

Granny popped up again. "Phil's still alive but that creep has a gun on him." In spite of the situation, Emma sighed with relief.

"And don't think about calling the cops," Leroy shouted from Gino's suite. "If I see one cop car or hear one siren, he's dead."

Emma turned to Gino, her eyes wide with fright. He was now at the top of the stairs, phone in hand. He nodded his understanding and slipped his phone into the front pocket of his jacket.

"Come out where we can see you, Leroy," Gino called out, coming forward to stand next to Emma. "And let us see Phil. We need to know he's okay."

There was some shuffling from Gino's suite and some curses and grunts of pain. Several minutes later, Phil appeared at the door. He was holding his left arm with his right and was obviously in pain. Blood, dark against his light gray jacket, was seeping from a wound halfway between his shoulder and his elbow.

Emma started to move forward, but Leroy put the gun to Phil's head. "Careful," he said. He was wearing jeans and a navy blue sweatshirt, different clothing than when he'd shown up this morning, and his face was dark with contempt, his large eyes no longer welcoming and friendly as they had been on the first day of their arrival. He seemed like a different person entirely.

"Please," Emma pleaded, her voice choked. "He needs help. He's bleeding."

"It's okay, darling," Phil told her with a strained smile. "It's just a scratch."

"Put down the fire poker, Emma," Leroy told her, "and kick it toward the wall, out of your reach."

Emma, who had forgotten that she was holding the poker, looked at it a long time before complying. Placing it on the floor, just beyond the runner, she put a foot on it and shoved it away from her and Gino. It hit the side floorboard with a metalic *thunk*.

"Great," Leroy said, infusing his voice with forced perkiness. "Now how about you two going downstairs, single file? Phil and I will be right behind you. If you so much as stumble, Phil dies and you right after him."

They walked, as directed, down the stairs, single file, taking each step carefully until Gino and Emma were at the bottom and Phil and Leroy halfway down. It was then Emma caught sight of Granny. She was hovering nearby, angry and agitated. "Leave Phil alone," the ghost shouted at Leroy.

"Head toward the library," Leroy told them, "but move slowly and stay in my sight. When you get there, sit on the sofa facing away from the windows."

Again, Gino and Emma complied. Once they were seated, Leroy and Phil moved closer. "Sit down, Phil," Leroy ordered, "next to Emma."

Gino moved over and made room for Phil to sit between them with Emma on Phil's left. Once Phil was settled, Emma turned in her seat and started fussing with his injury. When she started to help him out of his jacket, Leroy again cautioned them about any sudden moves. They took it slowly, not just to appease Leroy but to be careful of Phil's injury. Gino helped to remove Phil's good arm from the jacket on his side. Then Emma gingerly pulled the jacket free from Phil's injured arm, with him using his good arm to help. Phil gritted his teeth and made deep guttural sounds as they worked to rid him of the jacket. Sweat beaded on his bald pate and his eyes narrowed to slits.

Once the jacket was free, Emma did her best to make a compress out of it and press it against the still bleeding wound. Phil grunted with pain. Gino started to get up.

"Not so fast," Leroy said.

"There are clean dish towels at the bar," Gino explained. "I just want a couple to stop the bleeding."

"Sit back down," Leroy ordered Gino. "I know where they are. I'll get them."

Still keeping the gun trained on them, Leroy slipped over to the bar and retrieved a few clean and folded dish towels. He tossed them to Emma, but they fell short and landed at her feet on top of her muddy boots. She bent down to retrieve them. Working quickly, she unfolded one that hadn't hit her boots and refolded it into a square, thick bandage. She pressed it against Phil's wound over the sleeve of his knit shirt, which was soaked with blood. He flinched.

"Hold it there with your good arm," she told him. Once the bandage was in place, she went to work on another towel, folding it lengthwise into a long strip, but it was too bulky to tie.

Emma handed the towel to Gino. "Can you tear this into strips?"

Without a word, Gino took the cotton towel and tugged

on it until he was able to get a rip started, then he tore it into long narrow strips. As he got each one done, he handed it to Emma, who tied it around Phil's arm to tightly secure the square bandage. She used three strips before she was satisfied that it was secure and tight enough to stop the bleeding.

"Nice work, darling," Phil said, giving her a smile and a light kiss on her cheek. He still held his left arm with his right, but no longer had to hold the wound.

"Aww," said Leroy, sarcastically. "Isn't that sweet?"

"You leave them alone!" yelled Granny. She made a run at Leroy, but only succeeded in passing through him. As she did, Emma saw him shiver as if caught in a draft.

Emma wanted to talk to Granny, but couldn't openly. It also wasn't helping that the ghost was so worried about their safety, she wasn't thinking about how to help. Emma looked down and noticed the photo album that Fran had left open on the coffee table, and got an idea. But first she had to get Granny's attention. She gave it several tries, but Granny was so angry with Leroy she wasn't giving Emma much thought.

"That's him," came a voice from near the fireplace. At first it startled Emma but she quickly caught her reaction by fussing some more over Phil. Cutting her eyes toward the hearth, she saw Blaine Brown. "That's him, Emma," he repeated, pointing at Leroy. "He killed the man in Nana Abby's kitchen." Emma dipped her chin slightly to let him know she'd heard him.

"Leroy," Emma began, "we know who William Otis is and that you probably killed him, but what I don't understand is why you didn't take off right after we left this morning. You've had hours to get out of here."

"What are you waiting for, Leroy?" Gino said, his voice solid and authoritative. "Did you hang around to kill me? To make sure I couldn't tell anyone about the theft of *Broken Asphalt*?"

Surprise skittered across Leroy's face, but he quickly checked it.

Seeing he hit his target, Gino continued, "Yeah, we looked up Otis and he was very chatty on his website about the premise of his first novel. It sounds very much like one I wrote years ago, long before you came to work for me. One I keep in the file cabinet back home."

They could see Leroy thinking, measuring his options. "That gives you a motive for killing him, Gino, not me. Did you lure him here, then kill him?" Leroy chuckled. "Sounds like a bad plot in one of your trite, overblown books. At least you could have waited until these two were gone." He paused. "Or maybe you were using Emma and Phil as decoys, giving yourself an alibi."

"Like you used your trip to see a friend near Boston?" Gino shot back. "I know you never went there. In fact, you'd be surprised at what I know."

"You know nothing," Leroy snapped with contempt. "You have your head so far up your ass, you didn't even notice your wife was running around with that jerk Brindisi, making you a laughingstock."

"I knew about that," Gino said quietly. "And about her other indiscretions."

"When I found Leroy, he was upstairs ransacking your room, Gino," Phil said.

"My room?" Gino asked with surprise. He looked directly at Leroy. "Were you looking for another manuscript to steal, Leroy? I'd think after all these years you'd know I don't travel with them, except my current one on the laptop."

"He was looking for money," Phil said. "He'd found it just before I found him. It's stuffed in his jacket pocket."

Emma again tried to make eye contact with Granny, but the ghost wasn't paying her any mind.

"Oh, I get it," Gino said sarcastically. "Leroy here knows I always carry a wad of cash when I travel, not a bundle but a couple thousand for emergencies." He looked at his assistant again. "It's not enough you stole the book, you have to steal my petty cash, too? Didn't Otis pay you enough for the book?"

"Maybe that's why Otis was here," suggested Phil. "Was he here to make a payoff now that he'd finally sold it?"

Again a spark flickered in Leroy's big eyes, but he said nothing.

"It still doesn't explain why you're hanging around, Leroy," Emma said. "Otis is dead and you could have looked for that cash earlier today, right after we left."

"I'm telling you, Emma," Gino said, not taking his eyes off of Leroy, "he hung around to kill me. Stealing the money was probably something he thought about only recently, to make it look like a robbery. If you had gone off by yourselves today, I'm sure you would have returned to find me as dead as Otis." He paused as a thought occurred to him. "Were you going to kill poor Marta, too?" he asked, addressing Leroy again.

"Or was Marta Peele a part of this?" suggested Phil. "Was the plan that she go to her friend's while you take out the Costellos?"

Phil's questions caused Leroy to snort. "Marta wouldn't

harm a hair on Gino's head. She's devoted to him like a little lapdog. Not to mention, she's hardly smart enough."

"Okay, so that narrows the suspects," mused Granny. "I'll bet that nasty Vanessa is behind this."

"I'll bet your right, Granny," Emma said out loud, more to test Leroy's response. "Granny thinks," she said glancing sideways at Phil and Gino, "that Vanessa is behind this."

"Granny?" Leroy asked, slightly puzzled. Then his face broke into a sardonic smile. "Oh that's right. You're the ghost whisperer, Emma. So a ghost just told you that Vanessa is in on this?"

"Yes," she answered, "just as a ghost told me he saw you kill William Otis."

Leroy laughed and shook his head from side to side. "I'd like to see you sell that to a jury." He looked at Gino. "So you've finally gone around the bend, Gino, and believe in this B.S., too?"

"Who is he calling bull puckey?" Granny snapped.

"Calm down, Granny," Blaine told her as he watched with interest. "I think Emma's got a plan."

"Well," Granny said, "she'd better get that plan into gear or we'll all be haunting Misty Hollow."

Gino smacked his forehead with a palm, causing Leroy to aim the gun directly at him. "Of course, the meeting at the Plaza!" He looked at Leroy. "You really should be more careful, Leroy. I know a lot of people in New York. People who are happy to call me and let me know my wife and assistant were seen arguing in the bar at the Plaza." He paused and took a few deep breaths. Leroy said nothing.

"Granny, is Fran with you today?" Emma said openly

to the ghost, hoping that Leroy continued to think her medium skills were all a scam. Phil glanced at her like she was crazy, then his eyes changed, telling her he'd caught on to her plan.

"Of course she isn't," Granny said with surprise. "You know she's not dead."

"Too bad," Emma said to Granny. "I was hoping she'd be here to see this."

Leroy laughed again. "Who's this Fran? Another one of your imaginary friends?"

"Well, I'm glad she's not," Granny answered, her hands on her hips, "or she'd be in front of a gun, too."

Blaine floated over to Granny. "I think Emma wants you to find Fran and tell her to get help."

Granny looked at Blaine for a second, then she looked at Emma, who rolled her eyes in confirmation. "I knew that!" Granny snapped just before disappearing.

"Is that where you hatched all this?" Gino asked Leroy, returning to the theory about Vanessa. "Wasn't Vanessa offering enough cash to bump me off? Did you remind her that if I die, she becomes a very rich woman?" Gino shook his head and chuckled. "This is all making sense now. It's a very old and tired story line." He looked at Phil and Emma. "We have a prenup," he explained. "If we divorce, Vanessa gets a very nice settlement, plenty to keep her in style. If she's found to be unfaithful, that settlement can be halved. The baby would be proof enough for that without digging up other affairs." He looked back at Leroy. "But if I die, Vanessa gets half of everything. The other half would go to T."

As a horrid thought occurred to Gino, he slapped a hand over his mouth. When he removed it, his jaw was tight and his lips almost white with anger. "Please tell me," he said to Leroy in a low, menacing tone, "that you weren't supposed to wait until Tanisha got here and take her out, too?"

Emma tensed as the idea of both Kelly and Tanisha walking into a death trap coursed through her body like an electric current. She glared at Leroy, who remained smug and silent. Emma's body shook as she fought to keep herself from flinging her body at him in fury. Phil, sensing her wrath, put a hand on her knee and squeezed. It was a signal to sit tight, to use her head and not her emotions in the dangerous situation. Reluctantly, Emma worked to do just that, knowing it was the smarter course of action. In situations like this, clearer heads usually prevailed.

"Okay," said Phil, "that makes sense in a sick greedy way, but did Vanessa know about William Otis and the manuscript?"

"Vanessa knows nothing," Leroy said scornfully, "except for the latest in fashion and how to spend money." He fidgeted and pulled his phone out of his jacket pocket. He glanced quickly at it and frowned, obviously expecting a call.

"Yes, she offered to pay me to kill you, Gino," he said, returning his attention to his hostages. "She offered me a lot. She said she'd transfer the money right before she got on the plane to Italy."

"So," Gino said, joining more of the pieces together, "that's why you're checking your phone. You're waiting for the transfer to come through." It was a statement, not a question. "The thing is, Leroy, it won't."

Leroy narrowed his eyes at his employer, the skin pulled tight across his narrow face. "What are you saying?"

"I'm saying I'm no fool, Leroy. Vanessa took five grand out of our joint checking account yesterday, and ran up the credit cards. Then she bought a one-way first-class ticket to Italy. Right after that, I called the bank and locked everything down, every account, except for my personal account, which she can't access. If she didn't transfer the money yet, there's no way she could unless she has a secret account under her own name. And if she does, I guarantee she's not going to use it to pay you off now that the cash spigot has been turned off." He paused, then added, "And she's already somewhere over the Atlantic. She left this morning."

"No," Leroy snapped, "that's not true. You're just trying to mess with me, to get in my head like you do in your books." He sneered at his boss, but his feet shifted back and forth, telegraphing his faltering confidence. "But this isn't fiction, Gino. This is real. Very real. Vanessa told me she wasn't leaving until tonight, which would give her time to make the transfer." He waved the gun back and forth in front of them all. Blaine Brown made a grab for it but his foggy image went through Leroy instead.

"Sorry, Emma," Blaine said, and tried again with the same results. Each attempt only sent a slight shiver through Leroy.

"It's true, my boy," Gino told Leroy in a calm voice. "We spoke this morning. She even told me where she left the rental car, and I assured her that I wouldn't enforce the unfaithful clause in the prenup." Gino stretched his long legs leisurely, like he was simply relaxing with a few friends. "But this, this attack on my life will certainly change that."

Phil shifted on the sofa between Gino and Emma,

adjusting his hold on his injured arm. "But what about Otis? Was Vanessa in on that scam, too?" he asked again.

Everyone looked at Leroy for the answer, but he was unraveling like an old sweater, which made him even more dangerous. Every now and then Blaine tried to push him, but failed. Emma knew that if Granny got to Fran, help would be on the way, but would it be soon enough?

The room grew markedly chillier. Emma noticed it first, but soon everyone was fidgeting, trying to fold in on themselves to reserve their body heat. Leroy glanced up at the French doors, which had been left open when Emma and Gino had barged into the house.

"You," Leroy said to Emma, using the gun as a pointer, "close those doors. There must be another storm blowing through."

Carefully and without any sudden movements, Emma got to her feet and walked the few paces to the doors. It was a beautiful fall day outside, not a storm cloud in sight. As she closed the doors, she stuck a hand out. As she expected, it was noticeably warmer outside. If she closed the doors, and with no fire in the hearth, she knew the room might get even colder. With her back to Leroy and a small hopeful smile on her lips, she firmly shut the French doors and turned around.

As Emma expected, the room was filling with hazy figures, but only a couple were clearly visible. Blaine was standing next to Leroy as he'd been before. Abigail came into view near the bar and with her, Warren. The others, not much more than various clumps of shimmering dust motes, were scattered around the room, but as Emma carefully returned to her seat, she saw some of them materializing. Soon the room was filled with spirits, young and old, male and female. The figures all wore various styles of clothing from another era. A few she recognized from the photos in the album.

"My kin want to help, Emma," Blaine explained. "Tell us what we can do."

Emma needed to signal them but wasn't sure how. Would speaking to Blaine make Leroy more nervous, even though she was sure he didn't believe in her abilities? He had mocked her when she'd spoken openly to Granny. Granny was still gone and Emma hoped that she'd had enough contact with Fran to be able to find her. Maybe, Emma thought, if she tried to address Granny again, as if she were here, Blaine would pick up that she was really speaking to him. He was a smart young man and death hadn't seemed to diminish that.

"Granny," Emma said, looking directly at Blaine, "be patient, the time will come. Meanwhile, let's just gather around and wait." He nodded back to her.

Blaine gathered the spirits up. They closed in around Leroy like a delicate feathery cocoon, not with the purpose of protection but of capture. That done, Blaine looked to Emma, waiting for further instructions.

"You bet the time will come," Leroy laughed, trying to shake off the growing cold. "It won't be long before you'll be joining that old Granny you think you're talking to." Still unwilling to believe Gino about Vanessa, Leroy checked his phone again.

"Otis," Gino said, addressing Leroy and getting his attention. "Phil asked you about William Otis and Vanessa. Did she know about the theft of my book?"

"No, of course not," Leroy answered. "But she told me about it. I'd discovered it in the bottom of the file cabinet in a box about two years ago and asked her about it. Apparently, you'd told her your sad story one night after a few too many. She passed it off as just overwrought sentimentality on your end, and said you'd probably not even looked at the manuscript since you put it away."

"So you took it and had it copied?" Phil asked. "Didn't you think Gino would recognize it when it came out?"

Leroy shrugged. "Lots of books have the same plot. Bill and I worked it over, changing names and places. It could have been anyone's book. The publishing world is filled with copycats."

"Bill? You mean William Otis?" asked Emma.

"Yeah," Leroy, said. "We'd met years ago in a writing class and kept in touch. Like me, he's a good writer but was having no luck getting published, so we scanned Gino's manuscript and reworked it. And, boom, just like that we landed an agent." He grinned at Gino. "Your own agent, Gino. Obviously, you'd never shown Neil your manuscript because he didn't recognize it and immediately signed Bill as a client. Soon after, he landed him a nice fat publishing contract."

"So how do you benefit from that?" asked Gino.

Leroy shivered again and a dark, angry scowl covered his face. "Obviously, I couldn't put my name on the book, just in case you became suspicious. So we had an arrangement to split the advance and royalties. We were supposed to meet in New York. He had some sort of meeting there. He'd just gotten his first advance check and cashed it and was supposed to give me half, but he never showed. Later he called and said his meeting had been canceled and he'd never gone to New York, so we arranged to meet at the old farmhouse to make the money exchange."

"So you knew Vanessa was leaving me and heading to New York?" Gino asked.

"Of course I did," Leroy said with a smirk. "She started planning that when we were in Italy, but when I showed up at the Plaza, she didn't have the money she'd promised me."

"And that's what you were fighting about when you were spotted?" asked Phil. He tightened his grip on his arm as a spasm of pain shot through it.

"Yeah, pretty much." Leroy was getting more nervous by the second as it became more clear to him that Gino wasn't bluffing about Vanessa taking off and leaving him adrift. "Both of them stiffed me," Leroy complained. "First Vanessa on the hit money, then Bill with the advance money. I was going to use that money to disappear, start over somewhere on a tropical island where I don't have to lick the boots of a hack." He nearly spit the words at Gino.

"Ha!" taunted Gino. "I'm so much of a hack that *Broken Asphalt* sold immediately, even without my name on it."

Leroy shook the gun at Gino and everyone held their breath, expecting him to pull the trigger and get it over with.

"So you shot Bill Otis because he cheated you?" asked Phil, trying to diffuse the situation. It worked. The hand with the gun steadied and Leroy looked at Phil.

"When we met at the old house," Leroy explained, "Bill only gave me a thousand dollars. It should have been thirty thousand. He whined about taxes and expenses and promised more later. We argued but he only laughed, telling me to try and sue him and see what happens. He flipped me off, laughed again, and started for the door."

"So you shot him in the back for thirty thousand dollars?" asked Phil. "Small price for a man's life."

"Actually," Gino noted, "Otis died for a thousand." He looked at Leroy. "That's all you got from him, isn't it? Add that to the couple of thousand I had stashed away upstairs and you might be able to get a ticket to somewhere, so why not leave now and get on your way? We won't try to stop you."

Leroy let out a strangled half-crazed snicker. "I planned a little better than that, Gino. I just didn't plan on being suckered by Bill and Vanessa. Bill might be dead, but it will be easy enough to find Vanessa and squeeze her for what she owes me." He aimed the gun at Emma's chest. "I'll remind her that she got a deal, three bodies for the price of one."

The ghosts around Leroy stirred and swirled around him as the room grew colder. He shivered and the gun shook with him.

"No!" shouted Phil seeing the gun trained on Emma. "Please don't. Just go, Leroy, we really won't try to stop or follow you." Phil struggled to get to his feet, but Emma and Gino held him back.

"Now!" shouted Blaine to his army of ghosts. They pushed against Leroy as one just as he turned the gun on Phil and fired. The bullet went high, flying over Phil's head, shattering the glass in one of the French doors. Emma screamed and ducked.

"Again," shouted Blaine like a general directing his troops in battle. As a whole, the ghosts mustered their energy and quickly pushed against Leroy again. This time they succeeded in pushing his arm far to the side, just as he fired the second bullet. The shot shattered the mirror behind the wet bar.

Before Leroy could collect himself to fire again, Gino

hurled himself against his assistant, knocking him to the ground and dislodging the gun. Emma jumped up. Finding the gun, she held it on Leroy just as he untangled himself from Gino.

"Enough," she told Leroy as the winded Gino got to his feet. When Leroy tried to get up, she ordered, "Stay right there, facedown, hands flat on the floor above your head."

Phil got to his feet, but wasn't steady. His bandage was beginning to show signs of leakage. "Sit down, Phil," Emma told him gently. "We've got this."

Phil smiled at her and collapsed back on the sofa, taking deep breaths as he held his arm. "Better listen to her, Leroy," he said to the man on the floor. "She's a crack shot, unlike you."

The whine of sirens split the peaceful country air as police vehicles pulled up out front. "I'll go tell them it's all clear," Gino said. As he passed Leroy, he gave the prone man a good solid kick to the ribs, causing Leroy to scream in pain. "That's for my kid," Gino said. He kicked him again in the same spot. Again, Leroy screamed in pain. "And that's for Emma's."

Blaine sidled up to Emma. "Guess Granny managed to get to Fran, so if you don't mind, we'll go now. We're all pretty tuckered out."

Before Emma could say anything, including thank you, Blaine and his family were gone.

CHAPTER TWENTY-TWO

"HEDDY, Fran, I'd like you to meet my daughter, Kelly," Emma said proudly.

Kelly Whitecastle shook the offered hand of each woman and gave them a confident smile. "My mother told me about you last night when we arrived, especially you, Fran. Thank you for sending the police to help them." Kelly and T had arrived on Thursday, as planned, arriving just before supper. Emma and Gino had talked to their daughters after the police had finished questioning all of them about Leroy and Otis. They'd suggested that T and Kelly wait a few days before coming to Misty Hollow, but given the circumstances, the two worried young women wouldn't hear of it. It had taken everything to persuade them to at least stick to their original plan of arriving on Thursday instead of driving down sooner.

"Yes, it seems we have the same gift," Fran said,

returning the warm greeting. "But I can't take all the credit for the other day. Much of it goes to Granny. If she hadn't been so determined to get to me, I wouldn't have known to call the police."

Emma and Phil had arranged to meet Fran and Heddy at the turnout Emma and Gino had visited a few days earlier. It was the second turnout, the one closest to Mr. Dodd's property.

"No Gino today?" asked Heddy, surprised by the big man's absence.

"He and his daughter are spending some private time together," answered Emma. "But you'll meet Tanisha tonight at dinner." Emma hesitated. "You are coming to dinner tonight, aren't you?"

"We wouldn't miss it," exclaimed Heddy.

Emma let out a breath of relief. "Good, because Marta, Gino's housekeeper, is back and she's at the house cooking up a storm for tonight.

"She shouldn't go to any trouble," protested Fran. "We can bring a covered dish or two."

Kelly shook her head and laughed. "Don't worry about it. Marta is happiest when cooking for T and Gino. When I visit them in Chicago, I come home stuffed. After breakfast I heard her talking to herself as she planned the menu."

"Actually, Kelly," Emma said, "I think she's talking to Granny. Even though she can't see or hear her, Granny told me that Marta chatters to her like an old friend when she feels her presence."

"And she's not rubbing her crucifix any longer," Phil said, joining the group. "Have you noticed that?"

Emma laughed. "I have."

"How are you doing, Phil?" asked Fran, noting his left arm in a sling. "I heard you lost a lot of blood."

"Not too bad," he answered. "The doctor said I should be fine. The bullet didn't hit anything too important, like a main artery, but he recommended that I start physical therapy when I get home and see my own doctor."

Fran nodded her approval of the medical advice. "Sounds solid to me."

Emma started for the woods. "There's a small path over here," she told them. "But soon after we'll be trailblazing for a bit."

The small party made their way into the woods, chattering happily among themselves as they hiked to Alexander Dodd's property. Emma linked an arm through her daughter's as they walked. "So when are you going to share with me your plans for after college?" she asked.

Kelly gave her mother a sly look. "T and I are going to tell you and Gino tonight after dinner."

"T?" Emma asked with surprise. "So you two have something cooking together?"

"Something like that," Kelly said with a smile. "And we have a couple of surprise guests arriving today."

Emma stopped walking and pulled Kelly to a halt with her. "Guests? Does Gino know what's going on?"

Kelly laughed. "Don't worry, Mom, Gino isn't holding out on you and Phil. All T told him last night was that we had a couple of friends coming for the weekend and that we'd be making an announcement tonight."

"An announcement?" Emma was stymied. "Don't tell me you and T have both found love and are marrying best friends?"

"No, Mom, don't be silly. I don't have time for that right now."

Emma was relieved to hear that. She'd married right out of college and hadn't wanted Kelly to do the same before experiencing more of the world. "Does Granny know this secret plan?"

Kelly grinned. "She found out by eavesdropping on us. But T and I both know that Granny can take a secret to the grave." Kelly paused. "So to speak."

"You bet I can," said Granny, popping up.

"I thought you were back at the house visiting with Marta," Emma said to Granny.

"I was but I didn't want to miss this," the ghost explained. "Besides, you'll need my help getting those children to their family if you find them." The ghost turned to Kelly and winked. "By the way, your guests arrived."

"Oh come on, you two," Emma complained with frustration. "No fair."

Granny leaned in to Kelly. "I love it when she's like this. Kind of levels the playing field, don't it? Her being such a know-it-all the rest of the time."

Used to the banter between her mother and Granny, Kelly shook her head and started walking. The three generations of women, one dead and two very much alive, walked together, moving faster to catch up with the others.

When they reached the stone wall that marked the beginning of Dodd's property, Emma brought the group to a halt. "This is where I met Alexander Dodd," she told them.

She looked around but didn't spot the old ghost. After climbing over the wall, she walked around the area, "Mr. Dodd, are you here?" She called out a few more times, but heard and saw nothing. Spotting the exact place where Dodd had been sitting the day they met, Emma moved over to it. "Mr. Dodd, it's Emma. We met the other day. I was asking about those children."

"Did you have to bring the entire village with ya?" asked a disembodied voice. Slowly a ghost materialized a few feet away and studied the group.

"There he is," said Fran, pointing in the direction of Dodd.

"So you can see me, madam?" Dodd said, coming full into view.

"That I can, Mr. Dodd," answered Fran.

"Anyone else?" he asked the group. "Raise your hands if you can see and hear me?"

In response, Emma, Kelly, Fran, and Granny raised their hands.

"Good, now I know who I'm addressing." Dodd looked at Granny, examining her pioneer clothing. "I haven't seen you in these parts before. You're not from around here, is my guess. I'd remember a sweet-looking thing like you."

Emma couldn't tell if Granny was blushing, but her face did break into a wide smile. "I'm Ish Reynolds, Emma's great-great-great grandmother," Granny explained. "I hail from Julian, California. I lived there during the gold rush. Folks call me Granny. I travel with Emma sometimes. Kind of like a to-go ghost."

"Ah, gold. Yes, I remember," mused Dodd. "A lot of men ran off to the gold fields out west to seek their fortune. I might have, too, if I'd been younger."

"Mr. Dodd," Emma said to the ghost, "this is my daughter, Kelly, and our friend Fran. They can both see and hear you."

"Yeah, I saw their hands, remember?" the old ghost said.

"And this is Heddy and this is Phil," Emma told him, continuing with the introductions. "They can't see or hear you, as you noted by the display of hands." Emma moved closer. "We're all here to see if we can find those children I told you about. Have you seen them lately?"

Dodd scratched the stubble on his face, but it made no sound. "That I have. I told them a spirit woman was looking for them and they should stay in the area."

"This area?" Fran asked, indicating the immediate woods around them.

"No, not here," Dodd answered. "I saw them further up, at the other end of my property."

"Can you give us directions?" asked Granny.

Dodd addressed Granny with a slight bow. "For you, my dear, of course."

"Get on with you, you old fool," Granny snapped, yet still wearing a smile. "I'm a married woman."

"I was married in life, too," Dodd said, "but those vows were until death do part. I'm dead, so I figure I'm single again. You, too, you sweet filly."

"I'd like to hear you say that to my man, Jacob," Granny told him with a jerk of her chin. "We're still together even in the afterlife. So stop flicking your whiskers, you old goat, and tell us where those children are."

Emma heard giggling and turned to see Kelly, her head leaned close to Fran's, the two of them sharing a laugh. Heddy and Phil looked at each other, puzzled and eager to be let in on the joke.

Alexander Dodd made a big show of shrugging his shoulders and looking hurt. He shot a look at Granny only to see she wasn't budging on his overtures. Giving up, he said, "You follow this old wall here to where it ends. There's a smallish clearing there, just a few paces off, with a big old elm tree in the middle. That's where I last saw them children."

After thanking Mr. Dodd, the party started walking along the broken wall, stepping over fallen stones and around trees that had grown up among the rubble. They followed it as it wound through the woods and low brush. While they walked, Kelly filled Heddy and Phil in on their conversation with Dodd.

"So Granny's hot stuff," Phil said with a hearty laugh.

"Go ahead and laugh, cowboy," Granny said with a sniff, "but without me that old geezer might not have told you anything. I charmed it out of him." The three mediums broke into giggles.

They'd been walking about fifteen minutes when the wall abruptly stopped. Phil walked ahead a little bit to make sure the wall had ended and wasn't just broken in that spot. "Looks like this is the end."

They all split off and examined the area on both sides of the wall, looking for a small clearing and a large elm.

"I'm not even sure what an elm tree looks like," said Kelly.

"It looks just like that," said Heddy, pointing to a large tree. "That's an American elm, the state tree of Massachusetts." She walked a few more steps. "And here's another. And another."

"Yes, but here is a really big elm," said Phil from several yards away. "And it's in a clearing."

Everyone gathered around the huge tree. "This looks like a great picnic spot," noted Heddy.

"Or a grave site," added Fran, "which I'll bet it is."

"Shh," said Emma, a finger to her lips. When everyone grew quiet, she called out, "Chester and Clarissa, are you here?" She turned a few feet. "Chester and Clarissa Brown. We're here to take you to your family."

They all listened, hearing only the whisper of wind in the trees and the scurrying sounds of small living things in the brush.

"Chester and Clarissa," Emma tried again. "I'm the lady looking for you. The spirit woman Mr. Dodd told you about." Emma motioned again for everyone to remain quiet. They all stood there, Phil with his good arm around Kelly's shoulders, Fran and Heddy with their arms around each other. Emma and Granny remained in the clearing. They all stood and waited in silence. A minute later, Emma tried again. "Please come out, Chester and Clarissa. We're here to help you."

"There," said Kelly in an excited whisper. "There by that skinny bush."

They all turned in the direction Kelly indicated and soon the mediums and Granny saw two small images take shape.

"That's it, my sweets," Fran crooned to the hazy outlines, taking a couple of slow steps forward. "We're here to take you to your mother and father, so don't be afraid." The figures started taking on more definition and soon they could clearly see a boy and a girl. Emma recognized the Brown twins.

"You can call me Granny," Granny told the children. "I'm a spirit just like you." She turned to the others. "These good people promised your family they would find you and bring you home."

"To Momma and Poppa?" asked the girl.

"Yes, my sweets," Fran confirmed. Kelly and her mother joined Fran close to the ghosts. "Some of us can see and hear you, but some cannot," Fran explained, "but we're all here to help you."

"Are you Clarissa and Chester Brown?" Emma asked, wanting confirmation.

The boy nodded. "I'm Chester. This is my sister Clarissa."

"Where are you," Emma asked, "when you're not walking in the woods?"

Chester and Clarissa exchanged looks, then Chester asked, "Do you mean where do we sleep?"

"Yes, Chester," Emma confirmed, "that's what I mean."

Chester left his sister's side and floated over to the edge of the small clearing where low bushes were creeping toward the tree, trying to claim the clearing. He pointed down to the ground.

"Is that where the man put you?" Fran asked in a calm, soothing voice as she approached Chester.

The boy nodded again. "A bad man."

"A very bad man," Fran agreed. "Was it Mr. French? Did Mr. French put you there?" Again the boy nodded.

"Chester, Clarissa," Emma said to the children, "Granny is going to take you someplace away from here. She's going to take you to your mother and father. Is that okay?"

The little girl clapped her hands silently together, her ghostly face wreathed with joy. "Oh yes!" Her brother returned to her side, clearly just as happy.

"Come now," Granny said, going to them. "Come with me."

As the children started floating away, their images and

the image of Granny Apples started fading. Just before disappearing, Clarissa Brown turned around and waved to them.

"Where's Heddy?" asked Fran after the children were gone.

"I'm right here," came Heddy's voice from deeper in the woods. "I'll be right back."

Everyone relaxed in the clearing, glad their mission had come to a successful end. Kelly wrapped Emma in a hug. "Thanks, Mom. I'm glad you were able to do that and I got to see it. It was so awesome."

Emma kissed her daughter's cheek and returned the hug. "I'm just glad we were able to find the children. Their family probably saved our lives the other day." Kelly tightened her grip on her mother.

Heddy came out of the woods to rejoin them. In her arms was a collection of various small forest flowers and ferns. "Okay, now where did the children say they were buried?"

"Right here, sweetheart," Fran said, pointing to the spot Chester had indicated.

With grunts and groans, Heddy lowered herself to a kneeling position and started artfully placing the flowers and ferns across the small area. When she was finished, Fran helped her back to her feet. "Even though this make-shift grave is over a hundred years old," Heddy told everyone, "it still should be recognized and a word of prayer said over it."

Everyone joined hands and bowed their heads while Heddy said a short prayer over the grave.

CHAPTER TWENTY-THREE

EMMA squealed with delight when they got back to Misty Hollow and found Dr. Quinn Keenan in one of the rockers on the front porch. While she parked the car, he came down the steps to welcome them, much as Gino had just a few days ago. Both Emma and Phil gave him a hearty embrace, and so did Kelly.

Emma turned to Kelly with a wide smile. "Is this our surprise?"

"One of them," Kelly said.

"Hey, guys," Quinn said with a laugh, "you didn't have to hire a security team on my account. I'm sure my groupies would behave if asked nicely." He pointed to a security guard posted at the end of the drive. The guard stood next to a Jeep that had been pulled across the driveway after Emma had pulled in. There was also a guard at the old house and one patrolling the grounds on foot. Across from the guard were a couple of paparazzi snapping photos. The news vans had left the day before. It was the price of fame, especially when the media smelled a possible scandal or murder.

Quinn looked around, "Is Granny with you?"

"Not right now," Emma told him. "She's on a very special errand, but she'll be joining us tonight."

With Quinn was a tall, handsome young man. "Emma, Phil," said Quinn, indicating the young man, "I don't think you've met my son, Peter."

The young man held out his right hand to them. "It's a pleasure. I've heard so much about you from Dad and Kelly." Peter Keenan was as tall and strapping as his father, but with cocoa skin and black hair instead of ruddy skin and red hair, and with Quinn's rugged jaw.

"You've met Kelly before?" Emma was puzzled for a moment. "Oh, of course, you must have visited your father while Kelly was his intern."

"I did and am glad of it," Peter said. "We've become very good friends." He looked at Kelly and winked. "Even more than good friends." Now Emma was even more puzzled. She was sure that Quinn had told her that his son was gay.

"Hey, look who's back from ghost wrangling," called Tanisha Costello, coming out the front door. She yelled back into the house, "Marta, tell my dad he can start cooking. They're back and I'm starved."

"Gino's cooking?" Phil asked with concern. "Are we having bacon and eggs for lunch?"

"No," laughed T, as they all came up the stairs and headed into the house. "Dad is also great with a grill. He uncovered the big grill on the back deck and fired it up."

As she passed T, Emma stopped and leaned in. "Did you and your father have a good talk this morning?"

In response, T gave Emma a big hug. "Yes, about everything, including my mother. Thank you."

They were all seated at the patio tables enjoying grilled burgers, both beef and veggie, along with potato salad, green salad, and an assortment of cookies and brownies.

"Marta," Emma said to the housekeeper, who clucked over them like a mother hen, "I can't believe you had time to bake all these goodies."

"I didn't, Mrs. Whitecastle," Marta replied. "Mr. Costello picked them up at a bakery in town while you were gone. The rolls, too. They're good, yah?" Marta was not only happy that everyone was safe and sound, and Vanessa and Leroy were out of the picture, but she had received news that her friend was improving.

"They're wonderful, Marta," Emma told her truthfully, "but I'm sure yours are even better."

"I'm making a cake for tonight," Marta told her as she put down a fresh pitcher of iced tea. "Best chocolate cake in the world."

"I'll vouch for that," Kelly said with enthusiasm.

"And a big turkey dinner," Marta added. "But don't worry, Mrs. Whitecastle, there will be lobster and scallops, too. Mr. Costello told me you like scallops."

"Yes, but not fried, okay?" Emma said. "I think I've had my fill of fried food for a while. That last binge gave me heartburn." Everyone laughed.

"Okay," Gino said, getting to his feet. "I know the girls said they have a big announcement, and I know it has something to do with Quinn and his son, but I'll be damned if I'm waiting until after dinner tonight to get the news. So, T and Kelly, out with it." He sat back down.

Kelly and T put their heads together and whispered. Finally, Kelly said. "Mom and Phil, I know you're wondering why I've been dragging my feet about mentioning grad school, but here's the thing." She paused and looked at Peter, who nodded encouragement. "I'm don't want to go to grad school."

"But, Kelly," Emma said, interrupting her. Phil put a hand on her arm.

"Hear her out, Emma," he said gently, "then you can protest, or not."

"Okay, Kel," Emma said reluctantly to her daughter, "I'm all ears."

"Anyway, I'm going to Australia with Quinn on his next expedition." Kelly took a deep breath when she was finished.

"And I'm going with her," T announced.

"What?" Gino asked, totally thrown off guard.

"Me, too," added Peter, "and my partner, Roy."

The parents shot questioning looks at Quinn. "I'm going to Australia for at least a year to study the aborigines," he explained, "particularly one tribe deep in the bush known for their superstitions. The kids decided they wanted to come along and film it."

"You're an anthropologist now?" asked Phil. "I thought you were an archaeologist, a digger in the dirt."

"I am," Quinn answered with a grin, "but during my last stint in Australia I became interested in this tribe through a friend who is an anthropologist. This is really her project. I'm just tagging along to help and to learn things."

"And we're going to make a documentary about it,"

Peter explained. "We're forming a company, the four of us—Tanisha, Kelly, Roy, and myself."

"I'm going to be writing a lot of it," T announced, "and both Kelly and I can research ghosts and spirits and how they are integrated into the lives of the tribe, both then and now. We might even bring the paranormal into the piece in a more concrete way."

Emma leaned back in her chair, quiet for a moment, then she asked Kelly, "This is how you'd like to use your medium talents?"

"Um, yes, Mom," Kelly answered. "At least for this project. Is there something wrong with that?" Her voice held a slight edge of defensiveness.

Emma raised a hand to stop Kelly from saying anything more. "No, it's not that. I think research and education is an excellent use of your skills, and of Tanisha's. I'm just surprised. I thought you wanted to keep it all under wraps."

Kelly looked to Quinn, who smiled at her. "When Kelly was working with me," he said, "there were several incidents where her skills became quite useful, if not invaluable. When Peter came to visit, they became friends and kicked around the idea of doing a documentary about it as it related to ancient cultures for starters, and maybe later about people around the world who share such gifts."

"My background is in journalism, like T's," Peter explained. "But it's mostly been for TV, while hers has been in print. Roy is a gifted cameraman who has been on the crew of several award-winning documentaries. I think together we'll make a great team."

"We thought we'd start with Quinn's next expedition," added T, "and see how it goes. From there we could branch out and do other films, and not just about the paranormal."

Emma and Phil exchanged glances, then Phil asked, "And how long will you be gone and when are you leaving?"

"We'll be gone about a year," Kelly said, "and we'll leave in June, shortly after I graduate."

"That's only nine months from now, Kel," Emma complained. "I'd hoped you'd spend at least part of the summer with us. And I know your father will want to spend time with you."

Quinn cleared his throat. "We can push the departure until the first part of July, but not any further."

"May I say something?" Gino asked after remaining silent for some time. "After all, my daughter is part of this motley crew, too." Everyone turned to him. "Frankly, I think it's a good idea. If they are going to do something like this, they should do it now, while they're young." He looked at Tanisha, his eyes moist with pride. "Honey, I hope you spend more time than the occasional rushed weekend with me before you go, but even if you can't, I'll understand. You don't need my permission to go, of course, but for what it's worth, I heartily give my blessing and support." He paused. "But you know you're going to miss Marta's cooking."

T got up and went to her father, giving his neck a warm squeeze from behind. "Thank you, Dad."

"And speaking of support," Gino continued after the embrace ended, "how much do you need to fund yourselves for the year? I'd like to provide some of it."

"Oh, Dad," Tanisha said, giving him a big squeeze again. "Thank you. We were actually going to ask you all to buy shares in our company to help fund it. We have a business plan and everything."

"I have copies of the plan and the budget with me," Peter said. "We were going to do a formal presentation tonight."

"I've seen it," said Quinn, "it's very solid. I'll be buying in."

"Mom," Kelly said to Emma, "I know you and Dad have an account for my grad school. I'd like to use that for my share, if I can."

Emma and Phil conferred in whispers. When they were finished, Phil said to Emma, "So it's plan B?"

"Plan B," she confirmed.

"What are you talking about?" Kelly asked.

"As far as your grad school money goes, Kelly," Emma told her, "I'm okay if you want to use it to invest in this venture, but you'll have to get your father's approval, too. It's an account we started together for you. And Phil and I will look at your business plan and let you know before you leave this weekend about our buy-in share. We're definitely in, we just want to review the numbers." She shook a finger at Kelly. "But don't be shy about asking for your father's support, too. He'll probably be thrilled that you're going into the film industry, even if it's not the area he would have chosen for you."

"He won't be happy about my paranormal activities," Kelly said. "He's not happy about yours and you're no longer married."

Emma laughed. "No he won't," she agreed, "and I'd love to be a fly on the wall when that goes down."

The table erupted in laughter.

Gino stood up again and raised the beer bottle he'd

been drinking from. "A toast to . . . ah . . . ," he stammered, then looked at Peter. "Do you have a name for the company yet, son?"

"Not yet," Peter answered.

"Well, then," Gino continued, "a toast to Work In Progress. May it thrive and may none of our children catch any nasty diseases or parasites." Everyone raised their glasses and bottles in a raucous toast.

Once everyone quieted down, Quinn leaned across the table to Emma and Phil. "So what's plan B?"

Emma and Phil once again exchanged looks and smiles, then Phil said, "Emma and I have an announcement of our own. You see, we decided last night to get married in August, but with Kelly leaving the country, we're on to plan B. We're getting married before you all leave and everyone's invited. That includes Quinn and Peter."

"We can stop off in California on our way to Australia," Quinn said. "Get you two finally hitched and then take off."

"See," Phil said with a grin. "Plan B."

· CHAPTER TWENTY-FOUR ·

AFTER dinner later that night, Emma found Gino standing alone on the back deck enjoying his evening brandy and cigar. "A penny for your thoughts," she said to him.

"Ha!" he shot back. "I'm not sure they're worth that much, and even then my agent would take fifteen percent."

Emma chuckled. "It's been a wild few days. Are you okay?"

He shrugged and flicked some ash over the railing. "It depends on which topic you're asking about. Am I okay with this thing with the kids? Yes. I think it's a grand adventure, and one they shouldn't miss. And I love that they want to start their own business. As for Vanessa, I'll be okay with it. It's not like I didn't see the split coming, but I sure didn't think she'd resort to murder." He glanced over at Emma. "That, I will admit, shook me right down to my socks. I've had ex-wives wish me dead during fights, but I never thought one would actually try to do it herself." He squeaked out a sad chuckle of disbelief.

They watched as one of the guards left the guesthouse, which the security company had set up as a base on the property. He made his way with a flashlight along the edge of the lake across the lit path to the dock and up the other side of the property.

"How long will they be here?" Emma asked.

"Not much longer, probably just until you all leave. It's an election year," he explained, "with that and ISIS and global warming, my near murder and the theft of my book are already old news, but I don't want you all bothered for the rest of your stay."

"Are you and Marta staying on even after everything that has happened?"

He nodded, his profile silhouetted against the dim deck lights. "Yes. I really do like this place and once the paparazzi tire of standing outside on the road, it will become the haven I wanted. Although," he said, tossing his head toward the boarded-up French door, "I doubt I'll be getting my security deposit back." He turned to face Emma. "It will be a while before I go back to my home in Chicago, whether I stay here or not, so I might as well stay here."

"You and Marta are welcome to spend time at my home in Julian. It doesn't have a great view like this." She swept a hand toward the lake. "But there's plenty of room and it's empty quite often, although once Phil and I marry we'll make it our main residence."

"That's quite a long commute to LA for your show, isn't it?" Gino asked.

"You're not the only one with change on the horizon." Emma took a deep breath. "My show is being canceled come spring. I got an e-mail about it just an hour ago. Although I knew it might happen."

"But I thought the ratings were good," he said, surprised.

"They were, at least for a cable show, but the station is being sold and the new owners don't want to pick up a few of the shows, including mine. When I get back, we'll film the remainder of the season and then it will close down."

"I'm sorry to hear that," Gino said with sincerity, "but I'm sure something just as interesting will come along. Maybe you should write books like your friend Milo Ravenscroft."

"I'm looking forward to just having some time off. Shortly after the show ends Kelly will graduate, followed by our wedding, and then Kelly leaves. After that, maybe Phil and I can do some traveling." She leaned against the railing and looked at him. "What about you? Are you going to do that book about the 1800s serial killer?"

He nodded and smiled. "Oh yeah. I know a hot topic when I see one. Although I'm probably going to be tied up off and on for months with all this stuff about Leroy and Vanessa. You know, depositions, trials, the divorce, and other stuff. Hard to write when your concentration is scattered."

"What about *Broken Asphalt*?" she asked. "Have you heard anything from your agent?"

He laughed and sipped his drink. "Funny you should ask. While you were having your show canceled, Neil called me. He contacted the publisher for *Broken Asphalt* and filled him in on what had happened. Of course they agreed to yank the book from their catalogue and release schedule, but then they made Neil an offer. They want to publish it anyway, but with my name on it. With all the news and controversy, they're sure it will outsell all of my other books."

"But didn't Leroy and Otis change stuff?"

"Yes, they did, and I'm not about to publish something that's been tampered with, so I turned it down. I could finish my original manuscript and sell it, probably to my current publisher, but that book means more to me than a few more dollars." He looked at Emma. "You know what I mean?"

She nodded and placed an understanding hand on his arm. "Yes, I do."

He looked back at the lights stretching out onto the lake. "I'm told that every minute of every day someone in the world buys one of my books, so I'm pretty damn rich without it. I might spill my guts on the page, but I'm not selling my soul."

One of the French doors opened and Phil stepped out with one of the afghans in his good hand. He handed it to Emma. "I thought you might need this if you two are going to gab all night."

Laughter from the library drifted out to them. "What's going on in there?" Gino asked.

"A rousing game of charades," Phil answered with a grin. "Fran and Heddy are remarkably good at it and so is Marta. Quinn is claiming that Granny is helping them. He and Peter are losing big-time."

Gino took another sip of his drink. "Then I'd better get in there and help the men out."

"Emma," came a ghostly voice as Gino left. Emma

turned toward the patio table and saw Blaine. Behind him were several spirits, but none came clearly into view. Blaine stepped forward. "My family and I would like to thank you for finding Chester and Clarissa and returning them to us."

Emma gave the Browns a wide, warm smile. "I'm very happy we were able to do that for you. Will your family remain at Misty Hollow now that the children have been found?"

He shrugged. "Some might, but most won't. Now that the twins have crossed over, they will be happy to remain on the other side."

"It was an honor to meet you and your family, Blaine, and Phil and I want to thank you for saving our lives. We owe a great debt to you."

"That debt has been paid." With a polite bow, he and the other Browns disappeared.

Once they were alone, Emma put the afghan over her shoulders and held up one side, inviting Phil to join her under its warmth. He snuggled close and wrapped his good arm around her waist. "It's been one hell of a trip, darling," he whispered into her ear. "I can't wait to get back to Julian."

"Me either," said Granny, materializing on the deck a few feet from them. "I like action, but this has been exhausting."

1844